SLEEP OF DEATH

SLEEP OF DEATH

Philip Gooden

Robinson
LONDON

Constable & Robinson Ltd
3 The Lanchesters
162 Fulham Palace Road
London W6 9ER

First published in the UK by Robinson, an imprint of
Constable & Robinson Ltd 2000

A copy of the British Library Cataloguing
in Publication data is available from the British Library

ISBN 1–84119–146–9

Printed and bound in the EU

'For in that sleep of death what dreams may come, When we have shuffled off this mortal coil, must give us pause . . .'

HAMLET, 3, i

Prologue

*I*t was his custom in summer afternoons to sleep outside. He slipped through the back quarters of the house, through its passages and offices, and into the garden. The garden was walled. He could hear occasional cries from Mixen Lane, the distant splashing of the wherries on the river, the boatmen's shouts. The sun lay evenly across the gravel walks. He made his way towards a door in the far wall and unlocked it. Through the door was an orchard, doubly enclosed from the city beyond the outer wall. Once inside this inner space, he turned and carefully relocked the oak door. He paused and looked around, drawing a deep pleasurable breath. Tongues of leaves wagged at him in the breeze.

He traced a serpentine path through the apple trees and the pears and the plums, thinking of the way that, when autumn arrived, the massed scents and juices of the ripe fruit would be strong enough to overlie the river smells that now vaulted the wall. When he came to the hammock which was slung between two apple trees he paused again and glanced up between the glassy leaves of a nearby pear. From somewhere inside his house there was a shriek – of amusement, of surprise, he couldn't tell. It didn't matter. No one would disturb him now, when he was secure in his orchard. The servants had the strictest orders. Once he had been in the habit of bringing Alice here. Underneath the trees, *lying on mattresses of blossom or on the tussocky grass. The orchard trees were lower then. He could not remember when he and Alice had last visited the garden together. Alice with her oval, decided face, Alice with her hair still untouched by the years. For no reason – but he was deceiving himself, and knew that he was deceiving himself even as he denied there was a reason – the image of Thomas, his brother, slipped itself between him and Alice. A large jovial man, held in the world's regard, his brother Thomas. Equable, easy-going, popular . . . but a hollow man, without substance behind his fine, external walls. He hated him.*

Wearily, he levered himself into the hammock. The apple trees groaned under his weight. Segments of sky swayed as he looked up. A wall of white cloud was advancing from south of the river. He closed his eyes and waited for sleep. Something brushed his cheek. A leaf, no more. There was a rustle overhead. Pictures slipped through his head and then fell away from him like tumbling playing cards. King, queen, knave . . .

A few yards distant, the figure up in the pear tree shifted slightly. It waited to see if the man in the hammock was really asleep, whether he wouldn't respond to the creaking branches, the swishing leaves. But the man below remained still. The figure swung itself down from the tree. It landed on the tussocky ground, and crouched. There was a sound from the hammock, something between a snore and a sigh. The bulk of the man in the hammock could be seen, his dark humped mass straining at the cords of the netting. The figure slowly straightened up and then loped towards the sleeping man. By the hammock it paused again before withdrawing from a fold of its cloak a tiny flask of opaque glass. The flask was closed with a wax seal. The seal was prised off by inserting a long thumbnail under a protruding flange of wax. The wax came away as easily as a ripe scab.

2

At that moment the sleeping man shifted. He canted himself sideways so that he was almost facing the figure, which stood, breath stopped, over him. His eyes stayed shut. This was better, this was comfortable! The sleeper's bearded right cheek was laid nearly as flat as a plate. He might have been on the block, positioning himself for the executioner's convenience. The figure could see his enemy's bristles, the way his lips fluttered under each expelled breath, the whorl of his ear. His ear, that was what concerned the figure. There was a fringe of fine hair round the sleeper's ear, a poor defence, weak little whisker-palisades against what was contained within the opaque flask. The figure thought of the porches and alleys, the winding paths that lead off into the head's interior from this one hole. Of all the ways into the head this is the least guarded; it is the postern-gate which the treacherous servant leaves ajar for the besieging army.

The flask drew close to the sleeper's ear and was tremblingly positioned above the hole. At the lipped mouth of the flask a colourless bead of liquid gathered itself before being transformed into a thin thread flowing directly downwards. The thread insinuated itself into the man's ear, it burrowed its way down. In a moment the sleeping man stirred. He flapped a hand, as if to brush aside something that had disturbed him, another leaf perhaps or an insect. The figure clamped a hand over the side of the other's face to hold him in position. The spool unwinding from the flask ran faster, like the last moments of a man's life slipping out of his grasp. Some of the liquid began now to pool over the edges of the sleeper's ear-hole. The movements of his head became sharper, jerkier, and so the murderer pressed down harder, harder, with the left hand, while the right jiggled to keep the flask steady and to ensure that the final strings of liquid entered the waking man's head.

Done! Now the murderer didn't care if the sleeper woke. It

would be better if he woke, to see the cause of his death. The murderer stepped back, like a craftsman admiring his handiwork. The man in the hammock clapped a hand to his ear. His eyes, they flew open. They searched among the surrounding trees before coming to rest on a shape which, to be sure, had smutted its face and was wearing a short cloak of goose-turd green that made it hard to distinguish among the thick foliage. Would have made it hard even for a man newly awoken and without any suspicion of harm in this fallen world. But the man in the hammock was dying and had only seconds to grasp the sight of the shape in his orchard before a hot knife of pain skewered his head and was withdrawn, and then thrust in again and again.

ACT 1

"You know the play?"

This was said with surprise. Players aren't supposed to know plays, players are only supposed to know their parts.

"I've seen it," I said. "Last month. You were magnificent. No flattery. I have said that to many others since then, before I am saying it to you now."

Nerves were twisting my speech. What was intended as genuine compliment came out as clumsy buttering-up. And pompous, as well as patronising, considering I was talking to a man old enough to be my father.

Master Burbage shrugged but was graceful enough to smile.

"I've played with the Admiral's Men," I said, to change the subject. "Nottingham's, I should say."

"The Admiral's will do. That's what they were on this side of the river. How do they do in the north of the town?"

"Well enough," I said.

"Tactful, Master Revill," said Burbage. "The audiences are different over there, more respectable – and more respectful – than our Southwark spectators. But the Admiral's Men ran away when we appeared south of the river, essentially they ran

5

away, although Henslowe would claim that it was purely commercial."

"Everything is commercial with Master Henslowe," I said.

"All bearpits and brothel business, his enemies say," said Burbage.

"Henslowe sees plays and playhouses as a good investment, nothing more. At least, that was my impression," I said, eager to make a good impression myself, and to cancel out something of the clumsiness of my earlier remarks. I didn't really know how Henslowe saw things, but there was nothing wrong with running him down to curry favour with a business rival.

"What is the most important part of the playhouse?" said Burbage.

I hesitated before replying. This was undoubtedly what they call a "trick" question, designed to catch out the young and naive. What *is* the most important part of the playhouse? The author? No; everyone knows that the author doesn't matter. The flattering thing would be to refer to the company; no company, no play. The obvious answer would be to say the stage – no stage, no play either. A clever response might be to mention the seats, for though many spectators are happy to hand over their pennies and stand by the stage and smoke, the better classes pay more for their seats and the even better classes pay yet more for private boxes. With seating comes a discriminating audience, and a more sedate one. Instead, I plumped not for the flattering or the obvious or the clever answer, but the shrewd one. As I thought.

"The tiring-house," I said, gesturing vaguely. We were sitting in a room adjoining the tiring-house.

For where would the players be without their place to change in, and to shelter between appearances? The tiring-house is where reality and illusion meet in perpetual conflict, or so I would go on to claim if Master Burbage was good enough to ask my reasons. The tiring-house is a magical cave of unending transformations, where a player becomes a king in the flick of a costume, and a king may become a beggar when he turns his cloak inside out and smirches his face. I waited for Burbage's approval, to begin my rhetorical flight.

"If you don't mind my saying so, Master Revill," said Burbage, "that is a very stupid answer."

"The stage, I should have said."

"The part that matters," said Burbage, "is wherever the money is taken. That is the centre of the playhouse. That is why I would never join those who sneer at Master Henslowe for the way he makes his money, or how much money he makes or for his attitude to the making of money. In the playhouse, before you can make anything else, you must make money."

Burbage's reputation was unspotted. It was hard to think of him trading in whores and chained bears. He was happily married, wasn't he, with a large number of children?

"People cross the river in droves every day," said Burbage. "They come to see us, of course they come to see us. But they come also to see the bears and the bulls in the pits. They come to visit the stews and taste a different meat from what they get at home. In short, they want to see animals being tormented, men and women both, and the men, they want to exercise their pricks across the water. And sometimes they visit plays before or afterwards. The same people. So that is why I have never taken exception to the way in which Henslowe and Alleyn choose to make their money."

"I wasn't," I began, "I didn't mean . . ."

"Players are so contemptible," said Burbage, in a narrow fluting voice that had an echo of the pulpit in it, "that we might as well be whores. We show off what we have and people pay to watch us. What do they call us, 'caterpillars of the commonwealth', 'painted sepulchres'?"

"Puritans say that," I said.

"Not only them. It is a commonly held view. Even so, we are crawling very slowly towards respectability, very slowly indeed. Why are you on stage then, in this despised popular business?"

"I like showing off," I said without thinking. "I like being watched, I suppose," I said, more slowly.

"Good, Master Revill," said Burbage. "I like that. Remind me of what you appeared in with the Admiral's."

"I was in *Robert, Earl of Huntingdon* and a thing called *Look About You*. Small parts . . ."

"We must all start somewhere," said Burbage.

I said nothing; I had already said too much. A man slipped across the background of the room, and glanced curiously in my direction for a moment. He looked like Master Burbage, the same tapering beard, a similar brown gaze. I wondered if it was Cuthbert, brother to Richard Burbage and the one who managed the business. Burbage craned round in his chair and nodded, and then the man was gone. I must have looked a query.

"Our author," he said. "He is the Ghost."

Indeed there was something ghost-like about the other man's manner of slipping into and then out of the room, something almost insinuating. Not Cuthbert Burbage therefore.

"He is the Ghost in the play in question, the one we were talking about."

"I remember the ghost appearing, on the battlements," I said. 'Angels and ministers of grace defend us!' I said.

"Yes, it is a good beginning," said Burbage. "I cannot think when our, ah, congregation has fallen so quiet so soon at the start of things."

"And the ghost appears in the bedchamber too," I said, eager to show off my knowledge.

"Indeed he does," said Burbage.

"But only to Prince Hamlet, the Queen can't see him. I wondered why that was."

"You'll have to ask our author, even though I fear you'll soon find yourself – like the rest of us – too busy for that sort of speculation," said Burbage. "To business. We may need you for two weeks. That is the time Jack Wilson is likely to be away. His mother is dying in Norwich and not quickly, he has been informed. He left early this morning."

"I will take on all his parts?"

"Let me see. You'll do the townsman in *A City Pleasure* and Cinna in *Julius Caesar*—"

"Cinna the conspirator?" I interrupted. Here was a part with a little weight.

"Not Cinna the conspirator but Cinna the poet," said Burbage. "You appear and are promptly killed by mistake, to show the indiscriminate bloodlust of the mob. You will do the cobbler at the beginning of the same play and Clitus or Strato at the end, I forget which. The Roman play is two weeks away, when you will also have the part of Maximus in *Love's Sacrifice*. Despite the name the part is rather small, I'm afraid. Now this week, you are to be a clownish countryman in *A Somerset Tragedy* – you can do the voice?"

9

"Why, zur, 'tis where I was born. Zummerzet is the place of my naivety, you might say."

"Good," said Burbage. "Then at some point you must be a French count and an Italian Machiavel – but not in the same play."

He raised a hand slightly as if to prevent my showing my mastery of a French or Italian accent.

"And of course you will appear in the play about the Prince of Denmark this afternoon."

"As . . . ?"

"Don't worry, Master Revill, your parts are very small, you may grasp them in twenty minutes. You will appear in the dumb-show as the poisoner, and then again as the nephew to the King—"

I felt a tightness in my chest. My eyes swam.

"But that is your . . . I mean . . . you are . . ."

The nephew to the King! Everyone knows that is the principal part in the play! Master Burbage's part. He wasn't seriously expecting me to take his role, and anyway how could I? The scroll containing the lines would run across the floor of the room we were sitting in and then all the way up the wall to the ceiling! Hardly to be learned in twenty minutes even if I prided myself on the speed with which I could seize on a part. I was about to say something of all this when Burbage caught my panicked expression.

"Ah I see," said Burbage. "No no, I don't mean that nephew to the King, I mean the nephew to the King in the play inside the play. As such you are only required to come out, look dark, and rub your hands in glee. Essentially, you are repeating the process you enacted in the dumb-show a few moments earlier."

"I have lines?"

"You unburden yourself of a handful of couplets and of the poison which you are carrying. You can play this badly because the murderer is intended to be gloating and obvious. In fact, the worse you play this part of nephew to the player King, the better. It takes skill to play badly. Deliberately badly."

"Oh," I said, obscurely disappointed, but also relieved.

"Then you are interrupted by the King, the real King. He is naturally disturbed by what he sees on stage, on the stage which we are to imagine on the real stage, that is."

"I understand," I said, and I did, now that memories of the earlier performance I'd seen were returning crisper and clearer.

"It doesn't matter whether you understand or not," said Burbage. "You're only a player. You take part but that doesn't mean you have to know what's going on."

"And what else do I have?"

"An ambassador from England comes on at the end, you will recall. Ties up a few loose ends, tells us that a couple of people have been put to death, expresses general amazement at the scene of carnage which he's stumbled into. I suggest you put on the kind of look you wore just now when you thought you were taking my part."

"At the end I don't have the last word, do I? I don't remember the ending of the play clearly."

"That is probably because you were rapt by the beauty or the wit of my own dying words as Hamlet. The last word of all goes to Fortinbras. He's going to be the next King of Denmark."

"Ah yes," I said.

"Fortinbras writes finis to our tragedy," said Burbage.

11

"I would like to have the last word one day."

"Master Revill, when did you arrive from your Zummer-zet?"

"About two years ago, Master Burbage."

"I didn't hear it in your voice until you did your, ah, imitation. I can detect it now."

"We're not all bumpkins even if we do come from the provinces."

"No, though some of us ride in on our high horses. I was born here, but our author is from Warwickshire. He rarely goes back. And the companies you've played with, again?"

"The Admiral's . . . and . . . Derby's once."

"At the Boar's Head?"

"Yes."

"You've filled in during sickness, unavoidable absence, that kind of thing – but no doubt you're looking for a company which you can permanently attach yourself to?"

"Yes."

"Nothing is permanent in this business, Master Revill. We could be closed down like that." He clicked his fingers. "Plague, the Council, commercial failure, anything could drive us out onto the road and into your bumpkin provinces."

"I want only to act," I said.

"Well, Master Revill, let me say that the Chamberlain's Men are pleased to have you for the next week or three, or until Wilson returns from attending on his poor dying mother. Now to terms. One shilling a day is your pay. Which also happens to be the fine if you are late for rehearsal, while it is two shillings for non-attendance at rehearsal, and three entire shillings if you are late and out of costume when you should be ready for the actual performance. Larger fines, very much larger fines, if you remove a costume from this play-house. Remember that costumes are worth more than players and plays put together. Some of our congregation come only to see the costumes. And if you lose your part by dropping it in the street or leaving it in the tavern or by some whore's bed you will not only be drawn and quartered but your goods forfeit. You will doubtless know this from your short time with the Admiral's, but I always like to be clear where I stand with new players."

"I understand, Master Burbage."

"Good. Now go to the tire-man for your costumes, and then to Master Allison our bookman for your parts. Just tell him you're doing Jack Wilson's. He'll understand. And before you leave this morning check the plot in there." He nodded towards the tiring-house. "You won't appear as nephew to the player-King till half past three or thereabouts this afternoon, and we start at two, so you have plenty of time before you come on, not just for your lines today but for the townsman in *A City Pleasure*. And you might as well take a look at what you're doing in *Somerset Tragedy* while you're about it. Leave the French count and the Machiavel for today. We're rehearsing *Pleasure* on Tuesday, and you can try out your Zummerzet voice on Thursday when we're running through the *Tragedy* of that county. All clear? If it's not, get the details from Allison."

"Thank you, Master Burbage. I would like to say how grateful I am to be given the chance to work with the finest—"

"Yes yes, Master Revill. We're only players, remember, caterpillars of the commonwealth – though I suppose some caterpillars are finer than others."

"You are the Queen's caterpillars," I said, referring to the

13

well-known favour enjoyed by the Chamberlain's Men at court.

"And we shall see if you are Master of the Revels, Master Revill," said Burbage, referring to the well-known civil servant who made a packet out of licensing plays.

Richard Burbage hoisted himself from his chair. Son of a carpenter, wasn't he? Well, there were good enough precedents for that. There was certainly something solid, something oak-like about him.

I visited the tire-man and was kitted out with Wilson's gear, one thing that was villainous and another thing with a showy but leftover feel to it. From the bookkeeper I received half a dozen puny scrolls giving me my lines for that afternoon and for the rest of the week. From the plot hanging up in the tiring-house for the day's business I ascertained that I joined in a dumb-show as a poisoner, and then appeared a few moments afterwards as one "Lucianus, nephew to the King", for which I was required to carry a flask (containing poison) and, presumably, a face with black looks. All as Master Burbage had said, and all as my returning memory of the tragedy of the Prince of Denmark told me. Later, much later when almost all were dead and gone, I was cued to enter the court of Elsinore with news from England of even more death. So I was a porter of death and a messenger of death, I thought neatly, trying to make a pattern out of my little roles, and then I considered that I enjoyed this good fortune only because Master Wilson was attending to a dying mother in Norfolk. But in *Julius Caesar* I was myself destined to die, playing the part of the unfortunate Cinna, the poet torn in pieces by the mob for his bad verses. The other plays I didn't know, though *Love's*

Sacrifice and *A Somerset Tragedy* by their very titles carried the promise of death dealt with an open hand.

I left the Globe, almost skipping on this fine, late summer morning. I was only sorry that Dick Burbage had not wanted to hear out my stammering gratitude. For grateful I was. Outside the playhouse in Brend's Rents, the alley behind, I glanced up at its sides, sheer white like the chalk cliff of a gorge. Like a palace, like a cathedral or a castle – this playhouse was all these to me, a place of authority and splendour. I remembered my first glimpse of it on arriving in London, fresh and green from Zummerzet. The Globe shimmered in a heat haze on the south side of the river, unmatched for height or amplitude by any building in the neighbourhood. The flag was flying and the trumpet reached my eager ears even across the great stretch of London's water, and I knew that playing was about to begin, and I wished myself, at any cost, to be one among that company. When you are near this great edifice you can see a polygon, but so multi-sided is it that, from a distance, it appears to be a fine shining ring. It is, in truth, a magic ring, in which any apparition may be conjured for the delight and the edification of what Master Burbage called the congregation. The Globe playhouse was, to me, as fabulous as Troy.

Later after my arrival, when I had been in London a few weeks and was mixing with my playing kind, I learned the extraordinary story of the construction of the Globe, how Burbage and his brother, together with the other shareholders, had—

"I'll fucking have you!"

I broke from my recollections. Someone was shouting at me. An instant more and the same someone had smashed into me. A great sweaty face was pushed into mine, foul breath shoving over the sill of his lower lip. I fell down on my back, and the great oaf tumbled on top me and panted there as if he really was fucking having me. After a time he levered himself off. From his costume I recognised a waterman. I would have known him for one anyway, partly because every third man in this borough of Southwark makes his living on the river, partly because he had that look, half sea-dog, half hang-dog, which most of them've got and which they claim comes from having served with Drake or Frobisher or the Lord High Duck or some other sea-worthy sea worthy – but mostly I would've known him for a waterman because of the flood of cursing that gushed out of his filthy lips the moment he had righted himself.

"Fucking arse-wipe – bloody fucking shite – Jesus Christ – where the fuck's the fucking fucker gone . . ."

All of this was accompanied with gusts of sour air, heaves of his great chest and rollings of eyes that did not quite swivel together, so I had the unpleasant sensation that he was looking simultaneously at, before and behind me.

"Where'd he fucking go? Why'd you let him get away, you shitting turd?"

I took a couple of deep breaths and stepped back from my panting assailant. What was going on? Instinctively I grabbed for my purse. When you come across a fracas in the street, there's a fair chance that it is a put-up job, and that the tusslers are waiting for a ring of spectators to form before the third man or woman tiptoes round the outside and relieves the more agog of whatever valuables weigh them down. When this unofficial subscription has been raised, the fight will suddenly end with a handshake and the participants magically evaporate. My purse, however, had not gone. Most likely, if the oaf had wanted to get it off me he would have done so when we were tangled on the dusty ground. Looking at his fists, which hung down like bags of meat, I thought that if he'd asked me to surrender my purse I probably would have done so with only a token protest. After all, what was money? Other things were more important, like – Jesus! – my parts in the Globe plays. My hands flew back to where I'd tucked the scrolls under my shirt, near the heart. Still there. I breathed a quick and silent prayer of gratitude to the patron saint of players (one Genesius).

"I don't know what you're talking about," I said, brushing at my clothes, and growing more angry, even as the hulk opposite me seemed to be sailing into calmer waters. "In fact, I don't know what the fuck you're talking about, to adopt your terminology."

Three or four people had stopped in the street, drawn by the prospect of trouble. The large boatman had stepped back a pace or so, and I mistook the look of bovine stupidity that was now begining to usurp his angry features for sheepishness. "And another thing," I said, foolishly deciding to demonstrate my intellectual superiority. "What did you call me . . . shitting turd I think it was?"

"So what if I did, you arse-wipe."

"Interesting example of pleonasm is that shitting turd," I said as nonchalantly as I could manage. "Pleonast, are you?"

Both of the boatman's eyes trained themselves on me more or less at once. I had said the wrong thing, been stupid by being clever at the expense of a no-wit. He took a step towards me and I stepped back. Unfortunately that was as far as I could go. Now the boatman had me between his sweaty self and a flinty wall. A few more people had assembled in the hope of seeing violence done to one who was young and blameless.

"What's a fucking pleenast when it's at home?"

He had his arm rammed across my throat so that, even if I had wanted to correct the way he said the word, I couldn't have spoken. His beard, which was as clotted as a bunch of seaweed, tickled my face. I made ineffectual attempts to push him off but he pressed himself against me, and I smelt on him a mixture of riveriness and fishitude and it was not agreeable.

"I said, you bum-sucker, what's a pleenast?"

There was a real danger that if I didn't answer, he was going to crush me as completely as a fallen mast would have. But it was all I could do to drag air through a dented windpipe, let alone produce any explanation. The fine summer morning was flecked with orange spots and there was a roaring in my ears.

"Pleenast – pleenast? Fucking tell me. I'll give you plee-nast!"

I had time to think that this was perhaps the first occasion in the history of the world that anyone had died for the sake of a little word from the Greek, and time also to consider that if I were to have my life over again then I would learn not to be so foolishly clever as to try to impress those who are, by nature, unimpressible. And I had time to think that this business of dying took too long, as the half-circle of white faces looking at this spectacle merged into a blur.

"It's a compliment," came a voice close to one of my roaring ears. "Let him go, boatman. It's a compliment. Let him go, I say."

After a moment the pressure on my throat was lifted. I was too busy forcing air inside myself to pay much attention to the exchange which followed, but was able to reconstruct it afterwards.

"When you've released him I'll tell you what he is unable to tell you himself. That's better."

"All right, you tell me then. What's a pleenast?"

There was still aggression and injury in what the boatman was saying to the newcomer but, even in my preoccupied condition, I was aware of a retreat in the man's tone, as well as an absence of fucking, shiting and arse-wiping.

"Pleonasm," said the individual who had interrupted my throttling, "is a rhetorical figure by which more words than are strictly necessary are used to express meaning. For example, if I said that you were a fine boatman as well as a good boatman and an excellent one, then I would have committed a pleonasm."

"Fine . . . good . . . excellent," said the boatman, half to himself. I noticed that the number of people about us had grown, rather than the dribbling away of a crowd which usually occurs when the promise of violence has not been fulfilled. They too were listening to the explanation of a pleonasm. Something about the man's calm and certain speech drew them, just as it pacified the boatman. I glanced at my rescuer. I'd seen him somewhere recently.

"I think that what this young man meant by calling you a pleonast is that you are a person of linguistic means – that you have a full share of that wealth of language which is available to all Englishmen whatever their class – in short you know a lot of words and it pleases you to express yourself in full – even at the risk of some repetition."

I struggled for the irony in this speech, because I was afraid that if I could detect it then the boatman would pick it up too, but not a tremor of insincerity, not a streak of piss-taking, did I hear in the other man's tones. He appeared to mean what he was saying.

"I'll say what I fucking like," said the boatman, but in a docile fashion.

"To be accused of having too many words is a fine thing," said the other. Then I realised that it was the man who had slipped unobtrusively past Master Burbage and me as we were talking by the tiring-house, the man who played the Ghost in the drama of the Prince of Denmark, "our author", Master William Shakespeare. Well, he'd certainly saved my bacon.

"He got in my way, didn't he," said the boatman to the playwright, his beard wagging in justification. "My fare did a fucking runner, saving your reverence. I'd no sooner touched the bank than the bugger was out my boat and up the stairs like a parson's fart, gone before you can sniff it. So what d'you expect a poor boatman to do? It may be only a couple of pennies to a gentleman like yourself but to me and Bet and our five kids it's our fucking dinner. Me, I can't afford to let a fare get away like that, the bastard. So I took off in hot pursuit and this bloke got between me and my quarry. And he fell down and I fell down on top of him and then he accused me of that – plea-nasty – what was it?"

"Pleonasm," said our author.

"That one. So what am I expected to do, go home to my Bet and our six kids and tell her that I was rooked out of threepence by some cunt who was too slippery for me? Jesus, I tell you, I'd be in the doghouse from Tuesday to Doomsday."

The crowd had begun to disperse, recognising the man's

whinge, no doubt, and expecting him to whip out a wooden leg gained in the sea battle of El Dago as a means of enforcing their sympathy.

"Just now you said five ki—" I started to say before the playwright threw a warning glance at me. His brown eyes didn't look so benevolent, but when he turned back to the boatman he spoke softly, almost kindly.

"I know how hard it is to earn even a modest living in these times," he said. "I know how our business depends on you boatmen. Without you, I think we would not be here."

Our author spoke the truth. There was a constant traffic to our side of the river, for the playhouses, the bears and the whores, and the single Thames bridge was convenient only for the few who lived either side of it.

"What business would that be, sir?"

"The play business."

"Beg pardon, sir, I took you for a gentleman."

Now it was my turn to take offence. Despite my having just recovered breath and wits, despite my having escaped death by a hair's width, I was ready to take up arms on behalf of my calling. But our author smiled as if he agreed with the boatman – and the common opinion was with him, it must be said – that the playhouse was no place for a gentleman to work.

"Tell me who was the first gentleman, boatman," he said.

"I'm not educated in the way of answering questions of that sort, kind or shape, sir."

Our ferryman might have no respect for players in general but he seemed prepared to make an exception for the playwright.

"Then I shall tell you, master boatman. It was Adam was the first gentleman," he said.

21

"That's my name!" said the boatman, as eager as a child.

"A happy coincidence. Your ancestor and my ancestor Adam, Adam, was a gentleman, for he bore arms. You know it is the right of a gentleman to bear arms?"

"Most infalliably, sir," said the boatman, now thoroughly mollified.

"Adam 'ad arms, one might say," said the playwright, who appeared more pleased with his words than the circumstances justified.

"How's that, sir?"

"The Scripture tells us that he digged – and could he dig without arms?"

The playwright seemed over-amused at what I considered to be only a mediocre joke. A stale one too. I was sure I'd heard it somewhere before. But whatever I thought, the words seemed to work some kind of magic on the boatman. His mouth cracked open to reveal teeth like boat-ribs, while gurgles of laughter sounded like water in the bilges.

"Very good, sir . . . dig . . . yes, how could he . . . without arms . . . very good."

"Now, Adam, take this for your lost custom, and as a mark of my general respect for your profession."

The boatman's grin remained. He didn't glance at the coins; long practice made him familiar with weight, size, number, amount. Oh, he knew a gentleman when he saw one.

"Thank you, sir. And I'm sorry if I crashed into you . . . sir." It cost him an effort to speak to me in almost the same tone that he managed with our author. "I'll remember what it was you said. What was it again?"

"Oh, pleonasm," I mumbled, thoroughly embarrassed now and wanting to be shot of him and the whole business.

"Pleenasm," said Adam, and then to my rescuer, "And if you ever need a boatman for something special, sir, you just bear your old Adam in mind."

"We should all bear our old Adam in mind," said the playwright.

"Adam Gibbons you will ask for. On either bank they know my name and face," said the boatman, and he lumbered round and headed off in the direction of the river.

"On either bank they know my name and face," repeated the playwright, giving the words a tum-ti-tum lilt. Then, "Well, Master Revill, you have come to us from the Admiral's. I can never get used to calling them Nottingham's Men."

"I, yes, I . . . thank you for helping me just then. If you hadn't come along . . . I don't know what would have happened."

The playwright shrugged and turned to go. I was taken aback: he already knew the name of an insignificant jobbing actor, as well as the company I had briefly been associated with. Also, I felt that he would have been fully entitled to lecture me on the perils of crossing swords, or paddles, with a runaway boatman. He could at least have called me a foolish young man. Yet he said nothing. I was almost disappointed.

Unwilling to have him leave me so abruptly, I caught up with him in a couple of strides. This area around the theatre was criss-crossed with ditches, a little stirred by the tidal slop of the river. Because the bridges across them were narrow, hardly more than a few pieces of planking, I was compelled to hover at my rescuer's shoulder as we traversed one little inlet after another.

"You appear this afternoon?" I said, more to make conversation than anything else. Speaking was a little painful after the boatman's assault. I visualised a red weal across my throat.

"Yes," he said. "You have Jack Wilson's parts, don't you? He makes a good ambassador in my thing today but he has not quite the look for the poisoner in the play, I mean the play inside the play. There is something a little straightforward about Wilson – although perhaps that is the best guise for a poisoner."

"King Claudius seems straightforward enough, sort of a hail-fellow-well-met sort and he's a poisoner," I said, my words tumbling over themselves in my eagerness to impress the playwright.

"You know the play?"

The same words, the same intonation as Master Burbage's. Evidently, it was surprising that a mere player should show himself capable of judging characters rather than merely *being* them.

"I saw it a couple of months ago."

I would have gone on to say something to the playwright about how magnificent he'd been in the part of the Ghost, but the fact was that, although I remembered the Ghost, I couldn't remember *him* as the Ghost, if you see what I mean.

The playwright glanced at me, and seemed to approve.

"You have more of the saturnine in your face than Wilson. Remember that you must grimace."

"Master Burbage said that I should play, as it were, badly."

Master WS appeared amused. "That's typical of Dick, I think. I'm not sure I'd give anyone the licence to play badly, as it were, or in any other way – but it's true that I have made Hamlet say something about 'damnable faces', so perhaps he is right."

"And then I am Cinna in your *Caesar*," I said.

"Which Cinna? The conspirator?"

"The poet, I believe."

"Torn for his bad verses. Alas, poor Cinna. Of course we are all poor *sinners*."

It was a moment before I grasped the pun, which the playwright stressed in case I missed it. As with the joke to the boatman about Adam and his arms, I have to confess that I found his sense of humour a bit . . . well . . . obvious.

"Like Orpheus," I said, trying to elevate the conversation.

"Who is like Orpheus?"

"Your poet Cinna. Torn to pieces by the mob, just as Orpheus was torn to pieces by the Thracian Maenads."

The reference, intended to show my nimbleness of mind and range of learning, did not appear to leave its mark upon the playwright.

"I suppose so," he said. Then, "You are lodging near here?"

"Yes, in Ship Street," I said. In fact, we were walking in the opposite direction to that in which my squalid accommodation lay. I was so reluctant to leave my rescuer's company that I pretended to be sharing his destination.

"Then you will need to go the other way."

"What – oh God, how stupid!" I clapped my hand to my head in showy forgetfulness. "Yes it's the other way."

The playwright stopped on the far side of a little ditch. Behind him was the Bear Garden. Outside was the usual crowd of loiterers and ne'er-do-wells. Somehow, I was on the opposite bank of the slimy channel.

"Till this afternoon," he said.

"You're the Ghost," I said, but he'd gone already.

*　　*　　*

"Tell Nell," said Nell.

"They're quite small parts really," I said.

"Not like this part, Nick," she said. "This one is growing larger by the second."

"That's nice," I said, distracted by what she was doing, but more excited, to be honest, about my afternoon at the Globe. "As Master Burbage says, we've all got to start somewhere."

"Master Burbage? Dick or Cuth?"

"Dick. You don't mean to say that they come to you," I said, genuinely shocked.

"It's a funny thing about that company, the Chamberlain's, or most of the older ones at any rate," said Nell. "They're different from the other companies we've had round here."

"What's funny? Tell me, and just stop that for a moment."

You can see how serious I was about my new company, that I would stop Nell just as she was getting properly started on me, so as to listen attentively to any scrap of whore's gossip about the Chamberlain's Men.

"They're pretty well all married, and every one of them's got hundreds of brats – that Heminges for instance had a dozen or more when he last looked – and normally that's a sure-fire combination, marriage and kids'll drive anyone into the stews. But not the Chamberlain's. They're either hen-pecked or limp from so much fatherhood, or – I suppose it's remotely possible—"

"What?"

"Can it be? That they actually love their wives?"

"Uxorious," I said.

"What's that mean when it's at home, clever dick?" said Nell.

"Forget it," I said. "I've already been in enough trouble

26

over words today. All right, you can go on with what you were doing earlier."

"When did you become a paying customer, Master Revill? I will go on, but on condition you do this. See?"

"Oh that's how you do it? Here?"

"Clever boy. Ah. And while you're doing that you can tell Nell about your triumphs on the stage."

"I'm a poisoner in a sort of play within the play, if you see what I mean . . ."

"No. You'll have to go back to the beginning."

"Are you comfortable?"

"Bugger comfort, get on with the job."

"It's about this Prince, see, and he's the Prince of Denmark—"

"Hamlet?"

"Yes, and he's pissed off because his father who was King has just snuffed it, and he hasn't been made King. The man who is now King is the late King's brother. Hamlet's uncle. What pisses Hamlet off even more is that the man who's mounted the throne has also mounted his mother. Hamlet's mother, that is. His uncle has married his late father's widow and has gained the throne of Denmark. What makes it worse still is that only a few weeks have gone under the bridge between the death of husband number one and the marriage to number two. There's a joke about them using the leftover food from the wake for the nuptials. Economising at Elsinore. Is that too fast for you?"

"It's good, Nick. Get on with the story."

"I meant the story. So for the first half hour Hamlet mopes around until the ghost of his father tips up on the battlements one nippy night, in fact on several nights in succession, and tells his son that he didn't die as a result of a snake-bite in his orchard – which was the story that'd been spread around – no, the serpent that took his life now wears his crown and warms his wife, sort of thing. And then ghost tells him to revenge his murder."

"Out with his sword and into his uncle? End of play?" said Nell.

"We've hardly started," I said.

"I hope so," she said.

"I meant the story. Hamlet, you see, is a thinker, not a doer, and although he rages against his uncle and vows instant vengeance he doesn't actually do anything. He wonders whether the ghost was actually the spirit of his father."

"Who else could it have been?" said Nell, her breath coming slightly short. For myself, I was finding the narrative a useful distraction from an early (and, one might say, a dishonourable) discharge.

"A devil maybe. Out to trick Hamlet. A devil in the guise of his father spinning some cock-and-bull tale about a murder so as to provoke the Prince into killing a totally innocent man."

"Sounds like a lot of trouble to go to for that."

"Hamlet is thinking, but he's not thinking straight. He's looking for reasons to avoid killing his uncle, maybe."

"So the ghost is a real ghost," said Nell. "My mother saw a ghost once."

"The ghost is real – and Claudius is guilty as sin – move down a bit."

"Claudius? Like this?"

"Uncle, King, murderer, adulterer. Yes, that's good."

"Oh, him."

"Do you want to change round yet?"

"In a moment. When you've reached the end. Of the play."

"Luckily for Hamlet, who should fetch up in the Elsinore castle at this moment but a company of players. And he has the bright idea of getting them to do a play which will mirror the way his father died and be performed in front of an unsuspecting Claudius. This play inside the play'll have a King and a Queen in it—"

"Like most plays."

"—and the Queen will swear undying love to the King, et cetera. But then the poisoner steps out and knocks off said King. That's me, poisoner. I have six lines – 'Thoughts black, hands apt, drugs fit and time agreeing' – you get the idea."

"Put one of your apt hands right here – now."

"This is the twist. The poisoner – me – is announced as Lucianus, nephew to the King."

"When it should be the brother?"

"Precisely."

"That's deep, Nick."

"Good. This is a cleverness on the part of our author which I haven't yet fathomed. Anyway, the play inside the play works because just after my entry Claudius storms off in rage. Oh! He has seen something to stir his conscience. He kneels down to pray. Hamlet comes in. Ah! Hamlet won't kill him because he wants to catch his uncle when he's gambling or pissed or in flagrante—"

"In what?"

"In this. Though, now I come to think of it, that's a bit strange – because if Hamlet was catching the King in flagrante then he'd be catching his mother at it too, and I'm not sure that he'd want that . . ."

"Dirty boy. Him . . . and you too."

"Claudius gets in a state, and sends Hamlet to England. Yes! This is after Hamlet's killed a wise old fool of a councillor who was eavesdropping behind an arras on Hamlet and his mother – in the Queen's bedchamber."

"What was Hamlet doing in his mother's bedroom? Not in flag . . . what's that word?"

"Flagrante. No, he was just giving his mother a real ear-bashing . . ."

"That's all right then."

"So our hero gets shoved off to England in the company of a couple of old schoolfriends or snakes – you sure you don't want to change round yet?"

"Get on with it."

"And of course he's right not to trust them because they're carrying a warrant for Hamlet's execution the moment they reach the English court. Oh Nell! But Hamlet never makes England. On the way his ship's attacked by pirates and he is carried off after a daring single-handed boarding of the pirate boat—"

"The groundlings enjoy a good fight."

"We don't see the fight. Just hear about it in a letter. This is where Burbage is economising. Anyway pirates aren't important, they're a device to get Hamlet back to Denmark while his schoolfriends go sailing on."

"What happens to them?"

"Chopped."

"Ah!"

"Oh!"

"Finish it, Nick."

"This is where I come in. Literally. I come in and I say what's happened to the schoolfriends at the end. But before my appearance one or two other things have occurred – entailing the complete destruction of the Danish royal court."

"Get on with it. I don't mean the story."

"Nearly at the end – don't think I can hang on for you to turn round this time – in brief – Hamlet returns – the son of the councillor he killed is revenge-mad – will do anything – specially since his sister who Hamlet fancied – has gone round the bend – because of old man's death – King Claudius sets up duel between Hamlet and this Laertes – to make sure nothing goes wrong he – he – oh Nell – Laertes puts poison on the tip of his sword – sword – sword – Jesus, that's good – and the King drops poison – into goblet of wine – Hamlet's meant to drink out of – all goes wrong – Jesus yes – Queen drinks out of goblet – drops down dead – Laertes gets stabbed own sword – but Hamlet stabbed too – before Hamlet drop dead he kill King poison sword poison goblet poetic justice all wrapped up very neat – ohNellohyesNell . . ."

"Oh Nick."

"Nell."

"But you haven't come yet, come on, I mean."

"Oh that. I forgot that for an instant. You are a lovely oblivion. Let me get my breath back. That's better. But I do appear at the last moment, see, and almost the final words in the play belong to me. As the ambassador from England I stride on stage, diplomatically but confidently, to tell Claudius that his commandment has been fulfilled to the letter. The young men bearing the warrant are dead. Hamlet, you see, switched their names for his while they were on the boat. All this doesn't make such an impression because at my feet are a dead King, a dead Queen, a dead Laertes and of course a dead Hamlet. 'The sight is dismal'."

"That's nice, Nick."

"It's a grim story."

"Your arm round me like this."

"Funny thing is the spectators are cheerful enough when it's all finished and we are in the Company, too. I've noticed before, people's spirits are often lifted by a tragedy – while our comedies can leave them thoughtful, even disgruntled."

Nell grunted something herself but she was already halfway to sleep. Hard day for her too. I wondered how many clients she'd entertained, and, as usual, struggled to stifle the thought. With her snuggled into me, and the evening light slanting on the panelled wood above my bed, I was glad to have some time to myself. I went over the afternoon in the playhouse again, like someone savouring a meal in retrospect. Naturally, I could not claim the lion's share of anything in the way of lines, attention, applause. Rather than being the lion, I was the whelp. Still, the whelp remembers, and dreams of the day when he will take his rightful place at the feast.

While I was waiting in the tiring-house, much earlier than necessary, I'd seen our author dressed as the Ghost, that is, wearing armour – for Hamlet's father's spirit is in arms to signify that there is something rotten in the state of Denmark. I had it in mind to thank him again for saving me from the boatman that morning but he looked at me vaguely as if he were already making his transition to an incorporeal state. I went back to studying my lines for *A City Pleasure*: here I had a part of substance (at least eighty lines) as a man about town, and I was grateful that there'd be a rehearsal the next morning for we had to play the very next afternoon. Jobbing actors have frequently to step into sick or absent men's shoes, and their first acquaintance with the play might be when they find themselves in front of three hundred groundlings impatient for the Company clown or tragedian.

So, to taste again my beginnings, my first course, with the Chamberlain's Men.

My very first appearance in the tragedy of the Prince of Denmark is in the dumb-show that precedes the play inside the play, as Master Burbage termed it. I am the fellow that mimes the removal of the crown of the sleeping "King" and pours poison in his ear; voicelessly, I condole with the widowed "Queen"; without a word, I make ardent love to her. I put expression into my action: the grasping hand that fondles the crown is the hand that tilts the imagined phial over the sleeper and the same hand that reaches towards the breast area of the flaxen-haired apprentice boy who is playing the player "Queen". My hand is, I feel, a speaking hand. As this takes place I observe that Claudius and Gertrude are chatting together, while on the other side of the stage Hamlet is all eyes. I realise that Claudius must not understand too soon what is happening. And I see how tidily our author has, as it were, comprised all audiences in this royal audience: one half is always more interested in its own affairs even as the other forgets itself in the action. I do not notice this at the time but only as I think about it afterwards, lying in my bed next to my whore Nell. Then the riches of this play are laid open for me, right after Nell has laid herself open for me, and my unsleeping brain at once wants to throw a bridge across these two kinds of understanding or knowing . . . but I can make nothing of this at the moment.

After the dumb-show I reappear as Lucianus, nephew to the "King". And this is something else that baffles me, that I should play the nephew. But none of this matters because I am upstaged by the King Claudius rushing off, crying out for light. And we "players" are about to slink away because it is evident that we have displeased the King (the real King, that is), and then my lord Hamlet wrings our hands and claps our shoulders because we have pleased *him* greatly. And this is the fortune of the player in little! Up and down like a bucket in a well. Today a Claudius, tomorrow a Cassius, that's the way of it. In the tiring-house once more, after I've conned *A City Pleasure* I make a pretence of studying my part in *A Somerset Tragedy.* Here I am a rustic boor. But I am really observing my fellows in the Chamberlain's Company, and learning to put names to faces: Master Phillips, for example, or Cowley or Gough or Pope.

And before I know it I am out again as the ambassador from England, come with the news that Hamlet's old schoolfriends Rosencrantz and Guildenstern are dead. But, as I'd said to Nell, this doesn't go for much when rather more significant characters have bitten the dust. This time I am upstaged by Hamlet's one genuine friend, Horatio, who informs the newcomer Fortinbras that he alone has the truth to tell. And now Fortinbras, who writes finis to the play, takes charge of everything, including the throne of Denmark. His first and last royal act is to order a military funeral for Hamlet. Then, like in most plays, we end with a little dance so that everyone goes off happy to their next diversion. The sun is shining behind the tower and tiring-house which throw their shadows across the groundlings and the lower seats. Hats bob, tobacco smoke weaves its way upwards, limbs are flexed in time with us as we jig on stage. The spectators make their dispositions.

Nell stirred and rolled away from me slightly. I took advantage of this to get up for a piss in the jerry in the corner of the room. Sometimes after I'd been with Nell I washed my equipment in wine – there was no insult to her in it, she'd told me herself of this method of prophylaxis. Once I'd tried vinegar, but once only. Hard pissing being also recommended as a defence against the perils of venery – and in the absence of a jug of white wine – I pushed the stream out with all the force I could muster. Then, bare-assed as Adam, I went to stand by the window.

My room was on the third floor of Mistress Ransom's. She was a pale, crabbed woman and kept a filthy establishment whose only merit was its cheapness. By contrast the brothel where Nell toiled was quite spick and span. Mistress Ransom claimed to be scandalised by the proximity of the whore-houses, playhouses and taverns, and went round with a how-I've-come-down-in-the-world air. She kept her nose canted up. This enabled her to overlook the filth underfoot and also indicated that she was somehow gazing at a higher social shelf from which she'd been dislodged by a brutish world. When she discovered I was a parson's son, she could hardly wait to offer me a room. She was a little disappointed when I added that I was a player. In atonement, I made the mistake of hinting that my father'd left me a little fortune (said in such a way as to suggest that little was large) and that I was only toying with the stage. I wanted to ingratiate myself; I needed a cheap room. The fortune my father had left me was little indeed and now almost exhausted.

Mistress Ransom overcame her objections to players, how-ever, within a day or two of my arrival. She loosed her daughter on me. Where old Ransom was pale, young Ransom was on fire. Young Ransom had perhaps twenty nine years to her debit. Her flaming red hair was matched by her flaring face. The bumps and lumps on it flickered like embers. The husband of Mistress Ransom was dead, I was given to understand, though I suspected he had merely decamped. Dead or fled, he must have had a fiery trade, as cook, baker or smith, and stamped its impress on his daughter. Little Ransom, who was twice her mother's size, came to my room on various pretences:

i) to see if I needed anything;
ii) to know if I would take supper with her and her mother that night (an invitation, she was careful to tell me, not extended to any old lodger);
iii) to find out whether I'd recovered from the runs after said supper;
iv) to tell me the house was haunted (it was – by her);
v) to request a light (for her candle had blown out on the stairs and she was left darkling);
vi) to ask me to investigate the curious noise in the corner of her chamber.

On each successive visit she revealed a little more of herself by a careless disarray of day- or nightwear, beginning with scarlet shoulders and proceeding by way of ruddy breasts to hints of the fiery pit down below. I knew that it was her mother who had set her on, because the daughter kept me in conversation at my door as her eyes swung about, waiting for the ordeal to be over. Give him five minutes trying to catch sight of your nipples, Mistress Ransom had said, and see if he doesn't succumb to those ripening blackberries. She was too genteel or too unpoetic to express it like that, but there would be an understanding between mother and daughter as the former artfully rearranged the latter's stays, ties and laces before sending her up the stairs. Alas, the goods that she was displaying had lain much too long in the sun. I pitied Little Ransom, saw her as a sacrificial cow to her mother's matrimonial plans, but a cow nonetheless.

The crisis came when I went to her chamber to investigate that curious sound in the corner. Before I could even get near the dark (and silent) corner, she launched herself on me, hugely afire, and I went down before the smoke, flame and stench of her cannon. But, like Falstaff at the battle of Shrewsbury in our author's play of *Henry IV*, I considered that discretion was the better part of valour. I played dead, or asphyxiated. I lay limp. Poor little Ransom lay on top of me like an army that has overrun its adversary, only to find that the enemy has disappeared. She needed some trophy to take back to her mother to prove that she had indeed occupied my position. A consummation devoutly to be wished. A promise of marriage made in hot breath and blood. But all her rummaging and groping couldn't produce a spark, and at length she was forced to retire, whole and unwounded. We avoided each other's eyes. I was still sorry for her, and angry at the mother who I knew had set her on. I made one or two references to Madam Ransom, and stews and houses of ill-repute, in her hearing. She got the point. The daughter's attentions ceased. But I earned the mother's undying hostility, and if it hadn't been for the fact that she needed the couple of shillings rent a week she would have booted me into the street.

And now I gazed down into Ship Street, suddenly melancholy. *Post coitu omne animale triste est . . .* as the poet says. The evening sun rested on the roofs opposite, and caused me to squint. If I had craned out I would have been able to see the river, but I was Adam-naked and anyway saw the river frequently enough. Down below I could just glimpse my landlady taking the evening air, with her nose tilted up, as if she were too good for this world, possibly too good for any world. Lounging in the street opposite was Nat the Animal Man, so called because he made a tiny living from dropping into taverns and imitating a horse's whinny, a cat's purrs. For a penny he would do you a tormented bear surrounded by the yapping dogs in the pit, the climax to the whole battle proceeding from one man's mouth. I have even heard him mimic the strange cry of the camel which one pays to see in that house on London Bridge.

I stepped back from the window and felt Nell's hand on my shoulder and her breasts in the small of my back. She rubbed herself against me, then squatted down to pee in the jordan. What our author might have termed the Old Adam I felt rise at what I saw, and no doubt at the aroma too of our mingled wastes. And when Nell saw what I felt, my hoisted sail, a pleased expression tugged at her full lips. The object of many men's lust, and of the affection of a few, she reserved her love for me or so I thought. I put this down partly to my natural attractiveness but also to the fact that she came from the same part of the country as I. We were country lad and lass in London, both engaged in diverting the citizenry with our arts. I returned to my bed, a little small to accommodate the both of us but so much the better for any purpose apart from sleep. Too late I saw what Nell was about to do.

"No!"

"What's wrong? No one can see."

It was true that she was standing near the window without a stitch on. The lower part of her body was shadowed. The declining sun set her fair hair ablaze. Probably she could have been seen from the houses over the way. I wasn't bothered about that. Her left arm was extended over the edge of the window. She was holding the jordan, delicately tipping its contents into the street. Sleepiness or the mistaken belief that no one was down below had caused her not to check or shout the customary warning. I heard the dribble of the emptying pot, I saw the golden liquid catch the evening light. I heard the noise of my landlady. The shriek as she felt the wet descent, the scream as she realised what it was. I shut my eyes. I heard a donkey's bray, and realised after a moment that it was Nat the Animal Man, taking pleasure in Mistress Ransom's discomfiture, and most probably in mine as well, after his own fashion.

A City Pleasure, which was composed by one Master Edgar Boscombe (a name not previously known to me as one of the literary adornments of our stage), is a simple business. You know the story, or one similar to it. A young man from the provinces comes to London with his sister, looking for pleasure and edification. They are duped and gulled, but retain a curious integrity. The pleasure of the city is to ride them until they drop. They return home, sadder, wiser and poorer – only to discover that they never were brother and sister. They may marry; and they will marry. That was as much as I gathered from my eighty-five-line acquaintance with the drama. Unlike *Hamlet* I had never seen *A City Pleasure* through as a spectator. I played John Southwold, a citizen with ambitions to become an alderman and therefore I had to talk pompously and unplainly. There was no love lost between the players' companies and the City authorities, who were as much our enemies as the Puritans, and would have closed us down if their writ ran on this side of the river. So we seized any opportunity to take the piss, and I played the would-be alderman with satisfied self-importance.

The congregation in the afternoon was large, though not as large as for Master WS's *Hamlet* the previous day. I was preoccupied. My excitement at becoming one of the Chamberlain's Men, even if only temporarily, was overshadowed by the pressing need to find fresh accommodation. After Nell had emptied our piss over Mistress Ransom last fine evening, the landlady appeared at my door, still dripping and distinctly out of sorts. Nell was hiding under the bedcovers. Gallantly, I took the blame, along with my notice to quit. So it was goodbye to my pale landlady and her fiery daughter. For that relief, much thanks.

I could hardly put up with Nell at her place of work (*videlicet* a brothel), although she offered this, slightly reluctantly and in a spirit of contrition. There were, she said, holes and corners in Holland's Leaguer where I might shelter for a few days. But I did not, in truth, like to enquire too closely into the manner in which Nell earned her keep, and to be near her daily busy self would turn me into the hungry innkeeper forced always to see his meat eaten by others.

The problem of where I was to lay my head was solved, however, and most strangely, in the following way.

I made three appearances in *A City Pleasure*, two of them early on, and it was after the second of these that I was approached in the tiring-house by a member of our Company, Master Robert Mink.

"Master Revill? Are you on again soon?"

I shook my head. I wasn't due on for the better part of an

hour, to judge from the rudiments of my part I'd gleaned in that morning's rehearsal. In fact, I thought the gaps between my appearances unduly protracted, yet at all times I was mindful of what Seneca the tragedian said: "It is with life as it is with a play – it matters not how long the action is spun out, but how good the acting is." Master Mink's chins nodded at my head-shake. He was a fat man, yet surprisingly nimble. I had seen him moments before on the stage show the young couple who were not brother and sister how to cut a London caper. Now he pushed in my direction a piece of paper which was pincered between forefinger and thumb.

"Good. I have to enter again in a moment. Would you do me a favour, Nick?"

As a temporary member of the Company I wasn't in a position to refuse. I looked helpful.

"There's a lady in one of the boxes I wish to communicate with, but not to speak to. I wonder whether you'd be so kind as to convey this note to her. It's the seventh box along on the right. She will be the only lady there."

Costumed as I was, I made my way up the stairs to the galleries, wondering about the contents of the sealed note. Yet not really wondering at all. Despite what Nell had said about the restraint and the marital constancy of the Chamberlain's Men, there are always a few in any company who liked to spread their favours freely, and Master Mink had the air of one who basked in the assurance that women liked him. That is, he was fat and courtly.

The passage round the back of the gallery was empty. The doors to the boxes were shut. The quality resided here. From behind the first one came a clink of glasses and a giggle. Obviously there were other pleasures in the city than that

41

provided by the drama unfolding down below on stage. I was taking care to count my doors, not wanting to enter in on the wrong woman, or man, when from the fourth or fifth door along two figures suddenly burst out. A fellow in a leather jerkin and loose breeches collided with the opposite wall of the narrow little passage and then cannoned into me. Being barged into was becoming a regular occurrence, and I had my dignity as a player to consider. I stuck my foot out and he fell sprawling. Behind him was another man in a short black cloak, and wearing a tall black hat.

"Get him! Hold him!" he hissed.

Obligingly I knelt in the small of the big fellow's back. He groaned but made no effort to get away. Black Cloak knelt down beside me and ran his hands over the fallen man's jerkin.

"Ah, I thought so."

He held up a necklace that, to my inexperienced eye, looked valuable.

"Ungrateful bastard, Jacob," he said slowly and deliberately to the man who was face down on the floor. "And after the kindness of Sir Thomas and his lady towards you."

The other made a gurgling sound but still said nothing. Black Cloak looked at me and my evident costume. He had a long nose which was as sharp as a razor.

"You're a player?"

"I have a message to deliver." I was still holding Master Mink's billet doux.

"Never mind that. Sir Thomas will want to thank you in person for stopping this fellow from getting away."

He urged the man to his feet, tugging at his arm. I took the other and, like a couple of constables, we escorted him back along the passage. He was a lumbering individual, with a scrawny beard, almost a head taller than I. As we neared the door of the box from which these two had so abruptly exited, Black Cloak reached up and cuffed him about the head. This seemed unnecessary since he was as docile and cowed as a whipped bear. We crowded through the entrance to the box. Two men were sitting watching the stage. Beside them sat an attractive woman with an oval face and golden hair that reminded me a little of my whore Nell's. The dress of these individuals showed their wealth: the woman, for example, was wearing a jewel-encrusted farthingale and a low decolletage that uncovered a fine cleavage, a mode that was usually the sign of an unmarried woman. Seeing them watching the play down below, I was reminded that I was part of *A City Pleasure*, and no part at all of whatever was occurring among these spectators. I must return to the tiring-room within a few minutes. I cursed Master Mink for sending me to deliver the note now stuffed into a pocket. The older of the two men in the box glanced in our direction but he appeared little concerned with whatever had taken place in the box or outside in the corridor.

"Now, Sir Thomas, he is here," said Black Cloak to the older of the seated men, pushing forward the bear-like fellow into the centre of the little room. At the same time he flourished the necklace in a way that I can only describe as theatrical. The woman's hand went slowly, almost in a caress, up to her throat.

"I saw Jacob slip this from my lady's white neck" – he waved the pearl necklace so that it looked like a stream of milk – "oh so closely while all of you were attending to the play. He's a cunning one. He possesses subtle pickers and stealers for all his size. I saw it all from where I was standing behind you. How did he think that he would get away with it?"

In demonstration, Black Cloak seized the right hand of the larger man in his left and held it up to display to the others. I had the impression that, if he could, he would have detached each of the large man's blunt fingers and passed them around in proof of what he was saying. Yet I could see nothing delicate in these fingers that were supposed to have stolen. I stood, uneasily, at the rear of the box, puzzled because the large man made no attempt to wrest his hand away from the other's grasp. Nor did he speak. He merely hung, crestfallen, in the centre of this little group.

"He saw that I had witnessed all of it," continued the man in the black cloak. "My eyes are everywhere, you know, in your service, Sir Thomas. He tried to get away. I followed him out and, by good fortune, this gentleman was coming along the passage. Our friend Jacob bumped into him and fell. I overcame him and recovered the necklace."

Again he flourished the milky chain. The whole report was delivered in a clipped, dry style as if Black Cloak were recounting some military skirmish in which he had been modestly victorious.

"This gentleman is one of the players," he added.

I bowed slightly, and gave my name. Whatever the circumstances, I saw no reason why these good folk should not be acquainted with Master Nick Revill.

None of the three occupants of the box had yet spoken. Now the one who had been addressed as Sir Thomas stood up and came forward. I was aware of the play proceeding below, the buzz of voices, the answering laughter and noises of approval from the groundlings. These boxes were designed for privacy and whatever drama was taking place here would not touch on the absorbed attention of the rest of the audience.

"This is a sorry state of affairs, Jacob," said Sir Thomas, "and after I had kept you in my household."

He was, like Black Cloak, shorter than Jacob and had to look up into the thief's face. But he had an air of authority and spoke with easy assurance. I wasn't able to judge the expression on Jacob's face but I saw the shake of his head.

"What's the matter, Jacob?" said Sir Thomas. "Are you trying to deny what Master Adrian is saying? Much better to come clean over this business now."

The big man continued to move his head slowly from side to side, and I understood then that he was dumb. Bear-like not only in size and the colouring of hair and beard, but also in his inability to articulate his predicament. The man with the black cloak, who was apparently called Adrian, glanced at me, as if wanting a confirmation of everything which he had described. I knew that I should have to return to the stage within a few minutes. Although I couldn't have said exactly how I knew it, I knew too that Adrian was lying. Everything he'd said from beginning to end was false. There was something glib in his speech, and in the way he had protested too much. If he had been on stage, one would have perceived immediately that within this figure – with his black clothing, his showy gestures and his overstatement – lurked the villain. Most probably, it was he who had taken the necklace, and the hulking Jacob who'd pursued him through the door, rather than the other way about. The passage was so narrow and the two men so close that such a confusion between pursuer and pursued might have occured. Then, when the large man collided with me, Adrian – seeing it was all up with the robbery and needing a story to channel suspicion from himself – spotted his opportunity. He pretended to find the stolen item in the other's jerkin, having placed it there during his rummaging.

All this I saw in an instant, and yet I had not a shred of proof.

We must have made an odd tableau, standing or seated as if all six of us were blocked for the stage and waiting for someone to tell us what to do next. Although Adrian, whom I supposed to be some kind of steward in this household, had named another and lower servant as a thief, it did not seem to me as though the others were ready to act on his accusation. I noticed that the woman was looking at Jacob more in bafflement than anger. Her hand remained at her neck. The necklace dangled from Adrian's grasp, as if reluctant to be loosed. For some reason, this confirmed his guilt in my eyes. For certain, it was he who had filched the necklace; if Adrian had recovered it from Jacob's clothing, as he had mimed doing outside the box, he would by now have handed it back to the lady. There is a taint in stolen goods and no honest man will hold on to them. Sir Thomas turned to the second man who had remained seated. He was younger, a pale-faced individual dressed in black.

"What do you think, William?"

"I think that this gentleman from the players could say more if he wished."

He looked steadily at me. Sir Thomas nodded.

"No doubt. You have heard what Adrian has told us, Master . . . forgive me, you said your name was . . . ?"

"Nicholas Revill."

"Master Revill. Is this how it appeared to you?"

"I saw what I saw. These two men exited from your box in some confusion. One stumbled into me, the other recovered that necklace from him. I think."

Jacob now turned towards me. His large brown eyes were blank; he expected no favours from me or from anybody. His helpless air would have moved a savage to pity. And it may be, too, that a dumb man will remind a player of the treasury of his tongue, and cause him to thank God for giving him all his faculties complete. Adrian's razor nose quivered. He continued to hold up the necklace as damning evidence of the other servant's guilt. Rings glittered on his fingers.

"Well, Jacob," said Sir Thomas. "I fear I have no alternative but to to have you escorted to the Clink."

The Clink is one of half a dozen or so prisons in Southwark. Our lawlesslessness is well provided for.

"No," I said.

There was a pause while everyone swallowed the enormity of my contradicting Sir Thomas.

"No?" he said.

"I mean," I added hastily, "that Jacob did not steal this lady's necklace."

Like Caesar, I had crossed the Rubicon. No stepping back. I was about to be exposed as a fool, and a malicious fool at that.

"Explain, if you would," said Sir Thomas.

"Master Adrian, give me your hand if you please."

I spoke with all the assurance of the budding alderman that I played in *A City Pleasure*. Thinking of which, I glanced down towards the stage. Well, this too was a kind of act. Hurry.

The steward with the black cloak glanced at Sir Thomas, who shrugged, but in such a way as to indicate that Adrian should comply. Adrian held out his left hand, raising his eyes heavenward. He was a good player, perhaps a more subtle villain than I had at first assumed, but I was the better player, and, knowing this, I felt a sudden gust of certainty sweep through me. I gestured at the other hand, the one grasping the necklace. Even now unwilling to lay down the string of pearls, he transferred it to his left. I took his free palm between mine. It was a narrow, dry hand, and that must signify something . . . everything that we have signifies, everything is pregnant with indication. And now I was about to draw conclusions from this hand or, rather, from its accessories.

He wore several rings. From under one of them I slid something out. I walked over to where the woman sat by the rail of the box, no longer even pretending to watch the play.

"Forgive me, my lady," I said. I pulled taut what I held in my hand. It was a thread of hair. I placed it near her ladyship's golden, unbonneted head, trying to angle the single thread so that it caught the light. The hair was a match, or close enough for my purposes. The four men – Sir Thomas, the younger William, bear-like Jacob, and the sharp-nosed Adrian – held me with their eyes as attentively as if I were an alchemist who had just effected that magical transformation of base material into gold.

"This was under the ring on his middle finger," I said. "As you can see, it is from my lady's head."

I left the connection for them to make.

"This is absurd, a piece of playing," said Adrian. "What is he saying? He is saying nothing."

He still held the necklace, but I think that he would have been willing enough to get rid of it now.

William spoke. "This gentleman from the players is saying, I believe, that you removed the necklace, and as you did so a hair from my mother's head was caught between the ring and your finger."

William's words clarified slightly the relationship between the occupants of the box. Even so, the lady hardly looked old enough to have a son in his twenties. From my vantage point, a little to one side and above where she sat, I saw nothing but a head of gold untarnished by the years. Unlike many ladies of rank – unlike, for instance, our beloved Queen (whom I saw three days after I arrived in London, and from a mere eight yards off) – she wore no wig but rested content and justified in what Nature provided. Furthermore, her partly uncovered breasts were full and smooth and white. If she was William's mother, then presumably Sir Thomas was his father.

"Do you know what happened, Alice?" said Sir Thomas, appealing to her.

"I am not sure. I felt nothing." Her voice was low and resonant. "But this should be simple enough to prove. Let Jacob steal the necklace again. If he can take it once then he can surely take it twice. Give it to me, Adrian."

The steward, who now appeared to wish himself anywhere but in this box in the playhouse, returned the necklace to Lady Alice. Swiftly she reclasped it around the white pillar of her neck. Now she was the centre of the scene, and we five men mere bystanders.

"I am looking at this play once more, this – what's it called . . .?"

"*A City Pleasure*," I said.

"I am absorbed in *A City Pleasure*. I am all ears and eyes on the stage. The back of my neck is bare, save for the necklace, and I am quite undefended. You may do what you please with me."

She still spoke softly, but as she described what she was doing she suited the word to the action and, becoming a rapt spectator, bent her head slightly forward to expose the upswept golden hair and the contrasting snowy white skin and the clasp of the necklace.

"Now, Jacob," she said in a tone that was almost kindly. "You must remove this necklace from my neck. You must try your best."

Sir Thomas pushed gently at the hapless Jacob who, until this point, had been standing in the centre of the box. Slow and worried as he was, he nevertheless understood what he had to do. He shuffled a couple of paces forward to where my lady Alice was leaning over the balustrade. She gave no sign of being aware of anything except the play unfolding below. Jacob stretched out his arms, then seemed to realise that this was more a job for dexterity than force. He looked at his large hands, and tried to flex his fingers but they were quivering so much that he could get no control over them. These great paws, covered on the backs with reddish hair, approached the pale column of his mistress's neck, and he had the wit to realise that this was a kind of sacrilege, as well as the simplicity not to be able to conceal it. In the middle of her bare nape glowed the intricate clasp that secured the pearl necklace.

I glanced at the others. Sir Thomas was watching his ungainly servant advance on Lady Alice. Her son, the black-suited William, who had still not risen from his seat in the other corner of the box, was dividing his attention between the tremulous thief and Adrian. The latter had positioned himself near to the door. The steward caught my eye and shot me a look as sharp as his nose. It was apparent that he held me responsible for this little scene, even though this part had been his mistress's suggestion. His own version of events would have seen Jacob safely on his way to the Clink by now.

Jacob's hands arrived at Lady Alice's neck. They were shaking uncontrollably. For all her self-control, the woman tensed as she felt his fingers scraping and scrabbling at the clasp. After a few moments Jacob turned to look at his master, Sir Thomas. I do not think that I have ever seen such a combination of helplessness and entreaty. He made some strangulated sound in his throat. But speech here was quite unnecessary. All of our actions speak, and his dumbness was pitifully eloquent. Sir Thomas nodded, and Jacob let his huge hands drop to his sides.

Nobody spoke. It was quite evident to every person in that little room that Jacob could never have taken Lady Alice's necklace. For one thing, he was far too clumsy, barely capable of undoing the catch even had it been around his own neck and his hands absolutely steady. Certainly, he could not have performed the trick without her noticing. But a stronger reason was that his every movement, his every gesture, showed that he lived with a respect that amounted almost to reverence for this man and woman, his master and mistress. We had all witnessed how his hands shook as they drew close to her neck, how reluctantly his feet had dragged across the oak flooring of the box. He was attempting to be a thief only at the command of Sir Thomas and the Lady Alice. If they'd told him to leap out of the box into the area where the groundlings stood

51

below, he most likely would have obeyed. Nor was this a matter of acting. He was too stupid to act, but he was also – and this I saw suddenly – too *good* to act anything. Jacob was simply what he was, a single man and nothing more. For the rest of us in that box I cannot speak; we might all have been players, and even the poorest of players is a double man.

The silence was broken by Adrian. (I mean the silence in our little box, for all the time during this interlude the buzz and hum of stage business floated up to our unlistening ears.) But before he spoke, he smiled. A little lop-sided grin. Like Jacob he had a kind of wit, in his case the wit to realise that he was cornered.

"Player is clever," he said. "Player knows his business, as I hope I know mine."

I felt chilled, even though the afternoon was warm and I was sweating in my heavy town costume. But there was guilt in his words and in his crooked smiling face. Now Sir Thomas spoke, but with a peculiar reluctance which I attributed to the difficult task which confronted him.

"Adrian, this is not the first time in which you have been detected in some malpractice. Coming at this particular time of difficulty, when we have looked to you for integrity, what you have attempted to do – to your lady Alice, to poor Jacob – is unforgivable. I am mindful of the good service you have performed for this family over the years, and for that reason I will not set the law on you."

He paused, and I had time to be surprised at his leniency.

"But you will leave our company and this box now, and if ever I or any member of my household discovers you within our precincts again, then I will not hesitate to turn you over to justice."

"There are things I could say," said Adrian. "To you, Sir Thomas, and you Lady Alice and even to young William, but this is not the time or the place. To the gentleman player here" – the way in which he spoke indicated that such a description was for him a contradiction in terms – "I wish that he may always have such, ah, easy spectators for his performances, such eyes that are quick to believe, such ears as are quick to trust. *His* presence you are unable to bar me from. I can have him before me at any time by paying a penny and standing with the common people."

He slid from the box, with his short black cloak and his black hat somehow seeming to swell, an exit performed with as much relish as if he were taking the devil's part in some old Morality Play.

"Are you all right, my dear?" said Sir Thomas, turning attentively towards Lady Alice.

"Perfectly," she replied.

Sir Thomas patted Jacob on the shoulder in an avuncular way. This bear of a man appeared hardly to have recovered from the sacrilege of attempting to slip the pearls from his mistress's neck.

"I must thank you, Master Revill, for your part in exposing Adrian. It is of course obvious now that Jacob could never have taken my wife's necklace, but sometimes we need the obvious pointed out to us. Thank you."

I inclined my head slightly, grateful at his gratitude. Sir Thomas went to the door of the box, perhaps to check that the steward really had gone. Lady Alice beckoned me to her side. Her voice dropped even lower so that I had to bend forward to hear her. No hardship because I was only inches from the snowy slope of her breasts.

"I must thank you too," she whispered. "And I believe you have something to deliver to me."

I suddenly remembered the note from Master Robert Mink which had brought me up to the gallery in the first place. So this was the lady it was intended for! I fumbled in a pocket of my costume and passed it across. This was half secret and half open business. Her son, who had remained sitting in the opposite corner of the box, most likely saw the transfer. He had made no comment so far on what had transpired.

"Are you due to appear again?" he said. "I mean in this piece down below? Your part is surely not yet concluded."

"Jesus God!"

For the sake of the drama that had been staged in Sir Thomas's box I had forgotten the real drama in which I was appearing on the Globe stage. Jesus, perhaps I'd missed my cue. I thought of Master's Burbage's three-shilling fine. I thought more feelingly of the disgrace – the unprofessionalism – of missing one's entrance. My very brief career with the Chamberlain's Men rolled up and vanished before my eyes.

But I made it. I returned to the tiring-room moments before my final entry as the would-be alderman in *A City Pleasure*. Fresh from my private triumph in the box of Sir Thomas and his Lady, I gave my all. I was the foolish townsman John Southwold, who showed, by the absurdity of his language and gestures, that the hapless brother and sister (who weren't brother and sister) would be better off away from the falsity of the city. Only in a rural setting does virtue flourish. I have observed, by the way, that although many of our poets and satirists are ready to attack the town for its blackness and corruption, and to praise the country for its Arcadian innocence, few indeed of those same poets and satirists are willing to live up to their words and exchange the taint of corruption for the fruit of innocence. In short, they show no great desire to go out to grass.

My part in *A City Pleasure* was not that large but I flatter myself that my performance, with its little twists and flourishes, went down well with the groundlings (who always enjoy laughing at their betters) as well as with the quality (who are pleased enough to watch some upstart guyed upon the stage). Robert Mink looked at me afterwards in a puzzled way. No doubt he was wondering just why I had been absent on his errand for so long. But I merely nodded; I had done what he requested and saw no reason to unravel the confused business that had occurred in the gallery box. If he was friendly with Lady Alice – as the note presumably signified – then he would find out about everything soon enough, if she chose to tell him.

Later, sitting in the Goat & Monkey, I pondered on my role not just in the drama on stage but in the business in Sir Thomas's box. I considered that I had tilted the scales in favour of justice. True, I had my thumb in the pan. A little "unfair" but . . . There was no doubting that Adrian the steward was a nasty piece of work, while Jacob was a good-hearted, loyal and simple fellow. It is not often that right prevails. As for the steward's threats, I had no fear of those. I felt protected, secure. I had won the approval and thanks of a wealthy man and his wife, Sir Thomas and Lady Alice Eliot. I was, albeit temporarily, a member of the most prestigious company of players in London. My Nell provided for me free, and lovingly, what other men had to pay for, lovelessly. I was energetic, and as near being immortal as a sound head, lungs and limbs can make you at the age of twenty six.

This is the moment when fortune crouches lower as she prepares to pounce.

"How did you do it?"

It was William Eliot, Lady Alice's son. He slipped onto the bench beside me.

"Do what?"

"The trick with the hair. Dextrous."

"Ah," I said, and was glad to be given time to think by a tapster's interruption asking what we wanted.

"Tell me," said William, after he had ordered a tankard for himself and another for me. "It doesn't matter now, and Adrian was obviously guilty. So the right thing has occurred by indirection."

He was echoing my own thoughts.

"Do you, for example, carry around a stock of head-hair for just such an eventuality? It certainly wasn't one of your own. Yours is coal-black."

"It was from your mother's youthful head."

"The others may have been fooled," said William, "but I was sitting closer and the thread of hair you were holding was not hers. I know my mother's hair well. Quite a different tint."

"You're right," I said. "The hair wasn't your mother's. It belonged . . . to someone else. There were a few threads on my shirt under the costume I was wearing. I noticed them by chance as I was changing into it this afternoon. I suppose I didn't remove them because the thought of having some threads of this person's hair about me was pleasing. Nobody could see them. I'm not sure that I thought about it at all. But it was chance, pure good fortune, that the colour was close to your mother's."

"Then you pretended to discover it under one of the steward's rings, took it over to where my mother was sitting – and invited us all to jump to the wrong conclusion?"

"As you said yourself, the steward was guilty," I said, a little uneasily. "After all he admitted it, as good as admitted it."

"Yes, yes. I don't quarrel with my uncle dismissing him. Adrian is more fortunate than he deserves to be. He might be in jail. I was curious how you came to produce a hair that came from somewhere else, from someone else – and now you've told me."

"Now I've told you."

"It was a sleight of hand."

"Only a trick," I said, anxious to move the conversation on, perhaps anxious to rid myself of this superior young man's company.

"And I am interested too in the justice of tricking the truth out of someone."

"I imagine that those men in the Tower who have a confession wrung out of them on the rack would rather be 'tricked' into the truth, as you put it, if they were given the choice."

"I don't doubt it," said William. "I am more concerned with the idea in the abstract."

"Oh, the abstract."

"Suppose that there is a fixed quantity of truth, and that every word of ours, every action, great or little, adds to or subtracts from this quantity. This pile of truth. This truth-mountain. Our steward has been dishonest, he has stolen from my mother and then attempted to pass the blame for the crime onto Jacob. This cluster of false words and actions obviously represents a great subtraction from our truth-mountain. A veritable weight. But then you come along, and to establish what has occurred you pass a little falsehood among the rest of us. You pretend that a thread of hair from your sister—"

"Hardly my sister!" I protested, irritated at the man's high-handed manner.

"No, of course not. I must have been thinking of that play we saw this afternoon, where the brother and sister turn out not to be be brother and sister after all. What a transparent device to produce a happy ending! I do not think we shall hearing too much more of the author of that. Who was he again?"

"A Master Edgar Boscombe, I believe."

"I prefer Master Shakespeare myself. His plots are much closer to truth, however ridiculous they seem on the surface. Also he shares my given name. What was I saying? Oh yes. The hair that was secreted about your person. Well, if it didn't derive from your sister, it was from your wife or your mistress, it doesn't matter which. I don't think it was a boy's hair."

He waited an instant for me to respond. I said nothing.

"You do not look like a lover of boys, even though you are a player. My point is this. Your action in pretending that it was Lady Alice's, my mother's, also represents a tiny subtraction from the great mountain of truth."

"And you're making a mountain out of a molehill," I said. "What I did was to commit a little falsehood in order to secure a greater truth."

"Ah, so you are simultaneously taking away and adding to the truth-mountain," said William. "I wonder, is that possible? I enjoy speculating on these things."

"Very Jesuitical," I sneered, then looked round to make sure no one was within earshot. It was not a good idea to use that word in a public place. But Master William Eliot seemed in no way discomposed. Thoughtfully, he drained off the last of his drink.

"Anyway, I don't know what you're talking about," I said. "I'm just a player."

"A simple man and so on."

Somehow he managed to turn everything into a jibe or a sly insult. I determined not to rise to it.

"If you like. You said just now that Sir Thomas was your uncle?"

"Yes."

"But he's married to the Lady Alice?"

"My father is dead. After my father died, my uncle married my mother. This happened quite recently, as you may have been able to tell from his attentive manner towards her in the playhouse box."

The tapster came across again to take our orders, and one of those natural pauses ensued while the tankards were brought. I took the opportunity of examining William as he sipped at his beer. He was a tall, thin man, about my age or a little older. (Which would put his beautiful mother in at least in her mid-forties, assuming that she had borne him early.) He had an inward-looking, melancholic air about him. His clothes were a fashionable black.

"You are in mourning for your father?" I asked.

"'Tis not alone my inky cloak, good mother,
Nor customary suits of solemn black . . ." he began.

". . . I have that within which passes show –
These but the trappings and the suits of woe." I con-cluded.

We laughed in recognition.

"You know the play?" he said.

"I was in the play yesterday. Small parts, you understand."

"This is for my father in a sense," said William, indicating his black clothing, "because he did die recently. But I don't believe I bear my uncle any grudge for marrying my mother, and I don't despise my mother for choosing another husband, though one can never quite plumb the depths of one's own mind in matters like these. My uncle is a good and shrewd man, I think. He is certainly a shrewd one. And a lenient one too, as you saw this afternoon when he allowed Adrian the steward to go scot-free. My mother is a woman who knows her own mind. She is also a handsome woman. If she wishes to marry soon after the death of a first husband, what more natural than that she should turn to that man's brother? They are not unalike, my father and my uncle. No, I don't brood on my mother's remarriage. I am not Prince Hamlet."

But the little flood of words, the most this young man had yet spoken, showed that he had brooded, was still brooding over this very matter. Anyone who eagerly denies something, with a mass of accompanying reasons, concedes the case against him, all unawares. And also William Eliot's air, his dress, his professed pleasure in speculation, everything about him might have lead one to think that he was modelling himself on that famous character, the Prince of Denmark.

"And yet . . ." he said.

"What?"

"Master Revill, I understand that you have nowhere to lodge at the moment, is that right?"

I was disconcerted. William Eliot had obviously been talking to someone. One of the Chamberlain's Company?

"I had a disagreement with my landlady over . . . something. She has given me notice."

"I'm going to make you a proposition," said William. "But first I must tell you something that happened a few months ago, if you are willing to listen to a story."

I nodded but said nothing.

"A man went into his walled garden one afternoon. He was in the habit of going there to sleep on warm days. He alone possessed the key to the door that opened into this walled garden. It was his retreat, his sanctuary, a place where he could think or rest undisturbed. There was nothing unusual in these afternoon absences. When he did not reappear in the house by nightfall of this same day, however, his wife and their son and the servants began to grow worried. They called from the outer part of the garden, they rattled at the locked door. No response. Eventually one of the servants was sent over the wall on a ladder. What the servant found in the twilight caused the wife to order the door broken down. When the household – by now most of them were assembled – poured though the narrow entrance to the walled garden they found the head of the household dead in his hammock. The body was almost cold. He had apparently lain there since the early afternoon. There were no marks of violence, no signs of foul play. He had died naturally. What does this remind you of?"

"It's obvious enough," I said.

"Well?"

"It's what happens before the beginning of the play of *Hamlet*. Hamlet's father, old Hamlet, dies in his orchard one afternoon. The story's put around that it was as a result of a snake-bite. But the Ghost tells the Prince that he was poisoned

– and that the murderer is now on the throne of Denmark and married to Hamlet's mother."

"I said that Master Shakespeare's plots were closer to the truth," said William. "What I've just described to you is the manner of my father's death. Asleep, one afternoon, in his garden, in his house, on the other side of the river, his death apparently a natural one."

"Jesus," I said. "And then to have your mother remarry – and to your uncle. All this really happened, what you're saying?"

"It's easy enough to check it if you don't believe me. My mother or my uncle or any member of the household will confirm it. There was even a ballad made on the subject of my father's passing, how death comes for rich and poor alike or some such profundity."

"It stretches belief that your family's history should mimic so exactly the action of a play," I said.

"Yes. It is disturbing to find that nature is so short of material that it is forced to hold up the mirror to art, if I may vary one of the Prince of Denmark's own observations," said William languidly. "But consider these things, consider them separately. Then they are less surprising. My father was several years older than my mother. He had not been in the best of health. One might ask, why should he die then and there, one fine spring afternoon in a hammock in his private garden? But, to look at it another way, why shouldn't he? As good a time as any other. Death is not always the thief who comes in the night."

"You sound very, ah, unmoved about this," I said.

"I have thought long and hard about it. I have tried to be dispassionate. Then, I examine the sequel to this. My mother sincerely grieves, I think, at my father's death. That was no playing, such as Hamlet complains of when he calls his mother Gertrude a hypocrite. My uncle Sir Thomas too showed grief, though in a manly way. He is not a Claudius, surely, full of fine words as he secretly clutches the knife. Each of them, widow and brother, naturally turned to the other for consolation. Consolation soon – very soon – changed to love. Again, what's exceptional about that? We are told in Leviticus that if brothers dwell together and one of them dies then the widow should not be married outside the family to a stranger."

"That is the case when the wife has not produced a son," I said. "Then the brother should perform the duties of a husband. But in this situation there was at least one son, you."

William glanced at me in surprise.

"My father was a parson," I said. "Whether I wanted to or not, I soaked up Bible learning every day of the week."

"There is no great gap between pulpit and stage. That's why they're always at each other's throats."

I was beginning to warm to this fellow, for all his airs.

"My father wouldn't thank you for saying so. Like our City fathers, he held that the playhouse was the root of all abomination."

"And so *you* are drawn to it. Does he know how his son earns a living?"

"My father is dead. My mother also. The plague beast struck at Bristol a couple of years ago, and one of its tails or legs swept through our little parish."

"And now you are a player. Well, whether the words of Leviticus about the marriages of widows and brothers apply or don't apply, I'm sure that it is not so unusual for two people in such circumstances to find themselves attracted to each other."

He said this as if he were talking about *my* mother and father.

"Probably not."

"So, you see, these events taken separately – a death and a remarriage – are nothing out of the ordinary."

"But you don't actually think that?"

"To be more precise, I don't feel it. Without being able to say why, I don't feel that all's right with the world."

"There's a simple way of clearing this up," I said. "When did your father die?"

"The first week in May."

"And the first performance of *Hamlet* was in June, I think."

I struggled to remember when I'd seen the tragedy of the Prince of Denmark. It was a successful play and so had received more than a couple of performances; and now it had been revived in the autumn. My first appearance with the Chamberlain's Men had been on the previous day in this very production. But I was fairly sure that my first sight of it as a *spectator* had been in early summer. High white clouds scudding above the open playhouse. A sense of freshness in the air, even among the groundlings. Standing at the back I'd pulled my hat lower to shade my gaze from the afternoon sun as I witnessed the destruction of the royal court at Elsinore (little dreaming that I would myself be appearing within a few months on that very stage as the emissary from England, come to announce the deaths of Rosencrantz and Guildenstern to unhearing ears!). Yes, this was in June.

"It was June," I said. "I remember."

"Well?"

"Your father's death took place before the play of *Hamlet* ever appeared on the Globe stage. You're not suggesting that our author got the idea for his play from what happened to your father?"

"Of course not," said William Eliot. "I'd never accuse any playwright of making up ideas or borrowing from reality. They'd be justifiably insulted. Anyway, every educated person knows that there's an older version of your author's *Hamlet,* some crude stuff that's been around for years. And that rough version probably had an even rougher version preceding it. And one before that, and so on."

"So it's not a case of nature holding up the mirror to art, as you wittily put it," I persisted. "Your father's death occurred before the play was first performed. But it's not the other way round either. The play was not composed so far in advance of your father's death as to indicate that the author might have 'borrowed' from reality, even assuming that he'd be prepared to do anything so indelicate. The two things, the play writing and the death, must have been occurring more or less simultaneously. Why, he must have been at work on *Hamlet* in April or even during May itself if it was first staged in June."

"He writes fast."

"No more than average," I said, pretending to a knowledge of our author's compositional habits. But what I said applied to any playwright worth his salt. We had no patience with any author who laboured for weeks and then produced a few paltry scenes.

"So there's no connection between the events of the play and my father's death, you think," said William.

"Just coincidence," I said with a confidence that I didn't feel.

"You're probably right," he said. Then after a pause, "You remember that I had a proposition to put to you?"

"Yes."

He broke off to order another drink for each of us, and, when our hands were full and our mouths refreshed once more, said, "You've nowhere to lodge presently?"

"You know already of the difference of opinion with my landlady, apparently."

"I can offer you quarters in my house, that is in my mother's and stepfather's house. It's on the other side of river, not so convenient for the Globe perhaps, but in a rather better neighbourhood."

"I like it here," I said. "This is the players' district."

And it was true. Southwark was near to being lawless territory, outside the writ of the City authorities. Our one respectable building was the Bishop of Winchester's Palace. Otherwise we were all stews, playhouses and thieves' kitchens, together with an array of prisons from the Clink to the Marshalsea – the ultimate destination for many of our folk. Southwark residents tended towards the unrespectable: coney-catchers and bully boys, whores and veterans . . . and yet somehow I, the country parson's son, felt in my element down here in a way that I hadn't when I lodged north of the river.

"I didn't mean permanent quarters," said William. "I can see that there are advantages to living near your workplace. Though you're only temporarily with the Chamberlain's Men, I understand. There's a man who is off visiting his dying mother, is there not?"

Who had he been talking to?

"I'm not interested in your offer," I said. "I prefer to find my own accommodation."

"No offence, Master Revill. I have an ulterior motive in asking you to take a room in my house. I'm not in the business of looking after players who have been thrown out of their lodgings for covering their landladies with piss."

A smile took the offence out of his words. But I was busy wondering if he knew Nell.

"Master Eliot, get to the point."

"I would like you to help me find the murderer of my father."

I began to think that my new acquaintance shared more than clothing and a fashionable melancholy with that figure who had swept the London stage, the lord Hamlet. Master William Eliot, like the Prince, had a trace of madness in him.

"I thought there was nothing suspicious in his death."

"Outwardly, no."

"When you break it down into a series of events there is nothing particularly remarkable about it. Isn't that what you said – or something like it?"

"Yes."

"Well then?"

"Master Revill, when you see a play you watch as one scene succeeds another, and you will perhaps not at first understand how the scenes are linked, or that the play with all its disparate parts is nevertheless a whole – sometimes a ragged, clumsy whole – but still something complete unto itself. Whether the play is well-made or ill-made there is connection, there is a plan, a plot."

"You should not confuse a play with real life. If there is a plot down here in this world, it is not likely to be discerned by us poor mortals," I said, and then realised I was echoing the kind of thing my father would have uttered on Sunday (and the rest of the week).

"Surely you can see," said William, "that someone has already created that confusion? My father's death in some of its details, my mother's remarriage to my uncle and so on – all of this has been revealed on the stage not a few hundred yards from where we are sitting. You say coincidence, but I say coincidence is simply a word for what we don't yet understand. And if there is a plot behind Master Shakespeare's work, which there is certainly is, then why should there not be a plot behind what has happened to the Eliot family?"

I made no answer. There was some flaw in his argument but I was unable to identify it.

"So what am I supposed to do?"

"Accept my offer of lodgings. You would be received into the house as a friend who has done the Eliot family a favour and who is in need of accommodation for the time being. I can speak for my mother and I believe I can speak for my uncle in this respect. You will of course need to cross the river daily for your work at the Globe. But while you are in my mother's house, watch and listen."

"Watch, listen? For what?"

"I don't know."

"Goodbye, Master Eliot. This is chasing shadows."

I made to rise, but half-heartedly.

"Please wait."

He held me gently but firmly by the upper arm until I resumed my place beside him on the bench.

"If I were not being honest with you, I would claim to have seen something in those shadows. But I cannot say, I cannot see, if there is anything there or not. And that is tormenting me."

He spoke evenly, but the grip of his hand on my arm and the rigid set of his mouth showed that he was in earnest.

"You are casting me as Horatio," I said.

"Hamlet's friend." He laughed, but without much mirth. "Then you accept?"

"I don't know. You must say what I am to look for."

"Everything and nothing. I am an interested spectator, a biased one. I need a neutral pair of eyes to see whether there really is anything out of place."

"Out of place? How will *I* recognise what's out of place in your house, for God's sake?"

"You will know what you are looking for when you find it."

"Very cryptic, Master Eliot."

"William."

"It is still cryptic, whatever you prefer to be called. But do your clever words actually mean anything?"

"That is the very question I would ask about my father's death. What does it signify?"

"And why me?"

"Because you showed quickness and dexterity when you accused the steward of theft this afternoon. More important, you were right to act as you did. Because you are a player, and have a sense of the divide between what men say and what they are. And because you know the play."

"That play?"

"Yes, the play about a father's death and a mother's remarriage. Don't worry that I'm confusing what really happened with what is presented daily on the playhouse boards. But the connection is a . . . pregnant one."

"Very well," I said. "But suppose there is nothing for me to find or suppose that I am a less percipient spectator than you give me credit for? You must understand that nothing may come of this pregnancy."

"I hope it won't," he said. I did not believe him. He wished, as all of us do, to discover the worst. He continued, "As I said, I respect my uncle and I love my mother. I wish them well in their new life. Though they were married so soon after my father's death . . ."

Having made the arrangements for my reception into his mother's house and after a few more inconsequential exchanges, William Eliot left me sitting in the Goat & Monkey, bemused at this latest shift in my fortune. I couldn't deny that his offer of lodging was opportune. It would save me the cost of my rent, a not insignificant part of a jobbing player's insignificant wages. Putting up in one of the grand houses on the north bank would be a dozen times more comfortable than anything I could afford across the water here in Southwark. Most of all, it would be an introduction to people of wealth and influence – and if one is a poor and youngish player making one's way in the capital then that is something not to be sniffed at.

And I was curious. The story that William Eliot had recounted was so queerly parallel to events in our author's latest play that, sceptical as I was, I could not help being affected by what he said. My own argument, supported by dates and times as well as by common sense, was that there could be no link between what had happened in a private garden on the other side of the river Thames and the imagined events in an orchard in Elsinore in the Kingdom of Denmark. If dramatic logic or the parallel were followed, then Sir Thomas Eliot would turn out to be a murderer, the Lady Alice an adulteress possibly complicit in the death of her husband, and – before the action was concluded – her son William would himself have carried out a fair few killings.

Absurd . . .

My thoughts were interrupted by a series of repeated screams a few feet from my face.

"Jesus, Nat, you startled me."

It was the man who made his living by mimicking animals for a penny in taverns or the street.

"What are you? I don't recognise that."

He was a small grubby man and he now held out an equally small grubby hand. I handed over a penny.

"Laughing hyena."

"Never heard of it."

"Its cries are like laughter, sir. Hear me now."

Encouraged by the penny, he gave several more screeches in which, I suppose, there might just have been detected a species of maniacal, mirthless amusement.

And, looking back, that was a justified commentary on the predicament into which I was about to sink myself.

ACT II

*S*o a new man has entered the house. He suspects that
something is wrong, without being able to put his finger
on it. Or he has been told that something is wrong. But he
knows nothing, and certainly nothing about me. What do I know
about Master Nicholas Revill? He is tall and hollow-cheeked with
coal-black hair. He is young and eager, though he tries to disguise
this with a display of worldliness. He is a player. Well, I am a
player too. But I give nothing away by saying that. So are all men
– and women too; we're all players – on or off the stage.
Professional players, I have observed, are usually rather obtuse.
For all their vaunts about understanding human nature, most of
them don't see further than their noses. They are so concerned
with the self that the independent existence of others is a strange
concept to them. I know too that Master Revill is the son of a
parson in the west; I believe that both his parents perished in the
plague. He then came to seek his fortune in London, having
contracted from somewhere the desire to make an exhibition of
himself on the stage. This desire is as virulent – and almost as fatal
– a contagion as the plague. A period with the Admiral's Men and
now with the Chamberlain's Company. But still he plays the
small parts. Nothing will come of him.

Every so often, on the nights when I am unable to sleep, I turn *round and round the memory of how I swung down from the pear tree in the walled garden, and approached the sleeping form of my enemy. Sometimes I see this as I saw it then, from inside my own case of eyes. Sometimes I see it as if outside myself, as another would have seen it. A crouched, stealthy figure dropping from the tree, fatal fruit. Then, loping across the tussocked grass, an animal closing on its undefended prey. Am I condemned for ever to relive the moment when I stood above his still breathing body, the moment when I unsealed the phial and trickled its contents into his ear? The brief convulsions. The early silence. The wait before my "audience" gathered, the little group come to appreciate, to be horrified, to be struck dumb, by the spectacle that I alone had created. How I wanted to hasten their arrival, by shouting out or screaming, doing something foolish which would have brought them running to the garden.*

But I waited. And was rewarded. The discovery of the body in the evening. The uproar and grief.

And what was this all for? For nothing if I am discovered – not likely, I tell myself on those sleepless nights, not likely that the crime will be discovered. Master Revill, he will find nothing. The only danger I face is from myself, from betraying myself. Guilt spills itself in fearing to be spilt, as someone says. I expected to discover that I had lost my clear conscience, but I have discovered instead something more valuable: conscience is a cowardly bitch and will respond to a good whipping. Oh, she will keep her kennel.

*   *   *

The wind brushed across the water, bringing a scatter of yellowing leaves from the trees on the bank. I huddled lower into my cape. The boatman pushed off from the shore and plied steadily into the current and the early morning traffic.

Downstream, the silhouette of the buildings on London Bridge made an unbroken line with the houses on either bank, so that we seemed enclosed on a lake and not afloat on a mighty conduit to the sea. Other ferries scudded back and forth, taking citizens to or from their pleasure on the south bank or their business on the north. Eel boats and herring busses slithered among the swarm of smaller vessels, and we rocked and bobbed when we crossed their trails. It was too late in the year, as well as too early in the day, for any pleasure boat. Once, just after I'd arrived in London and near this very spot (and the very day after I had glimpsed our glorious Queen in procession in the street), I'd seen the royal barge, oars agleam, mastering the tide. Mistressing the tide, I should say, mindful of its occupant. This double vision of our Gloriana on successive days – though, to be truthful, I had not actually seen her in the barge – gave me the curious idea that I was destined to glimpse her every day that both of us were in London. Yet I have not seen her since.

Whenever I crossed the river, I thought of that extra-ordinary feat of the Burbage brothers and the other Chamberlain's shareholders when they transported the Theatre playhouse from Finsbury, north of the river. It was one of those stories to which we theatre folk are particularly receptive, because it presented us in a fashion that was both heroic and practical. It is not by chance that the figure who holds up the globe on top of our (yes, now I may say our!) playhouse is the mighty Hercules. For this shifting of an entire edifice was a truly Herculean labour. The epic move was the talk of the town for at least a fortnight. The lease on the Finsbury Theatre had run out. There was a disagreement with the landlord. The Chamberlain's Company had a right to the structure, perhaps, but not to the ground it sat on. The oaken main timbers, the beams and the staves and uprights, were gently prised one from another. Pegs were eased from joints which had hardened over time, numbers were chalked across the dismantled frame, relays of carts organised to take the lumber down Bishopsgate and into Thames Street beside the river. And then in the middle of the winter of '98, when the Thames had frozen solid, there began the great enterprise of ferrying this load of living wood across to the far side.

I envisaged the carts and the improvised sledges creaking under the weight of the frame of the playhouse – its bare bones, so to speak. I could see the panting breath of the men, the shareholder-players, as they tugged at their precious cargo, searching for a purchase on the ice. I envy these men who are now my colleagues, I envy them their part in the epic undertaking. Above them wheels all the starry heaven of a frosty winter night. I could imagine the urgency of the crossing, and the relief of reaching the far bank. Then Master Peter Street, the carpenter, had worked a near-miracle in putting together what had been taken asunder. And behold! As broken bones are sometimes stronger when they mend, so the Globe which arose, phoenix-like, from the remnants of the Theatre in Finsbury is a greater and stronger edifice than anything that is or that ever was before.

From the stern of the little ferry I saw the white playhouse on the far bank, a sight now grown familiar but still capable of making my heart beat faster. My boatman, blessedly silent apart from the occasional oath which is as necessary to the breed as breathing, thrust his oars into the stream. I hadn't seen Adam Gibbons again, the man who had collided with me and then nearly throttled the life out of me. There were boatmen by the hundred, by the thousand, plying this stretch of the river, it is true, but London, great as she is, is also in some sense a small place and one may be sure of meeting again those whom one has encountered once.

We were now halfway across the murky river, and my thoughts turned to the household of Sir Thomas Eliot and Lady Alice and William. If I had twisted round in my seat I could have glimpsed it, one of the fine mansions on the north bank. I had lodged there for some days now and been received kindly, if distantly, by the head of the house. William's story was that I was a player in temporary distress for accommodation. True enough. And, considering the good turn I had done the family in helping to expose the false steward Adrian and vindicate the good servant Jacob, it was the least they could do to provide for my needs while I searched for somewhere more permanent to lodge. So, William said, he had said to his mother and his stepfather-uncle. Of the more obscure reason for my being there – to observe whether there was anything "out of place" – he naturally said nothing. I was his spy or intelligencer, primed to uncover the secrets of others, and this was the secret between us.

While I am halfway across the river, and nothing of interest can happen (unless the ferry be suddenly overwhelmed or the royal barge swan into view) I will recount the first of my discoveries. In the same way I will set down at intervals in the rest of this narrative the other things that I discovered inside – and outside – Lady Alice's house. I will produce them accurately and keeping to the sequence in which they occurred or in which I found out about them. Though I now know what really happened, I will not anticipate my discovery of the final, strange truth by hinting at or foreshadowing the end.

I took my mission seriously. I even kept a little black-bound book in which I literally noted down what I had uncovered. And, to please myself, I kept it in the crude cipher which I had used once with a friend at school: that is, I simply transposed English characters into their equivalent in the Greek (so that an *a* became an *alpha*, a *b* a *beta*, and so on). To be truthful, this would not have concealed what I meant from many eyes, but it gave to my investigation an agreeably cabbalistic air. I mention all this to show how innocently I entered upon this business, as greenly as a schoolboy scrawling notes to a classmate. I wanted to please William Eliot. There is value in having a well-connected young patron – but also I had taken to him, and thought our acquaintance might turn to friendship. And I was attracted by what I might call the "matter".

To begin with the body.

I spoke to the servants. I found people were willing to talk to me. I had won some credit in the Eliot household in a twofold fashion: I had assisted the unfortunate Jacob, who tended now to trail about after me when not otherwise engaged on his daily duties. And I had been instrumental in helping to get rid of Adrian the steward. He, I gathered, had been feared and unpopular with the servants because of his high-handed ways and his slyness. The story of what I, Nick Revill, had said and done in the box at the Globe playhouse had filtered through the house.

I spoke to the servants, I say. In particular, the one who had been sent up the wall on a ladder to see what what had happened to old Sir William Eliot. His name was Francis. He was a small, wiry man with a creased brow. He found it hard to keep still, and jigged and mimed, for example, his mounting of the ladder. He needed little prompting to speak about that evening. It might be the most exciting thing that would happen to him in his life, and the story he told must have been repeated a hundred times in the servants' quarters. I was merely the latest questioner wanting to know about the mysterious and tragic death of Sir William Eliot.

I have here set down the things that I discovered in my investigation into Eliot's death as if I were interrogating witnesses in a court of law. In doing so, I have formalised my own questions and I have condensed answers – and probably given them a coherence they did not possess – but I have not materially changed what was meant. It may seem surprising that a mere servant such as Francis should speak so frankly about his master or mistress, but I believe it to be true of these large households that they are more like parishes where neighbours gossip to one another and speak openly of the parson or the schoolmaster or the lord of the manor. And among people who live all under one roof, although they will be respectful to their betters, there is often a queer sense of equality too.

Nick Revill: When did you first understand that there was something wrong in Sir William's house?

Francis the servant: Janet came to me, on Lady Alice's orders. She told me to bring a ladder into the garden.

N: A ladder? Now you surely thought that was odd, Francis ?

F: I thought one of the women had lost something. The wind had caught a hood or a bonnet and blown it into a tree, maybe. But, to be honest, sir, I did not think much. I did what I was told.

N: What did you see when you went out into the garden?

F: My lady and her son William were together near the door into the hidden garden.

N: The hidden garden. This is what you call it?

F: The secret garden or the hidden garden, yes. Or Sir William's garden. We still use that name sometimes.

N: Because he was the only one who went there?

F: No one else had a key to it. Not even Lady Alice.

N: And now it was she that you saw waiting by the closed door?

F: Master William also. Some of the other servants were standing there too. None of them spoke when I arrived with my ladder across my shoulders, so. [*Here Francis mimes the porting of a ladder.*] It was dusk on a spring evening. It had been a fine day, a warm day, but now the air was cold. And I felt my skin prickling, like, at the cold. I shivered, I remember that I shivered.

N: What were you told to do?

F: Lady Alice said something like, "Francis, I'm rather troubled about Sir William. He will get cold if he's sleeping in there. I think he should be woken up before it grows any later." But I knew that she was not just thinking of his sleep.

N: How did you know?

F: I have seen my lady Alice in many moods. I have seen her angry and soft, and gentle and uppish, and . . .

N: Yes?

F: I mean no disrespect to her, sir, but there is a saltiness in her looks sometimes – you understand what I say?

N: Yes.

F [*here the good honest servant starts to gulp his words*]: I mean even towards me, or so I have thought, sir. I am sure she does not know she is doing it but there is something salt in her, and it is leftover in her expression sometimes like the lees is left in a glass of wine, and her voice falls away all low even if she is giving me a command only, and I have to bend forward to catch her words, and I am uncomfortable, and I hope you can understand me if I have misspoken, sir.

N: Perfectly, thank you. What you are saying is that she is a lady of many – how shall I put it? – moods. But you were mentioning her appearance by the garden door . . . ?

F: I've never seen her look as she looked then. It was getting dark but I could observe her face and features sort of moving around, and she was troubled as she said, pacing about and twisting about.

N: Why do you think she was certain her husband was in there, in the hidden garden?

F: Where else would he be?

N: In the house?

F: I believe they had looked for him, sir. All about the place and around.

N: Outside the house then. In the town? Why should he not be anywhere from Westminster to Shoreditch?

F: But he wasn't, was he, sir? He was in the garden, and he was dead, and it was I who found him.

N: No one disputes that, Francis, but you miss my point. What I mean is, before you found out for certain that Sir William was in the garden, why was everyone else so sure that he must be there?

F: Janet saw him go across the outer garden and open the

door into his orchard, as was his custom. She saw him in the afternoon.

N: I see. But mightn't he have left the orchard again without anybody noticing it? Didn't he occasionally go out – on business or pleasure? He hardly had to obtain your permission to leave his own house.

F: Hardly, sir.

N: Well then?

F: This is a large household, Master Revill, there are plenty of people here, and it would be very difficult for Sir William to slip out without being noticed. And Sir William never slipped anywhere. He made proper exits and entrances, just like you players do.

N: But it's possible that he did "slip" out?

F: Almost anything is possible if you want to put it like that, sir. But none of his city clothes, not his cloaks or his boots, not a thing was taken, and that seemed proof enough to us simple folk that he hadn't wandered beyond these doors.

N: Very well. As you say, the garden is where he was found anyway. Now tell me what you did next.

F: I placed the ladder carefully against the wall. Then I climbed up it hand over hand, so.

N: What did you see from the top?

F: Nothing. I thought to call for a light from those down below—

N: They had torches?

F: I think not. When they first went into the garden it hadn't grown dark. And now it was dusk. The secret garden is bounded by high walls and shadowed by trees, and I was unable to see anything but shapes from my post at the top of the outer wall. So I straddled the wall, and Lady Alice, she says

"Well?" and I say to her what I've just said to you, which is that I can see nothing. And then she says "Go on, go and look for him, Francis, please."

N: Was there anything – did you notice anything – about the way she said that?

F: A strange voice, you mean?

N: Yes.

F: No. I did as she bade me. I turned about so that I might grip the top of the wall with my hands and I hung there for an instant before I fell off into the dark. Then I dropped to the ground on the far side and groped my way about the orchard. I felt that something was wrong. Lady Alice and Master William on the other side of the wall, they felt something was wrong too. One of the master's bitches had set up a great howling that afternoon, you see, sir.

N: Yes. Proceed.

F: You're very curious, sir, if you'll forgive me for saying so.

N: I'm a player, Francis.

F: I know, Master Revill.

N: We players are curious about everything. Human behaviour is, as you might term it, our lifeblood. *Humani nihil alienum.*

F: If you say so, sir.

N: Not I say so but the Latin author Terence. Go on with your story if you please.

F: Where was I?

N: In the garden, the inner garden.

F: I move slowly about with my hands stretched in front of me, and the branches and leaves, they brush at my face and clothes. [*Francis suits his actions to his words.*]

N: You should have been a player, Francis.

F: Is it a respectable trade, sir?

N: We are crawling slowly towards respectability. Please continue with your account.

F: Something rustles close to my foot and I stand stock still with my skin prickling and, though it is only a night animal, I wish that Lady Alice had not requested that I climb the ladder and jump down on the other side. The dusk is dangerous, sir. It confuses. In the dark of the night, at least you know where you are – even if you don't know where you are, if you see what I mean.

N: Ha, very good, yes.

F: I felt too that I was . . . not alone in the garden.

N: And in a sense you were not, Francis, for Sir William was there also.

F: I don't mean that. I felt someone was looking over my shoulder. I jerked my head round sharp, so, and I did it quick to catch them at it before I could grow afraid. But I saw nothing save the heads of the trees. Still my shoulder turned cold. This person . . . his eyes were up.

N: Up? Who? Whose eyes? What do you mean?

F: I don't know, sir. But Sir William, he was not up, not up anywhere. He was lying down.

N: What did you do?

F: At first I am afraid to make a noise but after a while I begin to whisper, "Sir William, Sir William", like this, soft as can be. In a while too I am able to see better, for it is not so dark as I thought. I can make out the apple trees and the pear trees although there are dark pools of shadow lying underneath them. I had been crouching a little as if I was going to meet an enemy and wrestle with him, but now I stand upright. I say "Sir William, Sir William" in a stronger voice.

Then after a time I hear Lady Alice's words come vaulting over the wall. She says something like, "Have you found him, Francis?"

N: Were those her very words? "Have you found him, Francis?" Are you certain?

F: Yes, Master Revill.

N: You're very sure.

F: I was there. I turned my head and shouted back over the wall, "No, I ha–" when suddenly I saw him and broke off speech. So that instant there in the garden is, as it were, branded in my memory.

N: Describe the scene, if you would.

F: My eyes were now much sharper and I could see almost as well as by day. Above me was a moon, new-risen and near full, and the evening star was balanced on a wall top. Between two trees was a hammock, and in the hammock was my master. He was only a shape, but who else could it be?

N: You realised he was dead?

F: Death and sleep are brothers – that's what they say, isn't it, sir? But to my mind you cannot confuse those two, however much they be kin. I knew that he was dead the moment I saw him there between the apple trees. He had not answered for all of our calling. And his poor body had heaviness and no heaviness, if you understand me.

N: I think so. What did you do next?

F: I was silent. The hammock swayed and creaked in some of the air that came creeping up and across the wall from the river, and for a moment I thought that Sir William was going to stretch and rise up from his resting place and greet me by name as he did sometimes, and the hair stood up on the back of my neck. I waited to see. But he did not rise. He had gone from us for good. Lady Alice, she cried out "Francis!" in a way that brought me back to myself. I crept closer, not frightened now but respectful, like. I touched him gently on his forehead with the tips of my fingers, like so [*Francis extends surprisingly delicate fingertips*], and he was scarcely warm.

N: How was he lying?

F: On his back but with his head to the left side, so, and one arm outflung. I could not see his expression but when they brought him into the house we saw a horrible grin on his face as if he laughed at all of us. The key fell from his person and onto the floor inside. It made a clatter.

N: What key?

F: The key to the door to the garden.

N: Let us go back to when you first found him. What did you think at that moment? About how he'd died for instance?

F: I didn't think anything, Master Revill. I was frightened, then I was excited, if you'll forgive me for saying so. It had fallen to me, you see, to make a discovery which would make a difference to everyone in our household. Later I was sorry, because Sir William was a good master. We shall not see his like again.

N: And then?

F: I shouted out something. I cannot recall what it was. I went back to the door. The others were still on the far side. I was very calm and also lively. I could hear them breathing over the wall. I said that I had found Sir William and that torches should be brought, and they knew what I meant, and then they broke down the door and came inside, and everyone went and stood about the body wringing their hands, and Janet ran all over the house beside herself, and my lady Alice and us servants, we were grief-stricken.

N: And Master William?

F: Him most of all.

N: And that was it? You saw nothing further? You did nothing else? You didn't touch the body, or rearrange anything before the others came into the garden?

F [*hesitating*]: No, sir.

N: And one more thing, Francis, if you would be so good.

F: Sir?

N: Sir Thomas Eliot, where was he all this while?

F: Sir Thomas?

N: Your old master's brother and now your new master.

F: He was about his business.

N: Where? Here in the house?

F: Oh no, I do not think so. He was away, in Dover, I think.

N: So when did he find out about the death of his brother?

F: The next day it must have been, sir. When he returned from Dover. My lady went to tell him as he came into the hall, but in truth he must have been able to tell something was wrong. Tom Bullock would have said as he arrived.

N: Tom Bullock?

F: He is the doorman. He says little, but even he could not keep his mouth closed around this.

N: Was Sir Thomas often here?

F: He dwells in Richmond. No longer of course. Now he dwells here with my lady.

N: But, before your old master died, he was often here?

F: I dare say so, Master Revill.

N: Out of love for his brother and sister?

F: It is said—

N: Yes?

F: – that he was near to bankrout before this marriage.

N: Thank you, Francis. And still one thing more. Can I ask you again about the moment when you saw Sir William?

F: Again, sir?

N [*sensing that even this simple man's patience is about to be exhausted*]: For my own private satisfaction. You touched nothing about Sir William's person in the garden?

F: I – no . . .

N: Well, I thank you, Francis.

[*Nick Revill makes to turn away, knowing that Francis has more to say on this topic and that a pretended dismissal, and an active conscience, will work best on this good servant.*]

F: Wait a moment, sir. You set me thinking now. I went close to the body and, like I said, I knew that he was dead straightaway, even before I put my fingertips out. His head was on one side and . . .

N: Yes?

F: It's a tiny thing, sir. But on the side of his face turned towards me there was a mark that ran aslant his cheek.

N: How did you see this? It must have been dark by this stage.

F: Like I said, my eyes had grown used to the dark, and there was a strong moon nearly at the full. The moonlight caught this . . . trail . . . as it will pick out the trail of a boat on the river. It was like a snail's trail, a silver track that stretched from his ear and down across the cheek before it disappeared in his beard. I . . . I wiped at the mark with my sleeve, sir, because I did not like to think that something had crawled across the face of my dead master. I had almost forgot it until this instant. Did I do wrong?

N: No, Francis. You showed respect towards your master. The sleeve you used to wipe Sir William's cheek, would that happen to be the one on the shirt you're wearing?

F: I keep it in my trunk beneath my bed. I have two shirts, and I have not worn that one since the night of the discovery. And if you were to ask me why, sir, I could not tell you.

We'd landed on the south bank by now. I paid off the boatman, adding a small tip, and was rewarded with a surly nod. Can you ever satisfy a boatman? Will Charon, who is to ferry us all across Lethe one day, be as bad-tempered as a London waterman? Impossible!

As I made my way up the landing steps and into Hopton Street on the way to the playhouse, I considered again what I had discovered. I must confess that the feeling that there was indeed something to find out – the feeling that this wasn't all a matter of a son's grieving imagination – had grown strongly upon me. William Eliot was convinced of something odd, even suspicious about his father's death. Now I was starting to believe the same thing. Even so quickly may one catch the plague! After talking with Francis and summarising our exchange in my little black book, I had noted (in my Greekified style) the following points for further reflection:

firstly: Why were the family, Lady Alice and William, so sure that Sir William was in the garden, that he hadn't, for example, slipped away from the house? One of the servants, Janet, had witnessed him entering the garden, to be sure, and no one had seen him leave – and his outdoor clothes were in place – but it seemed an absolute certainty with them that he was on the premises. Did this suggest that somebody knew he was there?

secondly: What did Lady Alice mean when she called out to Francis, 'Have you found him?' Why had she made that choice of words? Why not 'Is he there, Francis?' or 'Can you see him?' Lady Alice's query is what we call out to one who is searching for some thing or object – or for one who is no longer able to answer for himself.

thirdly: What caused the silvery streak which Francis had observed running slantwise across the cheek of the dead man? A snail or some other tiny creature? It was possible. I could understand why he had wiped it off his master's face. I could understand too why the servant had been reluctant to wear that same shirt again – although this, as well as the way he had described his action at the very end of our meeting, suggested that, rather than merely forgetting the incident as he had claimed, Francis had deliberately thrown earth over it in his mind. Why? Had he, by instinct or unawares, been frightened of something in that sticky track scrawled across the dead man's face?

fourthly: Had Sir Thomas really been away from the house when his brother died? Had he saddled up and ridden off a day or two earlier, claiming urgent business in Dover, only to return rather before the morning which followed the discovery of the body? Perhaps he had remained all the time in London. What did it mean that he was "near bankrout"? If this was true, then presumably he had been saved by an advantageous marriage.

What counted chiefly with me was not, however, the various pointers that I had picked up in conversation with Francis.

What convinced me that there was something wrong was a visit to the hidden garden, made in company with the dog-like Jacob.

The door was no longer locked since the old master's passing. It had secured his private orchard, and now he was dead there seemed no reason to keep it closed. On my second morning in the house I asked Jacob to show me where Sir William had been found. We traversed the larger garden and approached a wall that was pierced in the centre by the half-open oak door. An autumn wind was beginning to strip the trees. The grasses around the garden paths lay lank and untended. The door creaked when I pushed at it, with Jacob at my shoulder. Inside was a thick plantation of fruit trees. A few apples and pears lay mushed underfoot. A vine scaled the inner, south-facing wall behind us. The watermen's cries, the creak of the nearer boats and the slop of water against the bank floated over the riverside wall.

"Where did it happen, Jacob? Where was Sir William found?"

Jacob gestured, and lead the way towards the middle of the little orchard, ducking and weaving with suprising agility to avoid the low branches. Beaten-down areas of grass marked old routes among the trees. We came to a small open area where two apple trees faced each other. On the far side were a scattering of plums. Jacob stopped and pointed to the apple trees. They were old and gnarled. Their upper branches ran riot with each other but the lower ones had been pruned or altogether cut away. This was where Sir William's body had hung suspended in his hammock. Although the hammock had gone, probably taken away with the body, I could see, at about five feet above the ground on each tree, rings around the bark which were discoloured or abraded. I crouched slightly to avoid the dangling leaves and the apples. I ran my fingers round the indentations made by the hammock ropes; as one would expect, they were deeper on the sides facing away from the clearing, where the pull of a man's weight on the hammock supports would be greatest. As I was leaning forward something tapped me on the shoulder. I thought it was Jacob and looked around, only to see him grinning. Another windfall apple thumped on my outstretched arm. I retrieved it from the wet grass and bit into it. It was, if I am not mistaken, a Peasegood Nonesuch. I straightened up and stood flanked by the pair of trees, slowly chewing the fruit of one tree and pondering the fate of the man who had died suspended between two of them. Jacob, meanwhile, remained gazing at me with the patience and good nature of a dog which halts when his master halts but is ready to spring up the instant that he shows signs of moving.

Perhaps I owe my discovery to the Peasegood Nonesuch. It is a large and handsome variety of apple, and demands much eating. I stood there staring at, but not really seeing, the yellow and curling foliage of the orchard. Sir William Eliot had died here. Let us, I said, addressing myself in the plural, assume that he did not die naturally. Someone else had paid his fare to Charon for crossing the river Lethe into the underworld. Everything I'd heard indicated he was alone when he died. Janet had seen him crossing the outer garden and going into his private area. No one else possessed a key to the door. It was his custom of an afternoon to rest in his orchard, to think in this place – to sleep, perhaps to dream. This was his garden, his Eden. Yet Eden had Eve, as well as Adam. Did Lady Alice ever come here? Not on that day, certainly, otherwise she wouldn't have been so anxious over his whereabouts. And Janet's report had not mentioned Sir William's being accompanied by any other member of the household. No, he was alone when he opened the door and relocked it behind him, I was as sure of that as if I had seen him go through the door with my own eyes.

I pursued my thoughts. Eden was home to our first parents. Eden was also the serpent's lodging place. The snake in the grass. The serpent – or rather the serpent's malice – was not native to Eden. He crept in from the outside. I wondered, had anyone crept into the garden after Sir William had entered it? Through the door? That was locked, and Sir William had the single key. The key had fallen from his body as it was being carried inside, Francis had told me. Keys may be copied, though. Leave that thought for now. Apply the philosophic principle of Occam's razor, that entities are not to be multiplied beyond necessity. Assume that there was *no* other key. Then had someone come over the wall? But the walls were high. A ladder had been necessary when Francis had been ordered to get into the inner garden. An inner wall divided the two gardens belonging to the Eliots, while three exterior walls protected Sir William when he was shut up in his private garden. One separated him from his neighbours on the west side, one adjoined Mixen Lane in the east and the final wall opposed the river. Beneath this wall was a slick stretch of shoreline, exposed at low tide.

As I swallowed the last fragments of the Peasegood Nonesuch, I tried to put myself in the position of someone wishing to harm – even to kill – Sir William Eliot. I fashioned another self. I became a murderer; a simple transformation for a player.

Leave aside for the moment the question of how I gained

entry into the hidden garden. Leave aside too the question of where I came from, whether from the public lane or the neighbours' grounds or even from the outer garden of the house. (I discounted the river approach, as too difficult.) The point was, it could be done. Though the walls were high they were not insurmountable. I could have used a ladder, even if an accomplice to place it and then remove it while I was about my dirty business in the garden, would perhaps be necessary. I might have used a simple rope and hook to catch on the wall-top – this would do away with the accomplice. But, whichever method I employed, at what time would I make my entry? Knowing that Sir William habitually repaired to his orchard on fine afternoons in spring and summer, would I wait until I was sure that he was there, and then nip up the wall, drop down the other side and search the orchard until I stumbled across him swinging in his hammock? No. There were too many risks with this clumsy procedure. Sir William might not be safely asleep. He might be wandering among his trees even as I levered myself over his boundary wall. He might see me as I descended or as I threaded my way among his fruit trees.

No, were I the murderer, I would take my place *before* Sir William had entered his garden. I would be like those spectators who come early to ensure the best positions in the playhouse. I would wait until my mark was fixed and settled in sleep, and only then would I make my move. I would crouch in a corner of the wall like a cur. I would rise from the grass, as the false serpent does.

Or I would fall from above, like rotten fruit.

And now I remembered what little Francis had said to me, about what he felt after he had climbed into the garden but before he had found Sir William dead in his hammock – "Someone was looking over my shoulder, sir. Nothing there save the heads of the trees. My shoulder still icy. Their eyes were up. And Sir William he was not up, not up anywhere. He was lying down."

My skin prickled.

It came to to me then that the safest place to hide in a garden is up a tree. Were I the murderer, plotting this death long beforehand, I would prospect for a secure, leafy arbour a safe height above the ground, and once there I would watch and wait.

In my mind's eye and ear, I heard Sir William opening the door to his private domain, I saw him make his way gladly through his property, pausing to smell the fragrance of the blossom, to inspect the very beginnings of the crop of fruit that now hung from these trees or strewed the grass around. Then he reaches his hammock. Has he brought something to occupy his mind? A book? The household accounts? A letter requiring a careful reply? No, today he has come with nothing. He comes to rest, to sleep. Wearily, he lowers himself into the hammock. The cords groan slightly at the weight. He hears the shouts from the river, as I do now, and perhaps some noise from his own house. It's nothing. Just the shriek of a servant.

He settles himself down, gazing up at the bank of clouds advancing across the river from the south-west. He feels sleepy. But something disturbs him. Every time he is on the verge of falling asleep, a stray thought intrudes and jerks him awake. Up in my tree I, the murderer, wait. I have made a little tunnel for myself in the foliage so I have a direct view of the upper part of his body, most especially of his face. All I have to avoid is sudden movement. That might alert him. My perch is not comfortable, not after the hour or more I have passed in it, but a great ambition – and murder is a great ambition – demands small sacrifices. Sooner or later Sir William's eyes will close. Then I will fall softly to the ground, and creep and creep to reach him. I decide that while I am crossing his grass I will smile.

So . . . the vantage point chosen by the murderer has to be close to the hammock, close enough for him to ensure that his victim is sound asleep. It has to offer a secure hiding-place. These were my conclusions. With Jacob still looking at me, I made a tour of inspection of the trees in the vicinity of the clearing. Two or three of them were large enough to conceal a man, but the configuration of their branches seemed to offer no place where one might stay, let alone sit, with any ease. Then, a little further back, I came across a large old pear tree. Above my head, among the leaves, I saw several potential conjunctions where thick branches sprang from the trunk and where my putative murderer might sit, legs astride. I called Jacob over.

"Ever since I was a small boy, Jacob, I've enjoyed climbing trees. It's a taste I haven't grown out of."

So saying I jumped up and caught hold of the lowest branch. Swaying backwards and forwards, I soon gained enough force to swing myself astride it. Once up there, I manoeuvered myself into a sitting position, with the trunk at my back. I couldn't easily see the place between the apple trees where the hammock had been attached. In fact I couldn't see it at all. I shifted to a neighbouring branch. Ah, that was better! From among the leaves and the clusters of ripe pears (Jargonelle, I think, or possibly

Winter Nelis) I overlooked the tiny clearing guarded by the two trees.

"Jacob, would you go and stand where your late master was found? In the place where the hammock was. There, yes."

I pushed myself flat against the trunk. Of course, had I been a prospective murderer with my long-laid plans, I would have dressed for the part, worn something in goose-turd green, say, to give myself a tree-like hue. As it was, I was wearing a combination of russet and popinjay blue, and must have looked like some great flightless bird up in the pear tree.

"Now, tell me, can you see me?"

It was hard to remember that Jacob could not "tell" anyone anything. Instead he nodded and made a gurgling sound in response to my question. Yes, he could see me. Well, that wasn't surprising: I could see him. And I was wearing the wrong costume. But, unlike the dumb Jacob, Sir William Eliot hadn't been looking for anyone. When he entered the garden he believed that he was as alone as Adam. Why should he examine the trees to see whether they harboured strange creatures?

I gazed around. I was looking for a sign. Nothing. I gazed some more. What met my eyes was entirely natural, leaves, branches, a wasp burrowing its way into the holed surface of a pear almost before my face. You see how reluctant I was to abandon my idea that Sir William's murderer had been perched up aloft even before his victim came on the scene. But there was no proof of any of this. For all I knew I was chasing shadows, the very thing of which I had accused young William Eliot in the Goat & Monkey. There was no murder and no murderer. I had constructed a scene of treachery and murder out of smoke. I was, as one might say, barking up the wrong tree. The man had died a natural death, of the sort everyone is entitled to.

I swung both legs to one side of the branch and made to drop to the ground. As I did so I noticed a wisp of material caught at the juncture of a twig and my branch. The gods were smiling on me after all. I was about to be justified. I gently tugged at the thread. Was this the clue? No, it was not, for a moment's examination showed that this "evidence" came from my own jerkin. I raised my eyes upwards in exasperation, and then I saw it. Just at head height and two feet away from where I was sitting someone had carved letters into the trunk. Two inter-twined initials. My heart started to thump. I ran my fingers up and down the grooves of the letters. They were about an inch in height and appeared to have been cut into the bark hastily but firmly. Just as one would carve letters if one wanted to leave a message and was conscious that time might be limited. The carving wasn't fresh; already the letters showed weathering. Although they might have been there longer, these characters had definitely been incised at least a few months ago. Perhaps during the spring and before a man's death.

I launched myself into space and landed, in a crouch, on the turf below the pear tree.

"Thank you, Jacob, I've seen enough for the time being."

I left the garden in a brown study, Jacob devotedly on my tail.

The letters up the pear tree were a W and an S.

I wondered whether I was not already deeper into this matter than was good for my peace of mind or health of body.

I wondered whether what I had seen were the initials of our author, William Shakespeare.

* * *

And it was Master Shakespeare's Globe playhouse whose walls I was now walking alongside. His and the other shareholder-players'. This morning was a rehearsal for *A Somerset Tragedy* by Master Henry Highcliff. I put to one side speculation about those troubling initials, and concentrated instead on my part in the play.

A Somerset Tragedy is a simple tale of domestic lust and violence. It involves a land-holder and his younger wife, as well as a painter, the painter's sister, the man the painter's sister wishes to marry, the man the painter has arranged for his sister to marry (two different men, this), three hired assassins, a local lord, sundry servants and clowns, a brace of magistrates, a priest, an executioner. You get the picture. I didn't know the full plot, since I had received only the scroll bearing my own part, but I could guess what happened from a glance at the dramatis personae. Most likely it began with a rape: most certainly it ended with the rope. I was a yokel, with full-dress accent and boorish manners.

When I had glimpsed a little more of the play in rehearsal I would tell my Nell about it. She enjoyed hearing of my roles, or so I flattered myself. I had discovered that retailing the plot of a play while we were in bed together – as with Master WS's *Hamlet* or the infinitely inferior Master Boscombe's *A City Pleasure* – was an effective method of delaying my own journey's end, and thus of ensuring her own satisfactory arrival at that terminus. It was as if a torrent of words could temporarily dam up another sort of effusion. Sometimes Nell had told me of what her paying customers cried out when they were busy about her person, although this was knowledge that I wanted her to share with me only *in extremis*. I considered that my dramatic summaries showed a more refined temper than their cataloguing of her body parts, and what they were doing or intended to do with them and to them. I wondered whether I should mention to our author my interesting use of his Tragedy of the Prince of Denmark. I wondered what our author had been doing up a tree in the garden of Sir William Eliot. Unless it had been some other WS of course.

"Master Revill!"

It was Robert Mink, the fat player who had given me the note for my Lady Alice. We had coincided at the entrance to the playhouse. Together we made our way to the tiring-house, where some of the other Chamberlain's men were already gathering. Mink was clutching a much larger scroll than mine. He noticed that I was looking at the size of his part.

"I play a painter in the county of Somerset," he said. "I wish to marry my sister off for reasons that are obscure to me. When she does not agree, because there is another man back in the tiring-house, I turn murderous. I paint a picture of my sister which is so beautiful that the onlooker cannot help touching it. The pigment that I use in depicting her flesh, her nearly bare breast, is naturally poisonous to the touch. This picture will then be shown to the man I wish to kill. He will reach out to stroke her exposed, painted flesh, and so he will die. Have you ever heard of anything so unlikely?"

"Does he die? By touching the pigment?"

"Of course not. When did you ever hear of a murder plot going right in a tragedy?"

"Death in an orchard," I said.

"What?"

"I was thinking of Hamlet, and the death of his father, and how it does not look like a murder."

"Quite different," said Master Mink, his triple chins wobbling in disagreement. "Anyway that didn't go right in the long run, did it? The murderer never thrives. Master Shakespeare may stretch belief sometimes but there is a truth beyond mere fact, and he is in ample possession of it. But I fear that Master Highcliff with his Somerset farce masquerading as tragedy is another kettle of fish, a stinking kettle."

"Why do the Burbages put on this stuff then?"

"Because it draws in the crowds, dear boy. The spectators want to see sin in all its varieties, they want to see fighting and fucking and fury, and then they want to see all of this punished – otherwise they will not go home comfortable. But I tell you one thing."

"What's that?"

"We are right to look down on the authors of this stuff. We are right to pay them so little. Master Shakespeare, of course, excepted. Him and one or two others. But for the most part they are journeymen. Where would the writers be without the players? We are the men of value."

"I do not have such a low opinion of authors," I said, daring to oppose this large and experienced man of the theatre.

"Do you not?" he said. "There is no time to discuss this now, we are due to begin our rehearsal, but I would be glad to continue this interview this evening if you find yourself in the vicinity of The Beast with Two Backs. It's in Moor Street."

"Is that a pick-hatch?"

"Merely a tavern. Its real name is The Tupping Rams or some such. At the south end of Moor Street, if you should find yourself in that neighbourhood tonight."

After my participation in that morning's rehearsal, I had to agree with Master Mink. I did not think that we would be performing *A Somerset Tragedy* more than once, as I told Nell late that afternoon. We were in her room. This was barely more than a closet in Holland's Leaguer, not far from the bearpit. The women had their own rooms and were generally undisturbed as long as they paid an exorbitant rent to the madam and her one-eyed paramour (familiarly known as Cyclops). But the walls were thin, and cries and groans as well as intermittent thwacks penetrated our ears. The sounds were more reminiscent of Bedlam or one of the quarters of hell than a house of pleasure. I did not particularly enjoy meeting my Nell at her place of work, but for the moment my lodgings were on the far side of the river, and I had nowhere to roost on the south bank when I wished to see her. She had shut up her stall to the public for the day. Only now she had got her wares out again for a private browser.

"Why are you so sure you'll only play this play – whatsitcalled? – once?"

"*A Somerset Tragedy*. It's a poor piece," I said, with all the assurance of a few days in the Chamberlain's Company.

"You haven't played it yet for the public. Maybe they'll love it. You might have a great run, three or four performances."

"You get a feel for these things."

"As you have a feeling for this," she said, taking my hand and drawing it down.

"Ah yes," I said.

A while later, she said: "Nick, the title of your piece is strange, is it not? The tragedy of Somerset."

"Why?"

"I was remembering your father and your mother."

"But you never knew them, little Nell."

"But you have told me of them, Master Nicholas."

Such remarks reminded me how young Nell was. And indeed I have noticed that these women – our doxies, our trulls and rude girls – who spend their days catering to the depraved tastes of fallen man have, as if by compensation, a most child-like tendency in them sometimes. Nell had asked me before about my parents, the parson and the parson's wife, and encouraged me to talk about them. I attributed this to the fact that Nell had no idea who her parents were – or whether they were alive or dead. The woman she once called "mother" was a mere neighbour, if a good-hearted one. Accordingly, with none of her own, she took an interest in my mother and father. Mine at least you could be certain of, for they were united in death.

I was away from the village when they died. In Bristol. On business about my playing, trying to inveigle my way into one of the touring companies, Dorset's, Northumberland's, I have forgotten which. My plans didn't work out, and I'd spent a fruitless couple of weeks hanging around inn-yards trying to ingratiate myself with the players. My father did not approve. Players were parasites and crocodiles, double dealers and painted sepulchres. They were unnatural, because men are not intended by God to be other than they are, particularly not to play at being girls and women. The shows staged in inn-yards and other public places where players flaunted their filth were not only an incitement to disorder and lasciviousness in otherwise upright citizens, they were also a breeding ground for thieves, whores and knaves.

Needless to say, my father had never attended a play. But

he knew what he hated. He also knew, like all good men, that God hated what he hated and was busy with punishment, punishment everyday and everywhere. This punishment most often came in the guise of diurnal accident and disaster. Whenever a calamity overtook the village – a house-fire, a sickness among the sheep, the failure of a crop – he looked for the cause in the sinfulness of the householder, the shepherd, the farmer. For larger catastrophes like the Spanish threat, which had gone before I was grown, or the plague, which never goes, he looked to sinfulness on a grand scale. As a nation, we English were all deeply and doubly dyed with the devil's pitch. We teetered on the lip of the everlasting pit. The strangest thing with my father was that this sense of universal damnation went hand in hand with a loving-kindness towards his fellow humans, so that the householder or the shepherd or the farmer who had suffered calamity was certain to receive gentle words and a helping hand from him. He would thunder away in the pulpit, but when he descended from it he was the meekest, mildest fellow.

You may wonder that I can speak so lightly of what evidently weighed heavily on my father, this sense of sin – mine, yours, his, ours. But I have observed that an extreme course in a parent is likely to produce an opposite, though milder, response in the offspring. So a Puritan sires the whoremaster, while the rake begets a nun. If Nell were ever to discover her parents they'd no doubt turn out to be fine, upstanding citizens. Another explanation was that I'd heard my father's message too often. Listening to him roar and thunder Sunday after Sunday, and through the week too, inoculated me. What he saw as sin I see mostly as frailty, while what he considered to be a punitive providence I think of as unlucky chance. Most of all, my father the parson reserved his greatest wrath for what he knew least, players and the play-house. "The cause of plagues is sin, if you look to it well; and the cause of sin are plays; therefore the cause of plagues are plays." So he reasoned. All fell on deaf ears, however, for I don't reckon that above one in fifty of us had ever seen what he was so energetically condemning.

And when the plague came to our region who should it strike but those who would have no truck with players and playhouses? I mean the good, honest, simple folk of my village. My mother and father were included in that number.

I came over the brow of the hill. It was a fine spring morning. The last traces of frost lingered under hedges and in the ruts on the track, but the air was soft with the promise of better times. I had failed in my attempt to join the touring players and had been walking from Bristol since three that morning. I should have been returning tired and with my tail between my legs but, perversely, I felt fresh and cheerful. In the distance was the glint of the Bristol Channel and, beyond, the hills of wild Wales stood out in the bright air. Down below was my village of Miching. I wondered what my father would say to the prodigal's return. He would be glad I had not fallen among the sinful players but, humanly, he would wring my hand in sympathy at my disappointment. My mother, she would say nothing. I took one last look around from the heights and then plunged downhill. In the distance at the bottom of the valley was the cluster of cottages and huts separated by thread-like paths, the church and the manor house a little distant from the common people, the scattered farmsteads, everything that, together, went by the name of Miching.

I had made a few dozen downhill strides when, without knowing why, I stopped. There was something wrong. I paused, and shaded my eyes from the sun to see better. The village lay still. I even sniffed the air like an animal scenting danger. Nothing. I went another few steps and halted once more. Then it came to me: what was wrong was that there was nothing to see, nothing to hear, nothing to smell. On a morning like this, the beginning of a fine spring day, there should have been people moving in the fields or on the outskirts of the village, the occasional shouted greeting or question, the smell of woodsmoke curling out of the valley, the bleating of sheep. But there was absolute stillness and silence.

My heart beating faster, and with a sick feeling, I leapt down the path. At one point the track ran out of sight as it looped an outcrop of rock, and it was on the far side of this that I found a man sitting with his head in his hands. Roused by my panting and the thud of my feet, he looked up and I recognised him as my father's sexton, a thin bony man, an appropriate shape for his principal business, I had always felt. I spoke his name. After a moment he came to himself and saw who I was.

"Nicholas," he said in a spiritless voice.

"What's happened? Why are you here, John?"

He said nothing for a while but hung his head again, and pressed his hands into sunken cheeks. Then in a mumble he said, "Your father sent me here."

"Why? What for?"

But I knew already. There is only one cause for such a profound silence and stillness. The plague had struck villages to the east of us in previous years, and even Bristol had known it. It is a tide that creeps inexorably across the land, winter and summer, drowning without distinction young and old, rich and poor, though – unlike the tide – it leaves some spots and areas uncovered. So, in a city, one household will fall victim while its neighbour remains untainted. And yet the plague is a beast too, one that will abandon his orderly progress across country and suddenly overleap many places to land in a distant village or town. Then he will jump sideways or seven miles backwards, and all to confound expectation.

"I was stationed here to warn people away," he said.

How like my father, to think not only of his own flock but of the well-being of the neighbouring parishes.

"And to stop our own people from leaving," he said.

"My father . . . and my mother . . . they are helping those in distress?"

"You cannot go down, Nicholas. I am empowered to stop you and all travellers."

He spoke by rote. He could scarcely have turned an ant from its path. I was already past him. Then he called out my name, the clearest he had yet spoken, so I paused once more.

"You will go. But what you will see will be a sermon to you. It is a speaking sight, and the voice it calls us with is a loud one, to call us all to repentance."

I turned my back on him and went on down the track. As I neared the flatter ground I slowed down. I was desperate to see my parents, and to know that they were all right, but at the same time I was conscious of the risk I ran in entering a plaguey place. It was not self-preservation, or not entirely, but a more cautious mood overtook me as I grew breathless after my downhill dash. Nevertheless I proceeded past the outlying farms and cottages at the ends of fields. This was a well-known route from the earliest days of my childhood, but now it seemed horribly unfamiliar. The first promise of the morning light as I crested the hills above my home had been replaced by terror.

As I came nearer to my village of Miching I saw deserted streets; and as I came within sight of the first houses I found what I knew I would find: many of the doors marked in the centre with red crosses, and sometimes with the words "Lord have mercy upon us" set closely and neatly by the cross. Somehow this was the worst thing I had seen so far, not the crosses and the words themselves but their precision. There was no sign of haste or panic in the sign or the lettering. It was as if each sign had been painted by a craftsman with all the time in the world at his disposal. I paused in the main street. The church was around the corner at the far end. My parents' house was close by it. I waited to catch my breath. In truth, I didn't know what to do next. I wanted to cry out but no words came and I was afraid to break the silence.

Then I heard, off to my left, the faintest thump. A delay of perhaps half a minute, then the noise was repeated. I dithered. I did not want to go down the narrow muddy lane that led towards these sounds but, of course, I did go. On the way there were more doors with their neat crosses and pleas for grace. It was important to me to remember the name of this lane as I walked down it with dragging steps and I struggled to think, and yet I could by no means recall it. (Only now, lying in bed next to my whore Nell, do I remember what it was called by the villagers: Salvation Alley, and that not through any connection with the church but because there was a woman named Molly who lived at the bottom and who was reputed to sell herself. I do not know if it had a proper name.)

Beyond this muddy lane was an open patch of ground and when I entered on this area I discovered the source of the thumping noises. There was a cart on the far side of the green. A horse stood lonesome and patient between the shafts. By the back of the cart a great black pit had been dug. Three muffled figures were engaged in tugging and pushing at bodies heaped in the back of the cart. They used staves with a kind of cross-piece at the top. A corpse would topple into the pit, there would be a pause while one of the burial-men fiddled below with his stave – presumably to fork the body into a satisfactory position in the pit – and then another would be toppled down. Some of the bodies were swaddled in linen and some in rags only. Some were so loosely wrapped that they might as well have been naked, for their coverings fell away as they descended from cart to pit. Little did it matter to the corpses whether they fell clothed or unclothed into the common ground; little did it matter to the burial-men. But tears started to my eyes at this indiscriminate heaping together, as one might call it, of my father's parishioners. Prosperous and poor, reputable and ne'er-do-well, industrious and idle, young and old, man and woman and child (for some of the bundles were not full size), all made their brief passage through the air from cart to ground without distinction.

I must have stood there for some minutes, long enough anyway to count a dozen bodies being offloaded. At one point one of the burial-men looked up and caught sight of me standing at the mouth of Salvation Alley. He did not attempt to warn me away or to alert the others to my presence, he merely returned to his dismal forking of bodies into the pit. I was none of his business. He was none of mine. I turned about.

There was one more thing I had to do before leaving Miching. Following the back lanes, I came out by my father's church. The tower stood square in the morning sunshine. The doors were open but I did not look inside. Beyond the church, and the graveyard was the house of my parents, the largest in the village. Picking up speed and throwing a sidelong glance at the house as I went by, I saw what I knew I would see: that my father and mother's door too was crossed in red. And yet I did not falter but kept on. At the boundary of the village I turned aside from the road that would have taken me up the hill again and past the place where John the sexton was sitting. Instead I traced out a grassy path that ran alongside a stream. It was where I had often fished and bathed as a boy. Eventually I started to run, Then I ran, and ran, and ran.

Later, much later, a thought came to me that, had my father still been alive, I might well have told to him. It was the desire, the itch, to become a player which had saved my life. Without my profitless trip into Bristol to join Dorset's or Northumberland's Company, I would undoubtedly have been kicking my heels in the village when the plague came to Miching, thus ensuring that we all kicked our heels in unison.

I wondered what my father would have said to this instance of divine providence. But I already knew the answer: God had preserved me in order that I should do something. I had been saved from the plague for a purpose, and, in his eyes, that purpose was not playing.

"What?" I said.

"I said," said Nell, "do you often think of them, your parents?"

"I was remembering them now."

"I think of mine too," she said. "Even though I do not know what they looked like."

I drew her closer as she snuffled. She could be sentimental at times. And this is also a trait I have noticed in her, and girls like her. Their exposure to the sordid world, its cut and its thrust, has in some curious way softened as well as hardened them. They will shed tears over an injured animal, if it be small and young – though they still attend the bearpit, if only because it is a good place for trade. They will sometimes imagine that they would like a baby to fuss and cuddle – but if one comes by accident they are quick enough to farm it out and the more ruthless ones are prepared to abandon or kill it, because a new life puking up in the corner is bad for business.

"How's life over the river, in your grand house?"

She was slightly envious, I think. As she spoke there was a loud cry from a room down the passage, followed by a series of low laughs and dull thumps. For the life of me I could not have said whether these signalled delight or despair. Probably both, in which case the delight of the man most likely hinged on the despair of the woman.

"Better to be over the river than in the stews of South-wark," I said, cocking my head in the direction of the sound.

"Some men like the ladies to cry," she said. "And they pay better if they do. You should not believe everything that you hear."

If my Nell was sometimes child-like she was also, at times, very old. And now she was obviously indignant at the aspersions I had cast on her district and place of work, because she went on, "You would not think that life was so much better over there from the number of fine and mighty citizens who cross the river almost daily to visit us. These gentlemen seem to prefer it over here to keeping company with their wives, in their grand houses."

"That must be because their wives don't give them what they require."

"Some do say that," said Nell, "and it is true that I've seen high-and-mighty women from the other side of the water who look cold enough to piss hail. Hard enough too. But I prefer those men who make no bones about their needs. Whether their wives give them what they want or no, they still require more."

"A straightforward fuck, yes."

"There's honesty in appetite."

"Who said that, Nell? I've heard that said before."

"You did."

"When?"

"Does it matter? In the bed-time. When else do we talk? You see how I treasure your words. I'd write them down if I could write."

"I could teach you, to read and write. I did offer."

"You prefer me ignorant."

"Not so." But my denial did not ring true even to myself.

"Anyway, how much more could I charge if I was able to read and write? Would it be much? I think not."

"There's honesty in appetite," I repeated (apparently). "Very well, I suppose you remember too what I was doing when I uttered these immortal words . . . if we were in bed?"

Of course, I said this to draw her on. But it was true that she had a loving memory for my slightest words and actions, and was able to recall scenes with an accuracy that would be the envy of many a player. This hoarding-up of our encounters was deeply flattering.

"We were in bed in old mother Ransom's . . . and you had just . . . let me see . . . no, I was about to do . . . this . . . I think . . . or was it that? . . . it must have been one or the other."

"The other will do splendidly," I said.

After a time I said, "Nell, these gentlemen who come across the river so often—"

"What about them?"

"Have you been visited by any of the Eliots? Sir Thomas, or his brother Sir William – though he is dead now – or his son, also William? Sir Thomas, perhaps? He is a grave sort of man."

"And his dead brother is another sort of grave man, I suppose," said witty Nell.

"Oh Nell, you do not need to learn to read and write," I said, kissing her left nipple.

"They are mostly grave men at first. You may be surprised, Nick, when I say that they do not all give their names. Or if they do it is as likely to be Tom as it is to be Dick or Harry. And there are many of them."

I did not like to think of this.

"It is the Eliot household you are staying in?"

"Yes. Sir Thomas has recently married the widow of his brother, Sir William."

"So she is some crabbed bitch and he's likely to be scuttling across the Thames to get his end in over here."

"No, she is not crabbed."

"She is a young widow full of juice then?"

"Nor young neither. But she has some charms."

"Oh Nick, I see. That means she has many."

"Somewhere between my some and your many," I said, though an imp of honesty compelled me to add, "In truth I hardly know Lady Alice."

"But would like to?"

I kissed her other nipple. But Nell was not to be distracted.

"And her dead husband, Sir Something, he was old and she wore him out?"

For some reason I found the idea, unthinkingly as she had said it, offensive. "No, of course not."

"Because she's a lady? That doesn't mean she couldn't have done for him – in the bed, I mean."

"Nell, this is all imagination. Not everything comes back to the bed."

"You said that it did once, in the end."

"He died in the spring," I pressed on, determined to lay the facts before her. "He was found in his orchard. He had gone there to sleep and when he had not returned to the house by the early evening his wife grew anxious and sent a servant to look for him."

"These rich women never do anything for themselves."

"He had locked himself inside his orchard. It was where he used to go for privacy in the afternoon. Nobody else could get in. The servant had to climb over the wall. He found Sir William's body."

"And then the widow married the brother?"

"Very soon afterwards."

"I've heard that before somewhere. The death in the

orchard then the marriage to the brother. Something you were saying . . ."

' "The funeral baked meats did coldly furnish forth the marriage tables."'

"Not that. I have it! I always remember what you say. Something about a play."

"Yes, I know the play," I said, wearying of our encounter.

I made my way back over the river by the Bridge. A walk would clear my head after the afternoon's performance in the Globe and the subsequent performance in Nell's crib. It was the early evening. There were few people on the Bridge compared to the middle of the day, and most of them were probably returning, like myself, from their pleasures in the southern quarters of our great town.

I am a player. I am used to being watched, and like most players aware of others' eyes without seeming to be. I was about halfway across the river when the nape of my neck prickled. This has long been an infallible sign that someone is gazing hard at me from behind. I stopped by the building that was once a chapel (it is now a warehouse) and pretended to fiddle with my points. In truth, I had fastened them negligently as I was leaving Nell and they needed tightening. While I was doing this, and feigning irritation with the errant laces, I cast covert glances down between the houses that lined the bridge. A shopkeeper closing up for the day. A beggar swinging on his crutches. A fat, respectable-looking citizen who had most probably been about unrespectable business on the other side of the water. In addition, a knot of gallants was making its noisy way after me; one of them shouted an obscenity at a matron walking in the opposite direction. She pretended not to hear. I started walking again.

Within a few dozen yards I received the same sensation in the back of my neck. I felt angry. Convinced that I was being followed, my natural instinct was to face about and confront the man. But I could not turn round or even stop again without alerting whoever was behind me, and since the only advantage I possessed was that he didn't know that I knew he was there, I schooled myself against this. I suspected the beggar. As a class, hardly one of them is what he seems. As for his crutches, even if genuinely required, they were no bar to rapid movement. I have seen those fellows swing through the air when occasion called, their legs and sticks a whirring blur. At the far end of the Bridge I turned left into Thames Street, without changing my speed, and giving the impression of one who has a destination at the end of the working day but is in no especial hurry to arrive there. The south side of Thames Street is pierced by several alleys and crooked passages that run down towards the river. I listened hard for tell-tale footsteps after me, or more precisely for the rhythmic thud of crutches, but the street, though largely empty, still contained passers-by and the occasional grating handcart and I was unable to detect anything. I did not glance round.

After I'd walked the better part of a quarter of a mile – the prickling sensation remaining with me and my neck all this while, though slightly diminished – I turned down the wide slope that leads to Paul's Wharf. Once round the corner I checked to make sure that nobody was hard on my heels, then ran direct for the river. I covered the distance in a few seconds. The principal pier here is an imposing structure, the biggest landing place on this stretch, with stairs in one corner running down into the water at low tide. To the west side are the remains of an earlier erection that evidently proved inadequate to growing city trade, and has lain unused for many years. The wooden stanchions and cross-pieces of this pier are fractured. The planking where barrels and bales were once piled up is rotten and holed or altogether missing. It was low tide and I jumped from the street end of the main jetty onto the shingle. A couple of individuals were standing at the end of the pier but I do not believe they even turned round as I landed on the slippery pebbles. Crouching slightly, I made my way at a rapid walk to the shelter of the old pier, and slipped among the forest of posts that supported it.

The whole thing, from turning down towards Paul's Wharf to my concealment under the old pier, had taken less than half a minute. From my point of vantage I was able to see the top of the sloping way to Thames Street and, beyond that, the stone base of Paul's on which the great steeple had once stood. I waited. I drew back a little into the shadows and surveyed my hiding-place. There was a stench of river, to which, country-born and bred, I am not yet hardened. Pockets of light admitted themselves through the gaps in the planks over my head. Dead fish glinted at the bottom of the slimy piles, human turds had been left marooned by the departing tide, as had cartwheels and baskets, clothing and bed-hangings, fragments of rope and bottles, a portion of all the detritus of our great city. There was even a chest with a shiny clasp. But it was open and empty. Some of this truck would be gathered up as the tide rose but, when it fell again, more and fresh rubbish would be left. So it goes.

I turned back to the scene beyond my hiding-place. There was nobody on the new pier, apart from the men at the far end who were still gazing across the river. No sign of the beggar with his crutches. Perhaps I'd been mistaken when I had thought I was being followed. But then I saw that the two men at the pier's end were in fact three, and that the third who was now thanking them and walking away was the fat, respectable-looking citizen that I had glimpsed on London Bridge. He had been questioning them, evidently. "Did you see a young man come down this way, black-haired, in blue and russet? Bright blue? You couldn't have missed him?" "No sir, we've been watching the river, we've seen no one."

But I am inventing this exchange. I have no idea whether the respectable citizen said this or anything like it to the two loiterers by the water. What I do know is that my cit strolled back on the side of the new pier nearest to where I was crouched under the old one, and that on his smooth face was a mixture of bafflement and irritation. The sort of expression that would fasten itself on your face if you too had been pursuing someone and they had given you the slip. He paused and looked about, seeming to interrogate the air. Was that where I had gone? Into thin air? His eyes swept the underside of the old pier and I could almost see him admit, entertain and then dismiss – in the space of an instant – the idea that I had gone to ground underneath that filthy structure. He walked on, paused once more and looked back, then vanished up the slope into Thames Street.

I waited. I wasn't sure whether he might not have seen me and be waiting for me to re-emerge so that he could pick up the trail once more. I wasn't even sure that it was the same individual that I had glimpsed on London Bridge. If not, then he was an innocent man about his business on an autumn evening, and my imagination was away on business of its own.

Nevertheless I waited until the two loiterers had themselves abandoned their station at the end of the pier. Now I was alone on the scene. A chill wind ruffled the water. The houses on the other side of the river and on the Bridge downstream were turning into dark shapes, pierced here and there by a tiny glimmer of light.

I shivered. There is no moment so lonely as the first breath of evening, when business is done and pleasure's distractions not yet started. Under my hand I felt a slimy wooden post. Unless the old jetty was pulled down it would collapse soon of its own accord. On the stone base of St Paul's not far from me there once stood a great steeple shooting hundreds of feet into the air. Many years before, in the early days of our great Queen's reign, lightning had destroyed in a moment what men had laboured so long to build. Now the stone stump of the steeple stands as a monument to the temporality of all human things. Monuments, too, have their span. In time, the church would go, perhaps to be replaced by something else. The old pier which was sheltering me must crumble, and that in short time too. Even the great Globe Playhouse, our shining white building on the far bank, will fall one day to unremembered ruin.

The tavern named Ram, the plain and simple Ram – not The Tupping Rams, nor The Beast with Two Backs neither – was, as Master Mink had told me, at the south end of Moor Street in Clerkenwell. A light, miserable rain was falling. I made my way warily over the slimy cobbles. Not only for fear of slipping, but because this area of London, for all that it is the home of the Red Bull playhouse as well as the Revels Office, is on the northern fringe of the city. Like all borderlands, it has attracted more than its fair share of lawless resolutes, ready to deprive a man of anything about him that is detachable. But the only lurkers in tonight's shadows were a few stray dogs and cats; the human variety would no doubt be found, entertaining each other, inside the pick-hatch nearby in Goswell Road. Houses of sale, like playhouses, thrive on city fringes.

I wondered why Master Robert Mink had suggested a meeting here, away from the Southwark haunts. Within, The Ram was not crammed. Smoke and whispering and little barks of laughter emerged from a group knotted in one corner. Despite the paucity of lamps overhead, I easily spotted my co-player at a table on the opposite side of the room.

"Sit down, Nick."

He shouted to a young, feeble-looking drawer for another pint-pot for himself and an additional one for me, and, when the lad was slow to move, shouted again, "Quickly, before my friend dies of thirst. I have already passed on, and believe I must be in Purgatory now."

There was a single, sickly candle on the elmwood table at which we sat. By its smoky flicker, I watched the quiver of Master Mink's chins.

"You're doubtless asking yourself why I come to this hole when there are so many other holes south of the river, and close to our great Globe too, where I could be equally badly served."

I said that something of the kind had occurred to me while I slithered over the cobbles outside.

"I like sometimes to put a distance between the place where I earn my bread and the place where I eat it – or drink it. I also have an affection for this part of town. I once had a connection with the Red Bull. Boy, where is that drink!"

Out of the shadows, as if on cue, hobbled the puny drawer, no more than a boy, I saw now. One foot dragged slightly behind him, as if struggling to keep up. His mouth wrestled with some simple phrase – probably that cry of drawers everywhere, "Anon, anon sir" – but it was plain that he had even less command over his words than he did over his movements. His outstretched hands shook so that the two tankards which he was carrying slopped over onto the filthy flooring. He tried to place them in front of us but kept missing the expanse of the table-top. At each attempt, another ale-spurt leaped up and over the rims. Master Mink seemed split between deep irritation and high amusement at the boy's efforts, but finally he half rose, seized the tankards and put them on the table himself.

The boy stared.

"Avaunt thee, Gilbert," said Master Mink. "Avaunt, I say. In plain English, go. Shog off."

When the boy had turned and shambled away, a process that took some time, Master Mink said, "There goes a by-blow of the landlady's. Mistress Goodride is her name and that is her nature too. Well, the fruit of her loins shows all too clearly the mark of her sin. She bore him, and now Gilbert Goodride bears his mother's sin, I say."

"You sound like my father," I said.

"Was he a player?"

"A parson."

Though many men might not have been, Robert Mink seemed pleased by this comparison to a pulpit-pounder.

"Is her name really Mistress Goodride, Master Mink?"

I said, thinking that, like The Beast with Two Backs, this tavern-keeper's name might be another witty invention by my colleague.

"Robert you may call me. After all, we share a profession and a workplace, and have a licence to be familiar. As for the name of Goodride, it will do as well as any other."

I wondered how much to believe. I decided to revert to what we had been talking of before the arrival of the unfortunate Gilbert.

"You played the Red Bull?"

"A long time ago."

"That is the only playhouse I have not visited."

"I have played every one of them."

"But the Globe is the finest?"

"Yes, how can it be otherwise, with the Brothers Cabbage and Master Shakeshift and all, telling us that it is so."

I was a little shocked at the irreverence, and my face must have given me away.

"You have not been long at this game, have you, Nicholas?"

"Two years almost," I said.

"And you are from the west?"

I remembered how tartly I had answered Master Burbage over the matter of my origins, so this time I rested content with a nod.

"And now you are here, drawn by this siren?"

For an instant I thought that he was referring to Nell or some other trull or doxy.

"I mean London," said Master Mink. "I mean, to speak more precisely, the itch of playing. That is your siren."

"And so, if playing is my siren, I will not be pleased until I have dashed myself on the rocks?" I said, wanting (as I had with Master WS), to impress this strange man with my learning.

"None of us is pleased until he has dashed himself on the rocks," said Master Mink gloomily. "Do you think Odysseus could ever sleep happy again once he had heard the song of the sirens?"

"Do you remember Robert Greene?" I said, partly because I wanted to shift his mood and partly because I was genuinely interested in those giants, the playwrights and versifiers of the eighties and early nineties. "Though I know that your opinion of authors is not great."

"Oh yes, Greene I remember . . . and George Peele . . . Kit Marlowe . . . and Tom Nashe, Tom Lodge. Thomas Watson, too. Thomas is a good name for an author, is it not? That's what they were all called. *Thomas.* Thomas Kyd, him as well."

"Kyd of the *Spanish Tragedy*?"

"The very same."

Now this was like hearing that my interlocutor had walked with Elijah or spoken with John the Baptist. Men such as Kyd, with their blood-and-thunder tales of revenge, were the harbingers to our latter-day, refined masters like Master WS.

"Oh, Thomas is a good journeyman name, a good no-nonsense name," Robert Mink continued. "Boy, boy Gilbert, another drink for my friend and me!"

Mink's reminiscent, almost womanish, mood was replaced with a stentorian bellow as he called for more refreshment. So loud and abrupt was his shout that it not only caused me to jump, spilling some of what remained in my pot (Master Robert was drinking more rapidly than I could manage), but it provoked a stir in the quietly buzzing, gently smoking huddle in the opposite corner. One or two pale faces were even turned in our direction through the gloom.

"Where are they now?"

I said nothing; I can recognise a rhetorical question when I hear one.

"Dead and gone, in disgrace or in obscurity," said Master Mink. "Kit Marlowe stabbed in Deptford, Greene dying with nothing, so that his wife could not even afford a winding-sheet. Kyd tortured in the Tower and now gone too. You hear what I say about dashing oneself on the rocks? Do you think it was the sirens' song that Odysseus really wanted – or the rocks? Then there was that Thomas Nashe looking for sanctuary in, let me see, in . . . where was it?"

Out of the smoky darkness I could see Gilbert Goodride, the hapless drawer, commencing his progress towards us, clutching two more tankards which, brimming in the beginning, would lose much of their freight before the end of their journey.

"I have it!" said Master Mink.

"What?" I said, my mind and eyes on the hobbling little figure.

"Yarmouth! Nashe sought sanctuary in Yarmouth after he ran into trouble with the Council over *The Isle of Dogs*."

"What trouble?" I said, trying to distract Master Mink from Gilbert's advance. I had a nasty feeling that this was not going to turn out well.

"Lewd matters. Veiled attacks on someone in authority. Something that got up the Council's nose. Or most probably Mr Secretary Burghley's. WHAT DO YOU THINK YOU'RE DOING, YOU HALTING HALF-WIT!"

A combination of shaking hands and uneven gait notwithstanding, the boy had reached us with the slopping tankards. At the last moment, though, a spasm jerked the remaining contents of one of the pots over Master Mink. Now, my companion was, I had already observed, particular in the manner of his dress (unlike some players, who, appearing as kings, queens and princes during their afternoons in the playhouse, are content to pass for mechanics and handicrafts-men in their private hours). Even by the fitful, smoky light of the tavern corner, anyone might see that Robert Mink was well turned out; his doublet alone, Dutch-fashion and long-pointed, would have cost me two weeks' wages. Now his ample frontage was soaked in ale. Some of the liquid spattered his smooth cheeks and folded chins.

Gilbert Goodride, poor potboy, stood before us, shaking slightly, though whether from his natural condition or from fear of what he expected might happen, I do not know. This time, it was I who leant forward and relieved Gilbert of the tankards, placing them softly on the table.

"Now, now," said Master Mink, standing up and wiping his face with a fine cambric handkerchief. This "Now, now" may be delivered in several ways between the peremptory and the consoling. I was glad to hear from the other's tone that he seemed to condole with the unfortunate Gilbert. "No harm done, after all," he continued. "No offence."

So saying, he held out his hand, fleshy palm ajar, to the boy, as one offers one's fingers to be sniffed at by a harmless dog. The "now, now" had changed to a whispered "there, there". Master Mink might have been a good mother dealing with a child troubled with dreams. Gilbert was trying to mouth apologies but nothing coherent emerged. He seemed slightly reassured by Mink's soothing manner. So was I. But I was deceived. The plump, open gesture and the mild phrases lulled Gilbert Goodride as well. Suddenly, Mink's splayed fingers closed around the awkward right hand of the potboy. Why do we suppose that fat men are necessarily slow and clumsy? I should have remembered how nimbly my co-player could caper on the stage. Using only his fingers, he squeezed the boy's hand, tightening his grip like a vice, until the faces of both man and boy were contorted, Mink with the effort, Gilbert with the pain. Then, still holding on with the one hand, he forced open the boy's fingers with the other. He spread them, palm-side-down, over the guttering candle which sat, fatly, in the middle of the table. The boy gave a small scream, more from surprise than hurt, I think, although he must have felt that too.

Mink held the boy's hand above the dying candle for a instant before bringing it down hard onto the mess of wick and flame and smut and grease. When he released his grip, Gilbert sprang back from the table, shaking his hand in the air and making noises which were further from sense than ever. Then, still waving the offended limb, he shambled off towards the outer darkness, whining softly. From the table on the other side of the room came a bark of laughter. Somebody at least had appreciated the scene. More pitiful than the treatment of the boy was the way he seemed to accept it as his due, as if life could be no better and no different. I was reminded of a beaten cur slinking, without remonstrance, tail between legs, into a corner.

"Good," said Mink. "Sit yourself down once more, Nicholas. When I have recovered my breath" – though, by the by, he seemed not the least winded by his actions, while I (as I realised after a moment) had been holding my breath throughout – "I will try again for refreshment. This time maybe, we will be favoured with the mistress's attention rather than her idiot's."

"Perhaps she will be less than happy with you for treating her son like that," I said.

"That is as nothing to what she does to him herself. I have seen her beat him senseless when he was younger."

"But he cannot help himself," I said.

"That is why she used to beat him," said Master Mink. "That, and because he reminded her every day, in his misshapen way, of the heat of her reins. The quondam heat. She is no longer what she was, is our Mistress Goodride."

The terrible thought crossed my mind, not only that Robert Mink might have known Mistress Goodride carnally (this was more than likely, judging by his off-hand and faintly contemptuous manner of referring to her appetite), but that this poor drawer Gilbert might have sprung from his own seed.

"I must leave," I said. "I have business to attend to."

Then Master Mink became all sweetness to me. Putting a confiding hand on my arm, he spoke low, "Please stay a little longer, Nicholas. Be comfortable. I will not keep you long from your business. We have not yet come to the reason why I wished to meet this evening. I would value your opinion on a matter."

I had all this while been standing, but now I sat once more. His words were flattering. I was a still unfledged member of the Chamberlain's Men and – although I tried my best to forget the fact – only a temporary one. Naturally, I harboured the hope that, by my skill and willingness, I might so impress those he had called Master Cabbage and Master Shakeshift and the others that they would create for me a permanent space on their boards. Master Robert Mink was one of the most senior players of the Company; it was in my interest to pay him the tribute of listening, and of providing him with an opinion if he so desired.

Such arguments with oneself are always the easiest to win.

Mink fumbled in his fine-quality, ale-soaked doublet and retrieved a sheaf of papers. "One reason I grew angry with that foolish boy was that I feared for these."

He extracted a sheet, seemingly at random, and brought it up close to his eyes in the attempt to read. Now that the candle had been so summarily snuffed out by his own action, there was only a dim, swaying lamp suspended from the low ceiling. It was as ineffectual as a glow-worm.

"Never mind," he said. "I know them by heart."

"What do you know?"

"The Lover's Lament, I will begin with."

He cleared his throat. His slumped shape seemed to straighten on the bench.

'O lady coy, be not proud, be not proud,
To see thy conquest at thy feet implore
Thy favour. For, like to Actaeon's cloud-
y sight when, with heart all sick and sore,
He glimpsed the charms of Artemis,
As she did show to envious woods her—'

Et cetera.

I cannot go on. I had to sit through this stuff but that is no reason why you should have to. I will be merciful and draw the veil over Master Mink's effusions.

Robert Mink did go on, however. Declaiming, sighing, whispering, urging, as if on stage, he begged his mistress to have pity on him. He threw himself into Tartary. He exalted her unto the skies. He waded through a Dead Sea awash with naiads, and a forest-full of dryads. He called in aid the whole classical pantheon. But, like all true lovers in verse, he ended no better than he had begun, still lost and lorn, alas!

"Well?" he said when he had not so much finished as, for a time, dried up, like the kennel down a street in hot weather.

Naturally, I knew full well whose verses they were, while, inwardly, I marvelled that a player with all his experience of others' words should be so blinded to his own.

"Is it Master Thomas Nashe?" I said, all innocence and guile wrapped up together. "Is it he?"

"Oh no, not Nashe," said Mink, not yet ready to reveal his hand.

"Well" – I pretended to flail about for a suitable name – "it is Master Shirley then."

"Nor him neither."

"Marlowe? It had just a trace to my ears of 'Come live with me and be my love' – as the passionate shepherd says to his inamorata."

It had no such thing, of course, but Master Mink was inordinately pleased to have his versifying likened to one of the most famous poems of our time. I could see, even in the tavern darkness that swathed us, his bulk swell up with the pleasure of it all. Deciding, perhaps, that he was unlikely to top Kit Marlowe for comparisons, he decided to own up.

"I am no Kit Marlowe," he said, though it was plain from

129

his slight smirk – which I could not so much see in his face, as hear in his words – that he considered himself not so inferior. "Though it may be that I am as much of a passionate shepherd."

I could not square the man of soft feelings and elevated opinion with the impatient figure who had crushed and burnt poor Gilbert's hand; nevertheless, I continued to play my part.

"They are *your* lines?"

Nicely done, Nicholas, I thought, in its admixture of surprise and no-surprise.

"A poor thing but mine own."

"Oh not poor, Robert, but rich."

But something about my quick and facile rejoinder, coupled perhaps with my ready use of Master Mink's given name, roused his suspicions. No one is so quick to take offence as he who is easily flattered. He returned the sheaf of papers to his ample doublet.

"You do not mean it."

"I do, believe me."

"You do not mean it and I do not believe you. No matter, Master Revill."

He spoke mildly, yet I already had witnessed enough of Mink's mildness and what it might be a prelude to. Fortunately, he now gave me my dismissal for the time being.

"You have business to attend to, you said. Another evening, and you may hear The Lover's Triumph."

"I am at your service," I said, already rising from the table.

Outside, the cobbles of Moor Street were slimy with the rain that still fell, as steady and remorseless as Master Mink's verses.

Sleep of Death

Scene: The next day. The house of Sir Thomas and Lady Alice Eliot. During supper the conversation turns to plays and players, in particular the value of the company clown.

William Eliot: You have Robert Armin with you now, don't you? In the Chamberlain's Company?

Nick Revill: As successor to Will Kempe, yes. Armin is our clown and so the heir to Kempe's bauble, his thing.

Lady Alice: It was not such a little thing, Kempe's, unless I have been misinformed.

Sir Thomas: Kempe the jig-maker. Your only jig-maker.

Lady Alice: He jigged his way across more country than lies between here and Norwich, and more than country, I'll be bound.

William Eliot: "Successor" and "heir" are grand words for the company clown, though from the way that he spoke them I don't think Nick approves of the trade.

Nick: I wouldn't say this beyond these walls, but I don't believe clowns and suchlike are an ornament to the profession.

Sir Thomas: Profession, ha!

Nick: With respect, sir, that is exactly the reason why companies need to be careful in selecting their clown.

Sir Thomas: Explain.

Nick: We are no longer a bunch of tatterdemallions setting ourselves up on a wooden cart in some draughty inn-yard, there to play peekaboo with the Devil and God and Every-man, in a creaking Morality of vice and virtue. We are the voice of our age. We are the mirror of the times. We inhabit one of the finest buildings in the greatest city the world has ever seen, and in our little Globe is the greater globe contained, in all her passion and splendour and, yes, sometimes in her squalor too.

William: Well done, Nick! Some more wine?

Sir Thomas: Clowns surely have their place too in all this splendour and squalor?

Nick: But it is in the nature of the clowns to break bounds, to flow over their banks, to obscure the face of the play with their meaningless torrent of words and gestures. I believe that is one reason for Armin joining the Chamberlain's and Kempe leaving us. Armin is less . . . broad.

Sir Thomas: Oh, if you want broadness then I remember Tarlton back in the eighties. He was the one, a small hunched fellow with a squashed nose. He'd jig and he'd rhyme and do his faces, and then turn about and shake his arse at the crowd as if he was going to fart at them.

Lady Alice: Oh yes! And you have heard the story told of a lady that once offered to cuff him . . . because he was so impudent to her face.

Sir Thomas: What's that, my dear? Tell us.

William: He struck at her first?

Lady Alice: He was sharper than that. Words before blows. He agreed to the cuff – but only on condition she reversed the spelling.

Sir Thomas: Tarlton was the one, there is no doubt about it. There has never been a clown to match him. Tell me, Nick, you're the insider. It's not just my age but our clowns have grown more sedate. They roar less than they used, do they not? And, from what you've been saying, you must approve of this change.

Nick: What Master Richard Burbage calls the congregation loves them still, unfortunately, but they are no friends to our authors. The playwrights are of my mind, I think. They would muzzle them. Clowns hold the words of others very cheap indeed, and think nothing of mangling whatever the authors provide.

William: "Let those that play your clowns speak no more than is set down for them".

Nick: As the Prince says.

Lady Alice: Prince who?

William: The Prince of Denmark, mother.

Lady Alice: Oh, him.

William: Hamlet is giving advice to the players before they perform in front of the King and Queen at Elsinore, if you remember. He has a message that he wishes conveyed to his mother and step-father and he doesn't want the royal court distracted by zanies.

Nick: Though Hamlet speaks also out of a feeling for the players and their art, surely?

Sir Thomas: Art, ho!

Lady Alice: I don't like that play about Denmark. They all talk so much.

Sir Thomas: It was a painful experience for us to watch, as you may imagine, Nick.

Nick: I – yes, I – it must have been.

Sir Thomas: Here was a man done to death by his brother – and dying in an orchard too – with the brother marrying the grieving widow. My own brother goes to his eternal rest. Lady Alice and I go to the Globe for some recreation, a little diversion, the latest piece by Master Shakespeare, and what do we find? That some of the outward circumstances of our lives have been shadowed forth on the stage.

William: But what of that, uncle? Our withers are un-wrung.

Lady Alice: Unwrung withers, William?

Sir Thomas: A line from the play, my dear.

Lady Alice: Dear William knows that play so well.

William: It bears study, mother.

Sir Thomas: If I was of a suspicious cast of mind I would consider that Shakespeare had borrowed our clothes to flaunt himself in front of the public. That he was profiting from Lady Alice's widow's weeds.

William: Pure coincidence. The sad loss of my father and of your husband, madam, and your brother, sir, must have occurred even as the author was writing. The idea is not his, in any case. There is an older play of Hamlet, by somebody or other. No author worth his salt is going to use real life when there are so many books and plays to borrow from.

Lady Alice: What is he like, Master Revill? Master Shakespeare, who is he? Is he greedy and unscrupulous, ready to exploit a private tragedy? I have heard that he would be a gentleman but that he combines that wish with a hard head for business.

Nick: Then you know him better than I do, my lady. I find him hard to . . . describe. He plays the Ghost, you know, in this tragedy of the Prince of Denmark, and that seems a part which is especially fitted to him.

Sir Thomas: How so?

Nick: A ghost is everywhere and nowhere on this earth. He materialises and then vanishes, without a by-your-leave. You might *see* him but you cannot *seize* him. And when he speaks, we pay attention because he carries intelligence from some place the rest of us have never been.

Lady Alice: You mean to make your Shakespeare mysterious.

Nick: I hardly know him, as I say. I'm only a humble player. He is the author. But he did me a good turn recently when he rescued me from the attentions of a boatman who had his arm across my windpipe.

Sir Thomas: Then your company author must be a strong man, I wouldn't choose to wrestle one of the Thames boatmen. I have some respect for him now.

Nick: He overcame him with words.

Lady Alice: Oh, words.

Nick: There was a certain balance in the case, my lady, because the boatman had taken exception to one of *my* words, and was trying to throttle me because of it.

Lady Alice: A rude word?

Nick: Worse, my lady. A would-be witty word. I was stupider than I knew and our author rescued me from it. Tell me, Lady Alice, he has never visited this house, has he?

Lady Alice: Who?

Nick: Master Shakespeare.

Lady Alice: Would I have asked you about him if he had?

Nick: I thought perhaps . . . maybe . . . when your first husband . . . it might have slipped your . . .

Lady Alice: I know there is a fashion now for taking up with theatre people, and in the highest circles of the land too, but Sir William, my first husband, didn't really hold with them. He was rather set in his ways. I think he still thought of your kind as a – what did you call it? – a bunch of tatterdemallions in an inn-yard. So it's most unlikely that anybody from your world could ever have crossed our threshold. Not even Master Shakespeare. Why do you ask?

Nick: Oh, no reason, my lady.

Sir Thomas: That means that Master Revill here does have a reason – but doesn't want to reveal it.

Of course I had a reason. I wanted to know why the initials WS were carved into the tree where, I was pretty certain, a murderer had been crouching. I didn't want to think that a principal shareholder and occasional player in the Chamberlain's Men (let alone the leading author of our times) had somehow crept over a garden wall and secreted himself up a pear tree. Even less did I wish to contemplate the idea of this reserved, likeable man dropping down from his leafy perch, creeping across the grass and, in some manner as yet undetermined, putting an end to the sleeping life of Sir William Eliot.

True, Master WS was a proficient in the art of murder – just as he was in those other dark arts of lying, cheating and forswearing, of slander, theft, mutilation and mayhem. To say nothing of treasons, plots, conspiracies and stratagems, as well as the more homely gamut of envy, lust, sloth and avarice. Master WS was quite familiar with all these things because it was his job to sound humanity to its nethermost depths. He is a playwright and daily presents us with our vices and virtues, leaving us to choose whether or not to acknowledge them. Everything human is known to him; nothing, perhaps, repels him.

But knowing is one thing and doing is another. Master WS might show what passed through the mind of cut-throat or cut-purse as he lay waiting for his prey, but that didn't mean that he was either one of those creatures. All are at liberty to think murder, and some of us may speak it, but few, thank God, do the deed.

There must be other explanations. And now I cudgelled my

brains to come up with them. As: suppose that the "WS" I had seen inscribed in the bark stood for Walter Self or Will Savage or Wynne Sourdough. And then I thought that these initials most probably signified Wrong Scent, for I was becoming less and less convinced by my train of reasoning. Perhaps I had imagined those initials in the bark, I had been so eager to discover the mark of a lodger in the tree.

In my notebook and using my Greek lettering I had little to transcribe that night. I'd found out almost nothing from my supper with Sir Thomas and Lady Eliot and William, except that her first husband had disapproved of plays and players. Like many who lived to the north of the river Sir William considered them, considered *us*, a threat to good order. The theatre enticed apprentices away from their masters' service. The theatre encouraged lewdness and other low thoughts and bad acts. My lady Alice, however, differed from her late husband. She had a taste for the saltier comments of clowns – I recalled Tarlton's reversed "cuff" remark. I recalled too the low-cut gown that my lady was wearing. And then I shut my little book wearily, and considered going to William on the next day and telling him that my stay in his mother's house was fruitless, for there was nothing to uncover. In truth, I felt that I should move back to my side of the river, and return to my kind, the players and whores and ruffians, the super-annuated soldiers and sailors of Southwark. It was generous of William Eliot to have offered me hospitality, whatever his ulterior motive, but I could not repay him except with titbits of gossip about the Chamberlain's Men – and even here, there wasn't that much to tell. It was as my Nell had claimed: they were, with odd exceptions like Robert Mink, the most regular group of men.

There was a tap at my door, accompanied by a whispered "Master Revill? Nick?"

I recognised Lady Alice's low tones. I picked up my candle and moved to the door, scarcely a stride away. I was a guest but not an important one – a player, for God's sake – so my accommodation was at the top of the house in a tiny monk-like room. Lady Alice stood outside, dressed as she had been at supper and during the household prayers which followed.

"May I come in?"

She leaned forward as she spoke so that I caught a whiff of her breath, still scented with the meats of supper, and glimpsed her small teeth, not too discoloured and with only a few gaps, considering her age.

For answer I drew to one side. You cannot refuse the lady of the house. My room was small, as I have said, but even so she brushed past me closer than required as she entered and I felt the soft graze of her breasts. "William isn't here, I'm afraid," I said too quickly. Once or twice her son and I had sat up of an evening, discussing the philosophy of playing as well as exchanging gossip.

"I know. It was you I wanted to see."

She shivered slightly. There was no fire in the room and the casement was open. I made to shut it. From the window, positioned high up at the back of the house, I could see the river's black sheen.

"I thought that all country people disliked the night air."

I had been brought up to believe that the night air was indeed unwholesome but I felt that the remark was intended somehow to "place" me. I was no true Londoner, but a rustic.

There was a truckle-bed and a trunk in the room. I gestured nervously at the trunk which was covered with a thick cloth and served me as table. She sat down daintily. I perched uneasily on the bed, lower than her, and waited. She picked up my little notebook and glanced at its contents by the flickering candlelight.

"Why, this is not English," she said.

"It is Greek," I said, praying that she could not understand those symbols and not wanting to explain the feeble code I employed whereby each term was simply transposed into the letters of the Greek alphabet.

"An educated man."

"Within my limits, my lady. My father insisted that I learn Latin and Greek from an early age. He undertook my tuition himself."

"Did he intend you for a schoolmaster?"

"Possibly. That or the church."

"So you became a player."

"I did not set out to contradict his wishes."

"Then you must have been a very unusual son."

"My father – and my mother – are dead, but I like to think that he would not wholly condemn the place that I now find myself in, I mean with the Chamberlain's Men."

"Ah yes. We heard at supper just how highly you esteem the stage and your company."

I was slightly embarrassed by this reminder of my effusions at table, brought on in part by drink. I simply nodded in reply. I was aware too that, although I defined myself as a Chamberlain's man, I was only one for as long as Jack Wilson was away at his dying mother's. I resolved to be a little more sparing in future in giving the world my opinions on plays and players.

Lady Alice put down my little black book and leaned back on my trunk as if she were quite at ease.

"I was interested to hear what you had to say about Master Shakespeare. I have been curious about him ever since I read his 'Venus and Adonis'. You know that story ?"

Is there anyone the length and breadth of this land who can read, and does not know Master WS's 'Venus and Adonis'? That tale of male reluctance and a ripe woman's urging, whose theme is the chase – the hunting of the beautiful boy whose real wish is to hunt the boar. The book has been out in the world for a good few years now and kept our book-makers and our booksellers busy, for it has yet to slip into those Lethean waters which await all printed matter. How many young men have panted to its verses, as I have, and wished themselves smothered by the attentions of an older woman? How many unrequited lovers, boy and girl, have pored and sighed over its pages, seeing in the indifference of the chase-mad young man to Venus's overtures an image of their own rejection?

> "I'll be a park, and thou shalt be my deer;
> Feed where thou wilt, on mountain or in dale:
> Graze on my lips, and if those hills be dry,
> Stray lower where the pleasant fountains lie."

As she repeated these words from Venus's attempted seduction of Adonis, Lady Alice leaned towards where I sat opposite and a little below her. Either of us could have touched the other one without quite straightening our arms.

"If I remember it correctly," she said.

Again I caught the layered sweetness of her breath, but with a hint of something gross and yet stirring below. In the uncertain light of the candle her white front swelled out like a soft siege-machine, designed to tear away at the firmest bulwark. My eyes swam and I felt as if the earth had grown suddenly unsteady beneath the bed I sat on.

> " 'I know not love,' quoth he, 'nor will not know it,
> Unless it be a boar, and then I chase it . . .' "

Quoth I – but my voice was not altogether steady as I drew the lines up from the well of memory. But she was able to give as good as she got.

> "At this Adonis smiles as in disdain,
> That in each cheek appears a pretty dimple."

I only just prevented myself from reaching up to feel for the dimples (which I do not have). The smile, disdainful or not, was already fastened on my face. It occurred to me that this was the second time in twenty-four hours that I had listened to someone reciting verses of unrequited passion. The difference between Master Mink and Lady Alice, however, was as great as the difference between the latter's poetry and Master WS's. Rather than continuing with the exchange of lines from Master WS's V & A, I said, "You should have been a player."

"Boys make better women than we do. It is easier to believe they are what they pretend to be. A woman on stage would be a distraction."

I was surprised at the earnest reply. It was as if she had actually given thought to the preposterous idea that a woman could play a woman's part.

"One day perhaps . . ." She allowed her voice to trail away. "Now tell me, Master Revill, or Adonis, for you have something fresh-faced about you, something countrified, and besides a woman who is old enough to be your mother can be so familiar – tell me what is the boar that you're hunting here?"

"I'm not sure I understand, my lady."

"You do, but I will say it more plainly. Your presence in this house. Were you sent for? Is it of your own free will?"

"Lady Alice . . . your son heard that I was embarrassed for lodgings and kindly offered to put me up here . . . for a short while. In fact I was considering just now that I ought to return."

"Return?"

"To Southwark. When I have to leave the Chamberlain's Men I am more likely to find further employment south of the river than on this side of it. There are more playhouses there."

"Why do you have to leave the Chamberlain's?"

I felt myself reddening. Fortunately, the room was dim. Her face, with its firm, decided features, was suffused with colour too.

"Because I am standing in the shoes of a player who is absent for a week or two only."

"I see. I thought from the way you were talking at supper that you were one of the pillars of the company."

I blushed more furiously. To cover myself, I gabbled, "Jack Wilson's mother is sick. She is dying, I believe. In Norfolk. In Norwich."

"Perhaps he will not come back."

This was, of course, the hope that had passed through my mind, and more than once.

"No, no," I said.

"Yes, yes, you mean."

"Am I so transparent, my lady?"

"Not transparent enough, Master Revill, I think."

"I do not understand you."

"Have you found what you're looking for?"

"I don't know what I am looking for," I said, truthfully.

"That is as good as admitting that you are looking for something. Remember what happened to Adonis in the chase after the boar," she said. She reached across – we were still less than an arm's-length from one another – and cupped her hand above my crotch.

> "And nuzzling in his flank, the loving swine
> Sheathed unaware the tusk in his soft groin."

I was too surprised to respond for myself, although my member began to show a mind of its own under her near-touch. Lady Alice seemed pleased and also amused.

"What Adonis would not do for the woman who wanted him was, alas, done to him. Thus was Adonis slain."

She removed her hand, and so I was half relieved, half regretful.

"Not a word, Master Revill."

I wasn't certain whether this was an injunction or a question. Before I might have asked Lady Alice what she meant she had slipped away from my room.

This wasn't my last visitor of the evening, however. Moments later there came another tap, and my heart stirred for I thought it might be my lady returning to continue our discourse of 'Venus and Adonis'. Yet the tap was less confident. I went to the door, candle in hand, and saw the creased features of Francis, the wiry little servant who had been the first to discover the body of Sir William Eliot in the garden.

He looked troubled and began to gesture before he started to speak.

"Oh excuse me, sir."

"That's all right, Francis."

"You remember that you was asking me questions about Sir William and how I found him?"

"You were very informative."

"Thank you, sir. And now it's gone."

"I don't absolutely follow you, Francis."

"My shirt."

Here he drew out in the air a T-shape which I took to be the garment in question.

"Your shirt has gone? Ah, your shirt. The one you were wearing when you found your late master."

"Sir William, yes. It has gone from the trunk which lies under my bed."

"Perhaps one of the other servants in your room has taken it."

"I have asked Alfred and Will and Peter and they have said no and besides they are bigger men than me so why should they take my clothes when they would not fit?"

His brow creased like rumpled washing.

It seemed as though the unfortunate Francis expected me to do something about his missing shirt, even that he held me partly responsible for its disappearance, perhaps because we had previously discussed the item of clothing. It was curious, I thought, that the garment he was wearing when he found Sir William – and the sleeve of which he had employed to wipe away a silvery mark from the dead man's cheek – should apparently have vanished. Or it was not curious at all, and I was imagining all sorts of oddness where all was straight and even.

"I'm sorry to hear this, Francis, but I, er, expect your shirt will turn up again," I said, sounding to my own ears like some harried mother reassuring a small child. "It is a small thing, after all."

"A man like me may measure his worth in the world by his shirts, and one or two further items," said Francis with dignity. Having got this off his chest, he withdrew.

It must not be thought that, even while I was busy in the house of Sir Thomas and Lady Alice trying to discover something about the death of her first husband and growing more and more certain that there was nothing to discover, I was undutiful in my playing. Quite apart from Master Burbage's warning of the sanctions that waited on those who missed rehearsals, I had something stronger to urge me across the river every morning. My love of the profession, my hopes for advancement in it, both ensured that I was prompt in attendance. However small my parts, whether I was playing a respectable citizen or a boorish rustic, a Roman poet or a courtly poisoner, I was careful to have my lines off pat and not to trespass beyond the bounds of what I was set there to say and do. A licensed clown can carry out much of his own business, as I had indicated to Sir Thomas and Lady Alice, while the leaders of our company such as Master Burbage and Master Phillips have their own style which the crowd loves. But the newcomer does best when he holds quiet to his place while looking all about him. Besides all this, there was an air of intentness and responsibility which shaped everything that the Chamberlain's did, in contrast to my time with the Admiral's Men. It was as if we knew that we were engaged in a serious enterprise – why, we were holding the mirror up to nature.

True, the reason why many of our audience came to see us in pieces such as *A Somerset Tragedy* was because the plays were full of what Master Mink called fighting and fucking and fury. Burbage & co could not have afforded to turn their back on this gaudy stuff even if they'd wanted to. Nor do I believe that they would have wished it. To be a player, however elevated and respectable, is always to have the smell of the crowd in your nostrils, and that is a stench which you grow to love. Sometimes from the boards I would look out across the press, the sea of bobbing heads, bare and bonneted, the clouds of smoke wreathing upwards from dozens of pipes, the gallants who took their seats on the sides of the stage, the shadowy ranks of the galleries where well-to-do folk like the Eliots paid for their privacy and (perhaps) pleasures unconnected with the play. Underneath the lines being declaimed, I heard that continuous susurration which accompanies a crowd and which falls away altogether only when a prince dies or a courtesan gets her come-uppance. Out there in the press, bargains soft and hard were being negotiated, favours exacted, gossip exchanged, pockets plundered, ale gulped, pippins picked at by dainty teeth. Yet for all that, the press or congregation was with us and we with them. The Globe was like some mighty ship, and its glowing white walls were her sails, spread to take us into uncharted territory, while the utterance of speakers on stage and off, sacred and profane, was the breath that filled those sails.

And, no, even in the midst of these elevated thoughts, I did not forget my lines.

Two days after Francis had come to see me, anxious for his missing shirt, he was found face down on the muddy foreshore which lay between the wall of the Eliots' garden and the river. He had evidently slipped and struck his head on a large stone embedded in the ooze. The tide might have lifted him up overnight and carted the body off altogether so that he was never seen again, but he had fetched up against a rotten pile that protruded from water like a diseased finger. As the tide receded he had dropped into the mud again. He was discovered by a boatman who recognised his crinkled features and wiry frame as those of one of the Eliots' servants.

ACT III

*T*his was too easy.

   I arranged to meet him using Adrian as a go-between. Adrian is serviceable and malicious, and believes that he has a touch of the demonic about him. Hence the black apparel and saturnine gaze. He pulls his hat upon his brows, and looks and looks. He sees himself as a plotter, a cunning politician. Certainly he spent his time in my lady Alice's household lining his own pockets. It was only William's blindness to what was going on under his nose that enabled Adrian to remain so long in his position as steward – and it was only a matter of time before he was caught out and exposed. Our player had a hand in that business, and by his piece of legerdemain exposed the steward as a common thief. I am amused that Adrian considers himself to be an innocent in all this and blames the player for dishonesty. I remind him that he really did intend to steal my lady's necklace. He reminds me that it was I who suborned him to steal it. Nevertheless, Adrian hates our player (so do I) and is waiting for a chance to make him atone. This fact may be useful.

   In the meantime, Adrian is down on his luck despite all that pocket-lining, and for a consideration will carry out any small task, provided it be devious. I told him to accost Francis in private, and arrange a meeting between us. I did not want to see

Francis face to face myself. He would have wondered. He might have taken fright and refused me an interview. Adrian had to provide some vague talk about a shirt, and the offer of a little money if he would see me alone for a moment. Not too much money, mind, because nothing rouses a man's suspicions so quickly as an over-large reward for a small business. Without saying who was behind this, Adrian was to tell Francis that someone had important matters to communicate to him – to do with the shirt. With so little a thing may a man be ensnared. I almost wish that the shirt had been something slighter, perhaps a handkerchief. Why, a man's life might be laid down for a handkerchief.

The little servant came out of the side gate of the main garden. It was late in an autumn evening and a thin, insinuating mist had started to rise from the river. He did not like being out at this hour, no doubt believing, like many simple souls, that he would be blasted by the night air. If it hadn't been for the promise of money, and more importantly, the mention of his shirt I don't suppose he would have appeared at all. And oh the shirt! You would have thought from his anxiety that it had been woven of the finest holland rather than the coarse cheap thing it actually was – dowlas, filthy dowlas. I would not have have worn it on my back for ten pounds. Francis saw me standing in the shadows – or rather he saw my shape.

"Master—"

I could hear the apprehension in his voice. He was shifting around like an animal about to be slaughtered. I was afraid he was going to bolt back through the door, so I put on my calmest, most reassuring manner.

"No master now but a friend, Francis."

"I hope so, sir."

"Master Adrian has talked much of you and tells me what a fine servant you are."

"*I do my best, sir.*"

"*You were present when the body of Sir William Eliot was found, I know.*"

I had grown used to the dark and so, even with the mist swirling about us, I could almost see the start he gave at this unexpected subject. When Francis spoke there was a tremor of pride in his voice.

"*It was me who found the late master. In his hammock.*"

I resisted the temptation of saying, And it was I who put him there. Instead I said, "There are worse places to die than in one's hammock. To pass from a little sleep to a larger one."

"*Another gentleman spoke to me recently of . . . that same thing. He wanted to know how I discovered Sir William and other things.*"

"*Such as?*"

"*How my lady carried herself. What were her words that came at me when I was feeling the darkness on the other side of the wall. He had a deal of questions.*"

"*It is Master Revill that you mean?*"

"*Him, sir, the player.*"

"*Francis, accompany me, would you? I have something to show you.*"

"*Pardon me, sir, but could not this business be conducted indoors?*"

"*No house but has hidden eyes, Francis.*"

This reply seemed to satisfy him, for after a pause he continued, "Master Adrian, he said you had a shirt. It has gone from the trunk under my bed these two days. A man like me may measure his worth in the world by his shirts. I have little else."

"*You have hit on the very matter that I wished to talk to you about – your shirt.*"

"We are talking now, sir."

"Somewhere more removed. Why, this is almost a thorough-fare."

This was nonsense. Mixen Lane leads nowhere but to the river, and who would be going down there on a cold misty autumn night? The only passengers would be drunks who had lost their way or groping couples too poor to pay for a straw pallet in a flea-ridden leaping-house, and thinking to recline on the soft stinking banks of our Thames.

"Come Francis, I mean you no harm, and look what I have here — see!"

With a flourish that would have befitted the stage I produced the shirt from under my cloak. It seemed to glimmer as I passed it over, although for all that was to be seen in the misty darkness I might have shown him a piece of bed-sheet. Francis reached out eagerly and clasped the unwashed item. I believe he even put it up to his nostrils and snuffed his own scent. The question that would have sprung to my lips in such circumstances — why had I taken this garment into my hands? — did not occur to the simple servant or, if it did, he chose not to voice it.

"There are one or two other things I must discuss with you, Francis, and they concern the death of your late master. I have to tell you" — and here I leaned closer to him and whispered confidentially — *"that I suspect foul play was involved. I need your help. I need your head in this matter, but we must discuss it elsewhere."*

I took him by the arm and turned in the direction of the river. When you speak soothingly to an animal and caress it, the creature will follow you at heels, even though it is half aware that it goes to its doom; even so I urged Francis to accompany me with mild words and a gentle touch. He permitted himself to be *led by the nose. The lane sloped down towards the water and turned into a muddy slide. The tide was out, and the slime and stones that spend half their long lives under the filthy water were revealed to the nose if not the eye. I sensed rather than heard the river's black rush beyond the bank of the mist.*

"Here, sir?"

He was frightened again.

"This is away from prying eyes, is it not."

"It is night, sir, and quiet and misty. Who is see to us?"

"Just so."

He tried again. "It is not healthful to be out and about so late."

"We shall not be long. Anyway you are close to the house and that should bring you comfort."

Behind us, though unseen, loomed the garden wall. It was in there, over the wall, last spring that I had . . . And now here, almost in the same spot again, I was to . . . perhaps there is no end to this process once it has been begun. Murder breeds murder. It is the slippery slope, like the muddy chute which leads down to the banks of our river. It is even as the descent into hell, easy and easier still the further that you slide down. Facilis est descensus Averno.

"Why should I need comfort?" said Francis.

"It is a comfort to be close to the familiar, when one is in extremis."

Poor man, he did not understand exactly what I meant but he knew what was going to happen. I held him by the upper arm, but tenderly. If he had wanted to, he could have broken away, have slithered and scrabbled across the mud and pebbles up into the safety of Mixen Lane and the side-door of his master's house. Even in the darkness he should have found his path by the upward slant of the ground. He was a quick, nervous man, and might possibly have outrun me; but I knew he would not attempt to leave my grasp.

"You knew I was there, Francis?"

"I do not think so, sir."

"No matter. You my not have seen me but I have seen you. You jerked your head round, so, as you crossed the garden which lies over that wall."

In the darkness I mimed the sudden movement of the head which I remembered him making. His upper arm tensed under my grasp. Perhaps he was able to see me now. The mist on the river gave off a queer dirty yellow light as if it were sickening from within.

But if Francis saw me now, he had not glimpsed me then, on the day that I murdered William. Francis, the good servant sent in quest of his master, had turned his white face straight at me but his eyes were not accustomed to the growing dark and I was obscure among the budding foliage. To me, on that evening in early spring, the scene appeared almost light as day. I had owl-sight. The moon was up, and the evening star hovered atop the wall. Moments later I had heard him gasp as he stumbled across the body of my enemy, which swayed slightly in the airs of evening. Then there were torches and confusion; flickering lights while the body was hoisted from the hammock; a woman wailing, one of the servants and not my lady Alice. But before all that to-do I had witnessed the action which Francis performed: delicately, he extended his arm and brushed at the cheek of his deceased master. It was a gesture that spoke well for him, it was a gentle and gracious movement. It was also the gesture that would now ensure his death.

"You were up a tree, sir."

"Ha, I was like the owl."

" – *a less innocent creature I think.*"

"*What?*"

" *The worm, sir.*"

Although I realised that Francis was talking to delay the inevitable, I was minded to humour him, a dead man. I was surprised too at the firmness and composure of his voice.

"*The worm, Francis?*"

"*The worm that flies by night.*"

"*That is not altogether inappropriate, my friend, for as you know—*" *and here I swelled slightly as I spoke the words of Hamlet's father, the ghost, the late king –*

"*Tis given out that, sleeping in my orchard,*
A serpent stung me."

I have never been able to resist an audience, even of one. Francis seemed curiously relaxed when he said, "And you were that serpent, sir."

"*Just so—*"

He had taken me off-guard as I was reciting those lines, and tore his arm from my slackened grip. Nimbly he darted away into the mist. I was so startled that I merely stood and stared at the blank air. I listened. There were sounds of scraping and splashing as Francis made his frantic way across the mud and shingle. For an instant I was no longer sure of my own orientation, and where the river flowed, where the walls of the garden stood. I cursed myself for having brought this man down to the shore of the river and toyed with him, when I might have made an end of the whole miserable business in the lane by the side-gate and no one any the wiser. Now I was mortally exposed if he should regain the safety of the mansion.

From quite near at hand there came a dull thump and a drawn-out sigh, and I jumped nearly out of my skin because I thought that someone else was on my patch of bank. The noise was almost direct ahead of me. I stopped breathing. Now there was nothing to be heard above or below the sound of the gliding river.

I crouched down and whistled softly, as you might to draw on a frightened dog.

"Francis," I said softly, "oh Francis. Come back. I mean you no harm and never did."

Silence.

I groaned.

"Francis. I have injured myself. I need your assistance. Help me."

In front of me coiled the dirty yellow mist. To my left there was a plop and then a splash as small things returned to the water. But no human sound. I waited a few more moments and then, half crouching, I edged my way forward, hands splayed, feet slithering on the slime and stone.

He was closer than I expected, and face down in the mud. He had slipped as he was trying to effect his escape from me. Whether by accident or design he had made off in a direction parallel to the river rather than attempting to regain the little lane that ran up beside the house. In the darkness I was able to make out his shape – for who else could it be? – together with a black pointed object that sat next to his head. This I reached out to touch and then more quickly withdrew my hand. It was hard and slick, and not with river-mud. When Francis fell he struck his head on a rocky outcrop which might have been fashioned to brain a man, it was so sharp-pointed and so angled upwards.

Francis groaned. A tremor passed down the dark form at my feet. He was still breathing. With my nerves on fire, with a *buzzing in my ears, with a red curtain closing in front of my eyes, I straddled his prone body. I half raised him from the ground by his head, using my two hands as if I were lifting a small round boulder. His body seemed to make a motion to go after the head and to rise up between my legs as if to overthrow me, but it was light, it was tiny, it was like a tail to this round head clasped between my hands. Then I flung him back down again, head and all, so that the protruding stone might do its work properly. Something spattered my face. There was the same sound that I had heard earlier, of his head striking against the rock, but this time it was not followed by a sigh.*

I sat down on the bank of our Thames, careless of the dirt and other filth. Slowly my breathing calmed. Close by me ran the unseen river, with an innocent purling sound like a stream. I waited. In my hands, on my palms and finger-ends I could feel still the shape of Francis's head as I had raised it up from where he had lain on the ground. In size and texture it was like a ball of stone, but warm as if left out in the sun. In one place it was not smooth at all but soft and dented. I had the leisure to wonder whether I would ever forget the roundness, the warm smoothness of that other man's head before I threw it at the pointed rock. I gazed at my invisible hands, which were, I surmised, black with mud, with blood, with the night.

After a time I went towards the river. The ground grew softer and boggier. I thrust my hands into the water and wrung them together and it seemed to me that each hand was the enemy of the other, and I the enemy of both. The water was cold and continually tried to push my hands away from my body, and take them off downstream. Once I grew unsteady on my footing and almost toppled into the river.

Then I sat again and considered the matter. I had not done anything so bad. Francis was a figure of no account. He knew what I was, and for that reason he had to die. It was true that I had somewhat lost sight of my original aim in all this, and that I had been ushered down a path not of my own choosing. But I had made the best of the road I was forced to travel. Anyway, Francis slept. He was secure, secure as sleep. I was safe from him and he was safe from me.

I got up and laid hold of Francis's feet. I tugged and hauled, while he slipped and stuck in places as he was drawn unwillingly over the rough foreshore. It was several hours until high tide by my reckoning. I might safely leave the body on the water's edge, and by morning it would be carried away downstream to join the other detritus of our watery thoroughfare. The only impediment were the massive piers of the Bridge, and if Francis's corpse was smashed against them by the downsweep of the tide it would be even further disfigured.

I left him there, half in, half out of the water. And so an end.

It was only much later, after I was indoors again, that I remembered the shirt that I had given back to Francis.

*   *   *

I went to pay my last respects to Francis and was rewarded for my pains. His body was laid out on a table in an empty ground-floor room. There was no watcher, such as I had been accustomed to when people perished in my father's parish, but of course that was a country custom, and therefore most likely to be shunned in the great city. Francis had been in the water for several hours and received severe injuries to his head where he had struck a rock. But something of the old Francis remained still. Enough to show that he was as anxious-looking in death as he had been in life. He gave the lie, as plague victims do, to the idea that sleep awaits us on the other side of death, the bourne from which no traveller returns. I shuddered.

As I was exiting the room I collided with a tall, gloomy fellow whom I recognised as one of the Eliot servants. Behind him hovered the bear-like figure of Jacob.

"Master Revill?"

Jacob nudged him from the back. The two looked as if they were on a deputation.

"I lodged with our Francis in this house, I was his bedfellow."

"Yes, he told me of you . . . Alfred?"

"Peter."

"Peter, of course."

The mute Joseph again banged this skinny fellow in the ribs to prompt him, but it was apparent that he didn't know how to begin.

"I am sorry that he is gone," I said.

"Death comes for all," said Peter.

"Indeed," I said.

"To some he comes early," said Peter, evidently considering that the way forward was by remarks of riddling obviousness.

"The river is treacherous," I replied.

"Treacherous enough – but not as dark as a man's heart," said lugubrious Peter.

"No doubt," I said, curious as to why these two wished to speak to me, for they had the air of men with something to impart; but I was also – to be honest – growing rather tired of all these theatrical hints and whispers.

"Master Revill, Jacob here saw something . . ."

Jacob proceeded to sketch shapes in the air. His arms flailed

and he hopped from foot to foot. He pointed through the
door to where the dead man lay. He shrugged his shoulders.
He tugged at his shaggy hair as though trying to draw down
his brows. He stood in one place, then in another. It was plain
that he was enacting the roles played by two individuals, one
of them presumably being Francis. Unfortunately I hadn't the
least idea what he was trying to demonstrate.

I smiled and nodded, and that drove Jacob to ever greater
efforts at a dumb-show. I remembered his clumsiness in the
box at the Globe when he had shown how utterly incapable he
would have been in the business of stealing Lady Alice's
necklace. Suddenly a likeness occurred to me. The shrugging
of the shoulders was Jacob's way of fastening a cloak, while the
brow-tugging signified a hat being pulled down.

"Adrian the steward?" I said.

At this Jacob nodded furiously, and Peter said, "That's it,
sir."

"I thought he had been banished by Sir Thomas, on pain of
punishment."

"He's a sly one," said Peter, "as you'd be the first to know,
Master Revill."

It will be seen that the subterfuge which had resulted in
Adrian's dismissal had made me something of a hero, if I may
thus express it, to the staff in this household.

"What Jacob here is, ah, saying is that Francis, God rest his
soul, had dealings with Master Adrian?"

"Just so," said Peter, who had taken on the role of
interpreter to Jacob. Long association with the dumb giant
had given him a facility of understanding. "He saw them
together."

"When?"

Here Jacob went into further contortions. I turned to Peter for enlightenment.

"In the morning it was, yesterday."

"But Francis was a good servant, a loyal one," I protested with a vehemence that surprised me. "He wouldn't have gone against Sir Thomas's command."

Jacob nodded, not in agreement but in denial of what I'd just said.

"He was troubled by his shirt, sir," said Peter.

"I know, I know all about the missing shirt."

"No longer missing," said Peter, producing, with a flourish which might be described as theatrical, a battered, crumpled and dirty garment from under his own not very much cleaner tunic.

I reached out. It was made of coarse cloth and was damp. It smelt of the river. A sudden shiver ran through me.

"Where did this come from?"

"Why, off him," said Peter, nodding his head in the direction of the body on the makeshift bier. "It were wrapped round his middle, like."

"Who gave it back to him?" I said, half to myself. "You're sure it belongs to Francis?"

"Why, yes," said Peter. "Look at this mark here on the sleeve. He was wearing it on the night he found old Sir William and when he came back he took off the shirt and folded it and put it away in his trunk and never wore it again."

On the sleeve was a greasy smear. I raised it to my nostrils but the only scent was the river.

"Would you keep it, sir?" said Peter.

"Thank you," I said.

161

But I hadn't the least idea what to do with a dead man's shirt.

It was Nell who suggested an answer.

"Why don't you," she said, as she saw me peering and sniffing at the discoloured sleeve, "take it to old Nick?"

"Old Nick's got enough to do, surely, without troubling himself with dead man's wear. Why, he may have the man entire and all without the encumbrance of clothing."

Though, even as I said it, I considered that if Francis, the meek and inoffensive Francis, were destined for the undying bonfire, then which of us should escape a whipping for our sins? None, my masters, none.

"Not him, you fool," said Nell fondly. "Not that old Nick."

"Nor young Nick neither," I said.

"Nor you neither, you fool."

"Who then?"

"Old Nick off Paul's Walk," she said.

"That one. Oh."

"You know him?"

"Never heard of him. Who is he?"

And here my Nell came over coy and simpering so I guessed that this man was someone she had to do with in the way of business, the business of giving pleasure in her case.

"He is . . . he does . . . mixtures . . . preparations . . . compounds . . . in his shop . . . under the counter . . . They say that he . . ."

At this point my Nell whispered in my ear a secret concerning this individual, old Nick, and our glorious (but ageing) Queen. What she said is too dangerous to commit to paper but, if it were true, it might shake the foundations of our state, like all gossip.

"Can you introduce me?" I said. "To your old Nick, not the Queen."

Cartographers are accustomed to make Jerusalem the centre of this earthly world. But if they considered more carefully they would put our capital in the place of the holy city, for my money. And of all the places in London the very navel is Paul's and, to be more precise, Paul's Walk. Here is all of Britain in little, the gulls and the gallants, the captains and the clowns, the cut-throat, the knight and the apple-squire. Here the lawyer parades in front of the idiot, the money-lender walks with the bankrout, and the scholar accompanies the beggar (often one and the same in our poor fallen world). Here will you see the ruffian, the cheater, the Puritan, and all the rest of the crew. Why, you may even glimpse the odd honest citizen. Paul's Walk is a babel. One would think men had newly discovered their tongues, and each one of them different from any other. To my country eyes it appeared still a little shocking that such a worldly buzz, such a trade in flesh and metal, filled what was meant to be a sanctified place, the nave of a great church. I said as much to Nell.

"Religion is good for business, Nick. Devotion makes men randy."

I remembered the noises of my parents on a Sunday night after my father had given what he considered to be a specially fine performance in the pulpit. Perhaps she was right.

Now, late in the afternoon after the play, we made our way through streaming Paul's Walk, avoiding the peacocking clusters of the gallants, the reefs of the ne'er-do-wells. The men, I noticed, appraised my Nell, slyly or brazenly. Some of them might even know her. Some of them undoubtedly did know her. I did not like the idea of this.

We made our way across the churchyard and to a shop squeezed into a corner. It was the dingiest apothecary's I'd ever seen.

"This is the place?"

Nell didn't reply but pushed open the door. The light outside was strong and it took some moments for my vision to adjust to the gloom indoors. I hadn't had much to do with apothecaries since my arrival in London Perhaps I bought with me something of the countryman's distrust of new-fangled city remedies, as well as a suspicion that coney-catchers were to be found not only on the exterior in Paul's Walk.

Old Nick's place didn't hold out much promise. The shop had a squinting slit rather than a window, and little light was allowed in. Wooden boxes and earthenware pots were strewn on lop-sided shelves and the smoky walls were hung with sacs and bladders of animal and vegetable origin. Overhead a stuffed alligator swayed slightly in the draught from the door. I say that it was stuffed, but I believe that at two or three moments during what followed I caught it twitching its tail out of the corner of my eye. On a clear space of the wall behind the counter had been chalked various cabbalistic signs together with pointed stars and overlapping circles and, imperfectly rubbed out, a detailed drawing of a lady sporting a great dildo. There was a smell in the shop, not a completely agreeable one.

"Hello," Nell called, and then after a pause, "Nick?"

Silence. The alligator's eye gleamed in the gloom. I noticed that other impedimenta hung from the ceiling: a couple of large tortoises, a shaft of bone with a saw-like edge, a scaly tail (doubtless a mermaid's), a kind of tusk (a unicorn's for certain).

"This is a waste of time," I said. I wasn't sure what we were doing here anyway. The place made me uneasy.

"Wait," said Nell. "He will come when you call him."

"Yes," said a voice from the corner.

I looked towards the sound. I could have have sworn that the corner was empty when I first surveyed the grimy room. A figure seemed to come together out of the gloom, to assemble itself from patches of light and dark.

"I always come when my Nell calls."

The man who shuffled forward was very old. He looked like a plant root or stem that has been hung up in some dusty corner and forgotten. Despite his age his voice had a sweet, almost youthful quality, but it set the hairs on my arms bristling.

"This is also Nick," said Nell to the apothecary. "Master Revill, that is."

"Call me Old Nick," said the old man. "That is how I am known."

I made a very slight bow.

"He wanted to meet you," said Nell.

"But now he is not so sure."

I, by the by, had said nothing.

"Did you recover your ring?" said the apothecary.

"It was as you had said," said Nell. She turned to me, eager to convince. "I lost that ring – you know the one I mean. I came to Old Nick and he was able to tell me where my ring was. He reads his secret book and shuts himself away all in the dark and then he tells me that my ring is in the corner of Jenny's room, hidden in the dust."

Probably because he'd put it there himself, I thought.

"Master Revill is thinking that if I knew where your ring was, then it was because I had placed it there."

"No, no," I said too quickly. "I am lost in admiration at the skill of your friend, Nell."

"Master Revill needs convincing," said Old Nick.

He spoke slowly and his words spread in soft, sticky pools.

"And you tried the remedy?" he said to Nell. He was obviously establishing his credentials with me, through her. "Plantain, knot grass, comfrey—"

" – and powdered unicorn's horn, I suppose," I said.

"Nothing so fabulous," said the old apothecary. "There is no magic here, merely a newt's liver and sliced snakeskin. But it worked, Nell, it worked?"

"Oh, I am a new woman, sir," said my mistress.

I felt angry and jealous. What was this? I knew nothing of Nell's dealings with this man – and if anyone was in a position to make a new woman of her . . .

"But Master Revill still needs convincing?"

"Why should you trouble to do that, sir?" I said. I'd made a mistake coming here. Why had Nell brought me to this dingy shop? "I am only a player, a poor jobbing player, no gentleman, not worth the trouble of convincing."

"How is Master Wilson's mother?" said Old Nick.

"Who?"

"You are standing in Master Wilson's shoes, I believe, while he is away attending to his mother, who lies sick. For as long as he is absent and in Norfolk you will work with the Chamberlain's Men."

This time the hairs on the back of my neck prickled. But then I considered: Nell and this old man were . . . acquaintances (I wondered what payment she'd given him for revealing the whereabouts of her ring). What more likely than that she'd told him something about me?

"You didn't tell me that, Nick," said Nell to me, reproachfully. And this, I now remembered, was true. Nell had the notion that I had been taken on by the Chamberlain's more or less for good. I had not made clear the true state of affairs, for I wanted to impress. So she couldn't have told her friend Old Nick what she didn't know . . . therefore the apothecary must, surely, have other sources of information.

"How long do you wish Master Wilson to remain in Norfolk?"

"As long as possible," I said without thinking.

"I can bring that about," said this withered man. "An accident when his horse shies on his return or an attack by some wild rogues on the highway. Or, if you prefer, a sudden illness that will despatch him to keep his mother company. "

I was tempted – for an instant. To reinforce his point the apothecary added in tones of drawling sweetness: "All of these things I can procure. Accidental death, bloody gashes, a mortal sickness."

If you had asked me then for my dearest wish it would have been to remain with the Chamberlain's Men at the Globe theatre, part of the finest company of players in London and, hence, in the world. As long as Jack Wilson was kept at a distance I was safe. But when he returned to take up his – my! – post I would again be reduced to a workless, wandering player, scrabbling for a foothold in another company. So I was tempted, tempted by the vision of Jack Wilson thrown from his horse or bloodied after a bandit attack, or stretched on a bier. But as these images flashed through my mind there came with them also shame and a thrusting-away of any such underhandedness.

"No," I said firmly. "I do not know Master Wilson but he is a fellow player, and I wish him no harm."

"Then you are unusual in your profession," said Old Nick.

I saw then how clever the apothecary had been. For the first few minutes in his shop I had been a disbeliever. But the instant he dangled before me the vision of my unseen rival, dead or disabled, I took him at his word. Even if only for a moment, I believed that Old Nick could do what he claimed, bring harm over a distance, hurt with magic. I felt also unclean, somehow reduced to his level. More than ever, I wished that I had not agreed to accompany Nell to his workshop.

"Are you convinced, Master Revill?"

In the half-light on his crinkled face I could see nothing, not even a small smile. His words were drawn out, smoothly spread . . . *Maasster Reveell.* I inclined my head a little, and the alligator swayed in the corner of my eye.

"We need your help, sir," said Nell. I noticed her tone of respect, and that irritated me too.

"This is no business of Nell's," I said, "but mine only. Hearing from her that you are a man of science, I have brought you this for your – examination."

As Peter had tentatively given me Francis's shirt so I now passed it across to Old Nick, feeling rather foolish. It was, after all, only a shirt.

The apothecary reached across the green glass alembics and phials on the counter, and grasped the bundle of clothing. He turned it over in his hands, which were misshapen and yet nimble. He stroked the material. He seemed in the gloom to shudder slightly but this could have been my imagination or, more likely, the merest theatrics on his part. Old Nick raised the shirt, all that remained of Francis's earthly estate, to his nose. He sniffed, then snorted gently.

"I smell river."

Well, that took no magic powers of divination. I stayed silent, half hoping that the quack would trip over his own cleverness.

"I smell death."

"Because the man who wore this is dead." I was giving nothing away.

Suddenly the man behind the counter stiffened.

"Francis," he hissed.

Nell gasped, and my scalp crawled.

"Oh, Francis." Old Nick's voice had changed from the drawling honey note. Now there was something robust and commanding in it.

"Oh, Francis. Come back. I mean you no harm and never did."

But there was a world of harm in that voice. Couldn't Francis have heard that, even as I was hearing it now?

"Oh, Francis. Come back."

Yes, of course Francis had heard the harm in that voice. But he hadn't moved, he hadn't escaped. Why not?

"Oh, Francis. Come back."

Old Nick was pawing and sniffing at the shirt like a dog, pausing to turn his head up and utter these repeated phrases in a voice not his. I grew very afraid that Francis the servant might, by the force and command of these very words and urged by his habit of obedience, be brought back to life, might return to us all smeared with river slime, might at this very moment have entered into the dim apothecary's behind our backs.

"Stop!" Nell cried out.

Old Nick looked at her. He shuddered again, then looked at the shirt which he still held. When he spoke it was in his normal, drawling tone.

"It was night on the river. With me – and with him."

"Who?" I said. "Francis?"

"I have no names," said Old Nick. "One of them was frightened for his life."

"And the other?"

"I told you that it was night. I could not see clearly."

I remembered Peter's words: *"The river is treacherous enough – but not as dark as a man's heart."*

"Nevertheless," I said, struggling to recall the original reason why we had brought the dead man's shirt to the apothecary, "nevertheless . . ."

"There is no nevertheless, Master Revill. You described me as a man of science, and what I accomplish I accomplish without magic. I have a power, but it will not be commanded. I cannot tell you anything else at this moment."

"Yes, I have it again," I said, suddenly remembering that it was not Francis's decease that we were here to discuss, but the demise of old Sir William in his spring garden. "That shirt that you are holding, it was once, not long ago, smeared against a dead man's face, to wipe something away . . . by the sleeve . . ."

Old Nick examined each sleeve in turn. Once again he put the garment to his nostrils and snuffed. I was relieved when he took it away from his face without falling into the trance state.

"Yes," he said. "There is something amiss here too."

Yesss . . . amisss.

I waited.

"But, oh so faint, like the scent of apple blossom," said Old Nick. He again sniffed at a cuff of the shirt. "And this from a different time, another occasion."

"Can you tell what is on the sleeve? Does any of it remain?"

"Not here, not now, I cannot say. There are mixtures, preparations, methods. I may be able to . . . why does this signify?"

"Two men have died," I said. "One was the poor possessor of that shirt, as you know. He told me hours before he died that it had been stolen from him."

"And the other?"

I found myself curiously reluctant to say. "Someone I never met. But I think that his death may be tied with whatever substance remains on the sleeve."

"So I should use my science to discover this?" said Old Nick.

"Or magic. I care not. But I will pay."

"You shall pay, Master Revill. But that is not the point. I am not interested in your money."

"Then you are unusual in your profession," I said, in a feeble attempt to draw level to him.

The apothecary ignored me. Instead he said to Nell: "The same arrangement with you, mistress Nell?"

"Yes, sir."

Her deference to him and, more, her provoking "arrangement" with this man angered me. Now, jealousy is foolish in a man that loves a common harlot, one who must open her quiver to any man that has coin. And when was jealousy ever argued away?

"Good," said apothecary Nick. "Come to me in two days and you will have an answer. Not you, my Nell, but you, Master Revill, shall visit me."

I held my tongue until we were outside in Paul's again. Even as I spoke I knew that I should feign unconcern. What did it matter to me whether my Nell had an "arrangement" with the Lord Chamberlain, the Lord High Admiral or Old Nick himself (the real Old Nick, that is)?

"What arrangement, my Nell?"

"I'm everybody's Nell today, Nick. Your Nell, his Nell . . ."

"No evasions, Nell."

"Evasions? You must speak in plainer English if you want me to understand."

"The arrangement, Nell. The 'arrangement' which your friend in there mentioned. What do you do for him?"

"Look over there," she said suddenly. "See that fine piece of coney-catching."

A few yards off, stood a young man – obviously fresh up from the country by his dress and his general air of wonderment at our capital city – gazing about him. He was being greeted by a friendly, open-faced fellow, greeted by name. Master Russet or Master Windfall, or some such. The name, needless to say, would be wrong. Then our open-faced friend would make a stab at getting the country-dweller's county. Worcester, Gloucester? There too he was in error. Then he would essay a couple of the rustic's fellow-countrymen. "Why, sir, do you not have Sir Tarton Barton as your neighbour?" or "Doesn't Farmer Harmer live yonder over Pillycock hill, three mile from your place?" These names mean nothing to our fresh bumpkin, which is hardly surprising as the open-faced fellow has probably made them up on the spot. In exchange for these questions the rustic gives the following information: his name, his county and the names of a handful of his neighbours. He would have volunteered more, probably down to the name of his mother's aunt's cat, had not the friendly fellow apologised, thanked him and departed into the crush of people in Paul's.

Nell and I knew that in about five minutes our innocent rustic, or coney, or rabbit, would be greeted by another affable man. This second friend would, of course, know the name of the stranger, together with his county – why he would even be familiar with the gentleman's neighbours! "Goodman Windfall, have you forgotten me? I am such a man's kinsman, your neighbour not far off." My, the bumpkin would think to himself – reflecting on how he had been warned before he started off for Lon'n town that the citizens were cold and aloof, how they cared nothing for their country cousins, how they were even prepared to trick simple countryfolk – my, this is a regular turnabout. Here am I in this great city, the world's heart. And here I have been hailed twice in the space of five minutes by men who think they know me!

The sequel to this? The bumpkin's new-found friend proposes stepping into some nearby tavern, and drinking a toast to their shared county and joint neighbours. Inside the alehouse, a game of cards happens to be in progress. After a jar or two, bumpkin and friend are invited to join in. Bumpkin's pleasure at so speedily finding companions in Lon'n town is increased by the delightful way in which he seems to be winning more at the hands of cards than he is losing. But he is careful. He knows that luck has a habit of turning. Just as he is on the point of drinking up and leaving and finding somewhere secure to deposit his modest winnings, his friend, by now his fast and eternal friend, says "A fresh pint and then away. One more pint and another hand of cards . . . a last hand for friendship's sake . . ."

The coney will return to his country burrow a sadder man, possibly a wiser one and certainly a poorer.

As Nell and I turned away from the scene we saw and heard another man come up to our country visitor, sure enough addressing him by name – "Goodman Martin!" – and identifying him by county.

However often you have witnessed this operation in Paul's, or in other parts of the town such as Holborn or Fleet Street, you do not tire of the smoothness, the ingenuity of it. Perhaps it is because Nell and I were originally from the country ourselves that we always took pleasure in seeing our country cousins duped and fooled, although there was a small measure of shame in it, too. All the same, we reflect that we would not be caught out like this because we are worldly-wise. And, I also reflected as we continued through the throng, is not jealousy a somewhat, well, rustic notion? It is hardly worldly to be jealous, especially over a whore. So I assured myself, and I tried to shake myself free from care over Nell's secrets.

"What were you saying, Nick?"

"When?"

"Before we saw how many friends Goodman Martin has in this fair city of ours."

"I was talking about evasions but it doesn't matter. I do not wish to know about your 'arrangement' with an apothecary. And don't ask me what 'evasions' mean, either."

* * *

I returned to the hidden garden in the Eliot house after this excursion to Old Nick's in Paul's. Why to the garden, I don't know. Perhaps, like old Sir William, I saw it as a place of refuge from the taint of the world. I was alone in the house and grounds, for once without Jacob dogging attendance on me. The afternoon performance at the Globe playhouse, a thing set in Milan, full of Machiavellian dukes and cardinals and their mistresses, had gone well. But what remained with me on this fine autumn evening wasn't the recollected pleasure of how deftly I'd turned my villainous lines as Signor Tortuoso (the murderous creature of the Cardinal-Machiavel), or the compliment that Master Mink had paid me afterwards ("To the life, Nick, to the life"), but the more recent scene in the desiccated apothecary's shop. However wary of him I was, I knew he had not been play-acting when he snuffed up the secrets contained in Francis's shirt. There was much that was wrong here, and I felt resentment, momentary but deep, of young William Eliot for pitching me into a situation where I was expected to uncover dangerous truths.

As I have said before, the door to the inner garden was no longer kept locked. I traced my way among the laden fruit trees – for it seemed to be a consequence of the old master's death that none had been instructed to disburden the trees, and the area had returned, as will all things unregarded, to a state of nature, unweeded and now growing rank with fallen fruit – until I reached the place where Sir William had met his end. Once again, I surveyed the scene. A heavy, golden air hung about the garden. The rays of the declining sun struck across the wall and into my eyes. Blinded, I felt the grooves left in the trunk of the apple by the dead man's hammock. What did I expect to discover? Unlike the bowed trees, this revisiting of a dead scene was fruitless. Yet before I knew it, I was at the foot of the guilty pear. I hoisted myself aloft and into the fork in the branches where my man had been. And yes, there in the leaf-shadowed bark were the initials, clear WS, not new but not so old neither.

I think, until that moment, I had been hoping that I was in error. I had surely, as it were, misread my tree. But no, I had not.

WS. The playwright, he had sat up the pear.

I settled myself more comfortably. It was a warm evening. I may have fallen asleep for an instant, tired from being a Machiavel's creature, wearied by the encounter with Old Nick. Anyway, some very short period must have elapsed because I came to myself again with a start. Unthinkingly, I glanced down. At first I thought I was dreaming. I blinked, and blinked again. Then I permitted my scalp to crawl with horror.

There, in the long grass between the two apple trees, lay a dead man.

Now, I had never seen Sir William in the flesh, although I had studied his likeness in a picture in the Eliot household, but I could not doubt that here he was, in the very space (or, to be precise, just below) where his body had been discovered. Nor had I hitherto seen a ghost. Like most thinking men, I have sometimes questioned whether any of us can ever recross that boundary between the here and there. On the other hand, I have – also like most thinking men – felt differently on this question in the middle of the night. Yet this was the early evening, the light was good, and my sight was unimpeded. There lay Sir William outspread beneath the trees.

Then the ghost did something worse than merely lie there.

It coughed and scratched at its beard. And all became clear. For this was, of course, no dead Sir William but a living Sir Thomas, come to lay himself down in the very spot where his brother had been taken off. A strange practice. How could I have confused two men who were not, perhaps, so alike after all? With the image of the dead man in my mind's eye, I had imprinted it on the living one in the grass.

My first concern was to not reveal myself behind my leafy screen. But I hardly had time to wonder what Sir Thomas was doing there, and to ask myself whether it was brotherly or unbrotherly that he should position himself in the place where Sir William had quit this life, when the riddle of his presence was solved. From somewhere in the depths of the orchard appeared my Lady Alice. She was carrying an apple, a bright red apple. Possibly she had been searching one of the neighbour trees for one that was especially to her taste. Or to his taste. For now she bent low over her outstretched husband, who must have heard her rustling approach because he had already turned his head in her direction, and placed the apple, not into the hand that was proffered, but straight into his mouth. Before doing this, however, she rolled the ripe fruit two times up and down, up and down, the snowy slope of her breasts. She was wearing the same low-cut gown as on the evening when she had made the visit to my little room.

I don't know why, but I blushed, invisible though I was up in the tree, feeling as red as that apple which had just passed from wife to husband. I was spying on an intimate moment between a loving couple, like Polonius hidden behind the arras in Gertrude's bedroom and eavesdropping on mother and son. If so, better to blush unseen than to cry out loud and receive Polonius's penalty. Nor could I, ever the seeker-out of parallels, avoid the analogy between this apple scene and that of our first parents in a garden (I am not a parson's son for nothing).

Sure enough, the sequel to this apple-offering was reminiscent of what followed for Adam and Eve after they had shared the gift of the forbidden tree. Sir Thomas, pausing only to remove the fruit wedged in his mouth, reached up and pulled down his wife, who was bending low enough for her tits to be near tumbling from her gown, so that she almost fell on top of him. My view was good, only a little obscured by the leaves of the pear tree; indeed there was almost a pure rectangular space made by the branches and through which I peered as if into the heart of a picture. They rolled around on the grass for a time, laughing slightly, snorting a little. My face caught fire anew. These people were old enough to be my parents, for God's sake! I did not wish to witness several minutes of cut-and-thrust-and-shudder (though, if I am to be absolutely honest with myself and with you, I was not totally averse to witnessing it either).

But something happened to the couple in the grass, or rather didn't happen, as it does sometimes. After a few moments, without a sign of impatience or anger from either party, Lady Alice and her husband simply disengaged themselves and, while he remained lying in the long grass, she sat up beside him, rearranging her dress. I couldn't see the expression on her face, since she was turned sideways, but I could hear her voice well enough.

"Well, Thomas, this can wait."

"Hasty journeys breed dangerous sweats," said he.

"At our age, the bed is better," said she.

"My dear, I wonder whether it is because this was the spot . . ."

"I don't think of him."

"But you used to come here together?"

"You are too nice, Thomas, to remember what I told you once. You are too curious."

"You told me a great deal then, and not only in words."

Saying this, he raised himself slightly from the ground and gave her an affectionate kiss, which she returned, equally lovingly.

"Now we can speak plain. Then we had to do much in dumb-show," said Lady Alice.

"Like the prologue to a play," said Sir Thomas, rather grimly. "Tell me, why has your son invited this player to lodge with us?"

Up in the pear tree, I felt the sweat break out across my forehead.

"There is no harm in Master Revill, even if he does seem to be rather full of himself."

Had I been free to do so, I would have bridled at this comment of hers.

"What does your son want with him?"

"*Our* son."

"Our son."

"You know how he is drawn to the playhouse. If he were not a gentleman I believe that he might have turned player himself."

"I sometimes think William – I mean, William my brother – had the right idea about players and playhouses. To keep them all at arm's length."

"Hang him!" said Lady Alice, with a sudden, almost shocking burst of energetic spite. "He had no pleasures. He could not go, for certain he could not go."

"And you could raise the dead, my dear."

"Don't."

And she seemed, to my eyes, to shiver slightly as she glanced around. For a moment her gaze came to rest on where I sat aloft. Fortunately, I was not wearing anything gaudy, but in any case her mind was elsewhere.

"Oh, he had no pleasures," she repeated, in an abstracted tone.

" – except his habit of coming alone into this garden," Sir Thomas cut in. They sniggered together, like naughty boy and bad girl. A fresh wave of sweat poured off my brow.

"How useful that was," said Lady Alice, more calmly.

Was this not an admission of their guilt?

"To have him out of the way at the same time every day," said Sir Thomas, tickling with his fingers at the exposed bosom of his wife.

"Only if the sun shone," said Lady Alice, shifting a little in the anxiety of her pleasure.

"When it shone for him, it shone for us."

More low laughter. More sweating from the watcher up the tree.

An admission of guilt, yes. But guilt of what? Their words suggested that they had engaged in covert cut-and-thrust, perhaps in my lady's chamber, perhaps elsewhere in the capacious mansion, when the husband had been slumbering here in the garden in his hammock. This was not yet an admission of murder.

I waited for more, and more came.

"Of course, there were always your trips to Dover," she said.

"Oh, Dover is a good port, a good place of entry," he said.
They laughed together, still like bad children.

"Dover in Fish Street, that is," he said.

"I miss my visits to Dover," she said.

"There is no need to travel when you are well provisioned at home."

"But you still keep your lease on Dover?"

"A foxhole merely."

She did not reply, and by her shifting slightly away from her husband I could see that his last remark had not pleased her. Anyway, they spoke so low and were so consumed with amusement at their own doings, that I could scarcely hear them. But I had heard enough. I remembered what dead Francis replied to my question about Sir Thomas's whereabouts when his brother's body had been discovered. "He was away, in Dover, I think." Although the knight and his lady were speaking in a kind of cipher, it was one that was plain enough to read. Sir Thomas, in addition to his debt-ridden estate in Richmond, maintained some little lodgings in Fish Street (close to Paul's) to which he and his lady might repair for their diversion. When he went there he spoke of "going to Dover", a town sufficiently distant to account for lengthy absence. The phrase had evidently become a joke between the two. I wondered whether Lady Alice's displeasure at his retaining the rooms was because she suspected that he might now be doing with another what he had been acustomed to do there with her.

"My brother was a fool," said Sir Thomas, apparently thinking that the way back into her favour was to cry down the late Sir William. "To cultivate the ground here and to neglect the ground *here*." So saying, he dug his hand in between her breasts, as if he were some species of gardener. She yelped, and not entirely with pleasure, I thought.

"What wealth he missed, what a luxurious crop he neglected to harvest," pursued Sir Thomas, evidently pleased with his agricultural metaphors.

"What wealth *you* have gained," said Lady Alice, and from her tone I judged that she did not mean only her bodily self.

"Oh, we have benefited, my dear. This has been to our advantage," said her new husband.

"As the cat said when the farmer's wife rescued it from the well," she said.

But this proverbial analogy, rather surprising in the mouth of my Lady Alice, was not much to Sir Thomas's liking, for he now raised himself into a sitting position. The sniggering understanding between the two, the sense that they shared a history of secrets, had been replaced with a brisker mood. The first gusts of evening were blowing over the wall and ruffling the trees. My back was clammily cold with sweat. Sir Thomas got to his feet and then offered his hand to Lady Alice. But she raised herself up without his assistance and then, together but at a little distance from each other, they made their way towards the garden door.

I waited a good five minutes up the pear tree, to ensure that they would be safely across the larger garden beyond and into the great house, before lowering my stiff limbs to the ground.

Excerpts from my notebook:

I have changed my mind. I thought William's belief that there was something odd about his father's death was the result of his grief or, perhaps, of attending one too many performances of Master WS's *Hamlet*. But now the discovery of Francis's body in the river, the emergence of the shirt that was missing and then found wrapped round his corpse, the disturbing behaviour of Old Nick the apothecary and his vision of somebody talking to Francis, talking in an urgent, commanding whisper, talking him over to his death – all this compels me to acknowledge that old Sir William's death cannot have been natural.

Another point (under a sub-head, as it were): after Old Nick had taken hold of Francis's shirt and was speaking in that strange, tranced manner and using words and a tone not his own, it seemed to me that the voice was familiar. There was in it something faint, but recognisable.

So I must conclude that Sir William was murdered.

What follows from that?

Where, when, how, who? And why?

These are the questions which follow, as the night the day.

Let us start with an easy question. *Where?*

Response: in his orchard, where it was his custom to sleep on warm afternoons. This was no secret. Anybody wanting to take him at his most vulnerable would choose that moment, particularly as they knew that he regularly went there *alone*. No one else had a key to the secret garden, Francis told me. I have established this from other servants too.

Another question, almost as easy: *When?*

Response: at some time between the beginning and the end of the afternoon, a gap of perhaps four hours. Francis says that the body was scarcely warm. Even allowing for the coldness of a spring evening he must have been dead some time. Also: his wife and his son and other members of the household came out to search because they were worried at his absence. This too indicates to me that the murder occurred earlier. If he'd been in the habit of staying in his orchard for hours, until it grew dark in fact, they would not have worried.

A harder question: *How?*

This may be broken down into several smaller questions as, how did our murderer get into the garden, how did he conceal himself, how did he kill Sir William?

Response: I don't know. Or, rather, I know only what I think I know. When I reconstructed the crime in the garden, attended by the faithful Jacob, I was at first sure that I had found the hiding place of our murderer, up in the old spreading pear tree. Then I doubted. But the discovery of those initials, WS, has in a manner confirmed my suspicion – yes, this was an "occupied" tree – while throwing me further into confusion. Both times I felt in my bones that I was crouching, uncomfortably, up in the branches where our murderer had crouched, that I was in his bloody shoes. My confusion comes from what those initials may stand for. Here I waver, shuttling between doubt and certainty. At one moment I think: The playwright sat up the pear. The next I tell myself: It cannot be that the foremost author in the finest playhouse in the greatest city in the world skulks in trees, waiting to drop down on an unsuspecting knight so as to put him to death.

As to the other part of the "how" question, that is how did Sir William actually shuffle off this mortal coil, what precisely procured his exit? That, too, I don't know. But I have some hopes of the apothecary.

Question: *Who?*

Who wanted Sir William dead? (If I leave aside Master WS.) Who benefited from his death?

Look to his family.

Lady Alice I know from my own experience to be a woman with, as Francis expressed it, a saltiness in her looks – and not just in her looks. Witness the behaviour of the couple which I had spied from the tree in the evening. That they were bed-partners before the death of Sir William was hardly to be doubted. Suppose, however, that the occasional stolen afternoon, when the sun shone, or when she might go and see him in his lodgings in "Dover", was not sufficient for her, or for him. Suppose that she wanted Sir Thomas for a husband, now and for next week; suppose that Sir Thomas wanted her for his wife, also now and for next week; and therefore they would not wait for mortality to strike the first husband down but must needs give him a thrust. Suppose that Sir Thomas wanted control over more than his brother's human relict; that he wanted the fine mansion on the edge of the Thames? I have heard it whispered, and not just by the unfortunate Francis, that Sir Thomas was near bankrout; he was heavily in debt, he was about to lose his estate in Richmond. What had she said in the garden? "What wealth *you* have gained." Isn't this enough to make them plot together – lust and avarice conjoined – to get rid of the first husband? (As Gertrude and Claudius *may* have plotted together in Master WS's *Hamlet*.)

Or perhaps the plot was all Sir Thomas's, and Lady Alice merely accepted the result without enquiring into it too closely, as women are always inclined to take what fortune drops into their laps.

On the other hand, young William Eliot has informed me that both his mother and his uncle were, in their own ways, genuinely distressed by the death of a husband-brother. What I'd witnessed of them from the tree didn't suggest that their grief had lasted long. Just so do Gertrude and Claudius appear to be genuinely distressed. They are good players at grief. So too is Hamlet, good at grief. Who is to say what is real and what is play? I go round in circles. Each argument meets a counter-argument. In this real-life drama it is William Eliot who is playing the part of Hamlet, the son of a mother recently married to an uncle, and of a father dead in strange circumstances. What reason might William have for wishing his father dead? A voice whispers to me, and I am almost afraid to commit this thought to paper: haven't all sons, in some hidden part of themselves, a wish to see their fathers dead?

Who is guilty then? All? None?

A final question for myself: Why compare everything to a play? Why should I hold every incident up and see whether it matches something in Master Shakespeare's imagination?

Response: Because it seems to me that the play is the answer – the play's the thing. This starts with *Hamlet* and it will end with *Hamlet*.

As it happens, the next afternoon we did *Hamlet* again. It was a sure crowd-puller and -pleaser, so the Burbage brothers had put another performance on the schedule in two days' time. The tragedy of the Prince of Denmark was to be leavened by the little satire of Boscombe's *A City Pleasure,* performed on the middle afternoon. After the Sunday break, we were to revert to our diet of crazed Milanese dukes and cardinals, and murderous painters and rustics in the county of Somerset. Such is the player's round. So dizzying is it that one scarcely knows on any one day whether one's first line should be "Buon giorno", or "Good den, zur", or "Greetings, my fair dame". And while these plays, together with WS's *Hamlet,* were going forward, we were preparing for the next batch which included *Love's Sacrifice* (the minimal part of Maximus) and *Julius Caesar* (the disposable part of the poet Cinna).

But that afternoon it was, as I say, *Hamlet*.

After I had delivered my lines as the English ambassador, after Fortinbras of Norway (which, being not a very big part, was taken by Samuel Gilbourne, who had been with the Chamberlain's only as many weeks as I had days) had spoken nobly over the remains of the Prince, and after we had all done our little jig and the audience gone home happy, I retired to the tiring-room, surrendered my costume and, exchanging a few words with my co-players, exited into Brend's Rents.

I was not surprised to see William Eliot outside. We fell easily into step together and, skirting the Bear Garden, made to enter the Goat & Monkey, the tavern where we'd first encountered each other.

"Sir, sir!"

"Not now, Nat."

The dirty man was lounging at the inn-door, hoping to be invited to do his animal-noises in exchange for pennies which he'd promptly convert – oh alchemy! – into ale's muddy gold.

"I will do you a bear fight, death and all, sir."

"No, Nat."

"Four dogs dead and the bear mortally wounded – all for one penny."

"Piss off now."

"Can you do a unicorn?" said clever William.

"No sir, for though it is not widely known, the unicorn is mute," said clever Nat.

"There's a penny for your pains," said William, and Nat scuttled ahead of us into the Goat & Monkey to spend the coin quickly. While William and I were talking, he would

187

glance at us from his corner from time to time, raising his tankard to his new patron.

"I thought you would most probably be at the playhouse," I said.

"Yes. It is like an itch, that play. I must keep scratching at it."

"We do it again the day after tomorrow."

"You have nothing to report?"

"From your mother's house? No, apart from the initials up the tree which I told you of. And the strangeness of Francis's death."

"Which we have also talked of."

Although it had been William who first inveigled me into the Eliot mansion with the promise or threat of something "out of place", he now seemed inclined to dismiss my findings as insignificant. Initials up a pear tree? Nothing; children, and lovers like Master WS's characters, carved their names into trees, not murderers. The death by drowning of the servant who had discovered his father's body? People died in the river every day by the bucketful. Not quite true, but he had a point. I had not yet told him about my visit to the apothecary's for fear that he would laugh at my credulity. Nor had I told him about the two occasions when I had seen his mother in a less than respectable light, once in my room and once in the garden. What was I to tell him? That his mother and uncle had been bed-mates before his father went down underground? That in every argument with myself I went round in circles?

"I am sorry," I said, "that we are so little advanced in this matter."

"My fault, Nick. I should never have asked you to do this. I thought that a fresh pair of eyes, ones not half-blinded by family affection or dislike, might see something which I had overlooked. No matter. I have enjoyed having a player for a lodger."

"Your parents too?" I said, remembering the exchange between Lady Alice and Sir Thomas.

"There is much coming and going in our house. They are civil to their guests, as befits a knight and his lady. And my mother has a real taste for the playhouse. She always did. My father, he—"

" – despised players," I cut in.

"I don't know that it was as strong as that. But he was suspicious, certainly. He felt that no man should pretend to be what he was not, even in play."

"My father also."

"So we have that in common."

I saw William's gaze slide to one side of my face, even as I felt outspread fingers slipping under the hair at my nape.

"Nicholas," a soft voice whispered in my ear. I knew the warmth and sweetness of her breath. "Shift up."

Nell pushed onto the bench between William and me.

"I thought I'd find you here, in your favourite hole," she said.

Finished with business for the day, she must have been. That is to say, by now she had earned enough to pay the Madam, with a little left over to provide for daily necessaries. The life of the whore is even more precarious and provisional than that of the jobbing player. As ever, I wondered who – and how many – she had been with that day. And as ever, I tried to strangle the thought at birth, just as I stifled the notion that she was looking for new trade in the Goat & Monkey. Nevertheless, I was glad to see her.

William smiled at my mistress. He did not ask who, or rather what, she was. He would know that no lady should walk alone into a Southwark tavern. And her dress of flame-coloured taffeta most likely told him a story too.

"Who's this, Nick?"

"William Eliot, a gentleman who dwells across the river."

"Eliot. Is that . . .?"

"One of the most distinguished families in the city, yes," I said quickly, considering that William would not have been overjoyed to know that the secret matters of his family were the property of a trull.

"A drink, mistress?" said William, all courteous and courtly.

"Nell," said Nell, simpering slightly. I wished now that she had been sat not between us but on my side only, since she wriggled and snuggled herself in his direction. "Thank you, sir."

"Call me Will. Sack or sherry, Nell?"

"Plain ale, sir – Will."

My heart sank, not only at this display of familiarity but because my Nell could not drink without becoming light at the heels. She drank, not ladylike in little sips, but in great gulps. In that state she was liable to offer for nothing what she customarily exchanged for cash. I knew this because it had been how our acquaintanceship started. I poked her with my elbow but she ignored me. William called out to the potboy and gave his orders. Did he know what she was? Probably. Did he care? Probably not.

"You are not from our city, are you, Nell? I can hear it in your voice."

"From our country, Will."

"Have you shut up shop for the day? Are your customers all gone?" I said, in a none-too-subtle effort to inform William that he was dealing with a common whore and in case he had not been alerted to this fact by her dress or manner.

"You keep a shop, Nell?"

She was all eyes for him, and he for her, and I was away on the edge of their vision and out of their minds. She was throwing back the tankard of ale and, in between gulps, no doubt casting up her eyes at him from under their lids.

"In a manner of speaking, Will."

"And what do you trade in?"

"Dainties . . . and sweetmeats . . . and suchlike."

"I expect you are well patronised."

"I always have room for another customer."

"No, you are never full, are you Nell?" I said. "No matter how many crowd your parlour."

"Even so, I dare say that your stock goes fast," said William, ignoring my interjection.

"So fast that it must soon be exhausted," I tried again.

"It is always fresh, every day it is fresh," said Nell, also ignoring me and draining her pot to the last drop.

"Another?" said William Eliot. "And Nick, you as well?"

"Thank you, I have not finished," I said, with what I hope was a bad grace. It seemed my fate to be accompanied by quick drinkers. I remembered the other evening in the Ram with Master Robert Mink and his love-lorn lyrics.

"And whereabouts is your shop situated, mistress Nell? Where does a country girl set out her stall? I ask in case I should wish to inspect your wares."

"You should ask directions at the place which was my Lord Hunsdon's mansion." (This was, by the by, a piece of coy

191

indirection on the part of Nell, for the house she referred to was the place now known as Holland's Leaguer.) "They will be able to tell you where I am to be found."

"I thought so," said William. "I have seen other vendors in that street, but none, I think, that may match you."

"Thank you, sir."

By this time, Nell had almost finished her second pot, and I felt myself growing sick at heart.

"Excuse me," said William. He went out into the yard, no doubt for a piss.

Nell turned to me. I was staring into the bottom of my tankard to avoid meeting her gaze.

"Come, come, Nick," she said softly, laying her hand upon my knee. "It is all business."

"No pleasure, all trade," I said angrily.

"Which would you prefer it to be? My trade is their pleasure. But it is my business, as yours is to tread the boards. We are all beholden to men from over the river."

"My trade is rather more respectable than yours, I think."

"You have not said so before."

"I have often thought it,"

"I shall make it up to you," she said. "I shall restore you to good humour. Who can restore you as I can?" she said softly but urgently, with ale-freighted breath, as she saw William Eliot returning.

I said nothing, but was a little mollified at her whispered words. It was true, who could restore me as she could? And considering all this afterwards, I had to concede that my Nell had some right on her side and that I had little excuse to interfere in her business. It was more that I did not care for it to be conducted under my nose. Nor could I be angry with

William. He was only acting as I would have acted. There is also, I have observed, a little core of sweetness at the heart of jealousy. For, I think too, that I was for the first time fearful of losing her, I who had always taken the girl's heart for granted whatever she might do with her body.

William joined us again but did not resume his position on the bench. He announced his intention to cross the river to return to his mother's house and suggested that we share a ferry. I was relieved, for it meant that he did not intend a rendezvous with Nell at that moment, even were she willing. It meant too that, had I chosen, I could have returned with her to the place that she had described as Lord Hunsdon's mansion. There she could make it up to me. By her little movements against my flank, that was what she seemed to have in mind. Meantime, William stood somewhat impatiently over us waiting for my answer.

"Thank you, William," I said. "I am tired after a day's play and I have parts to scan. I will go with you."

I could sense my Nell's disappointment, and was glad, and then wondered if I shouldn't after all have accompanied her so that she might do her worst with me.

I have just now talked with the doorkeeper of the Eliot house, and I must this instant write down what he said. It is the only way to order my mind and to set things in their proper sequence. This fellow's name is Tom Bullock and he fits it, being thick across the forehead, the shoulders, the chest, etc. Unlike in my interview with the unfortunate Francis I do not have to straighten out and tidy up his words. What Bullock had to say he said, and no more besides. And, when I had heard him, I almost wished the questions had remained unasked. I was seeking to discover whether anybody unknown or unexpected had visited the house on the afternoon of Sir William's death. The doorkeeper has a small cubby-hole by the main entrance and anybody wishing to enter the house – or leave it, for that matter – must pass him. Perhaps Bullock sees himself as a man of a somewhat philosophical turn of mind and thinks that the greatest wisdom shows itself best in the fewest words.

Nick Revill: You remember the day of Sir William's death?

Tom Bullock: Of course.

NR: You were on duty here?

TB: Where else would I be?

NR: When were you aware that something had happened?

TB: Something?

NR: I will be more precise. When did you first become aware that the master of the house was dead?

TB: Let me ask you a question, Master Revill.

NR: I am at your service, Master Bullock.

TB: Why are you asking me these questions?

NR: You have probably heard that I am a player.

TB: I have heard.

NR: From your tone I can see you have no very high opinion of our profession.

TB: Everyone must have a living.

NR: I am with the Lord Chamberlain's Company. We play at the Globe on the other side of the river. Indeed, I was privileged to meet the master and mistress of this house at one of our performances.

TB: It was there also that you met Adrian the steward, I am told.

NR: Yes.

TB: And discovered him for a thief.

NR [*thinking that I had glimpsed the reason for the door-keeper's hostility*]: It is true that I had a hand in that business. I did not dismiss him, that was your master. I merely helped to expose him.

TB: I am no friend to Adrian. He got what he deserved. He is a dishonest and high-handed man.

NR: Well, we are in agreement.

TB: If you think so. But you have left my question by the wayside.

NR: Your question?

TB: Why do you wish to know about the old master's death?

NR [*forced to pluck some explanation out of the air*]: I have it in mind to compose a tragedy, a deep respectful tragedy of the domestic sort, like . . . like *Arden of Faversham*.

TB: Is he an author?

NR: It is the name of a play, a famous play, about – about a death in a household.

TB: I do not attend the playhouse.

NR: I thought not. But I am interested in the tragic events which happened in this house because—

TB: – because you wish to put them on stage?

NR [*seeing that I am venturing into deeper and deeper water*]: No, no. I am interested because – because "Humani nihil alienum".

TB: I don't understand your words, Master Revill. Plain English is good enough for me. Nevertheless, if you must ask some questions for private reasons of your own, do it and be done with it.

NR: Thank you. When did you first become aware that Sir William had died?

TB: I heard the cries and wailing from the other side of the house after they had brought his body in from the garden. One of the servants, Janet I think, went running around the house in tears and, all those that did not know, she told willy-nilly.

NR: In the afternoon of that day you were at your post here?

TB: I have already said so.

NR: Were there any visitors that afternoon?

TB: Most likely.

NR: Can you call any of them to mind?

TB: One was of your kind.

NR: My kind?

TB: A player.

NR: A player?

TB: Or a – whatd'youcallit? – author, I forget which.

NR: How do you know?

TB: He told me. Just as you told me a minute ago that you were with such-and-such a company at such-and-such a playhouse, he told me that he was an author or a player. Perhaps there is something about the gentlemen in your profession, you cannot hold your tongues but must be telling all the world your business.

NR: Did you admit him to the house?

TB: No.

NR: You turned him away?

TB: No.

NR: I don't understand.

TB: It is simple enough. Listen. I was sat here as I am with you now, and this "gentleman" knocked and announced himself as a player or an author I forget which – as if he expected I would fall down backwards in amazement at his greatness. But before I was able to say anything to him there was a great commotion in the street beyond the gate and so I went to see what was happening.

NR: The commotion was to do with the gentleman?

TB: Nothing at all to do with him. It was some apprentices who had uncovered two lurking foreigners and were scoffing and laughing at them. The boys made a ring about them and were mocking the foreigners' hats or the foreigners' manners or their foreign words.

NR: You knew they were foreign?

TB: I heard their words and I did not understand. I only know plain English, Master Revill.

NR: What did you do when you saw these apprentices and these tormented foreigners, Master Bullock?

TB: Do? It was no business of mine. Let them that be a-cold blow the coals.

NR: Of course. What happened?

TB: The foreigners received a blow or two and a hatful of curses before they managed to run away. They got off lightly – but I think the boys meant no harm.

NR: So you stood outside the gate.

TB: I guarded the house. If they had run in my direction I would have shut the gate against them.

NR: The apprentice boys?

TB: The foreigners.

NR: Then you returned to your post in here?

Philip Gooden

TB: Just so.

NR: And the visitor, the, ah, gentleman?

TB: Gone.

NR: Where? Into the house? Back into the street?

TB: Into the street.

NR: You're sure? You saw him?

TB: No. But he would not have dared to enter the house, so he must have returned to the street.

NR: While you were watching the apprentice boys and the foreigners.

TB: While I was doing my duty, guarding this house.

NR: You've never seen him since that day, the afternoon of Sir William's death?

TB: Many people visit this house. The Eliot family is a great family and they are accustomed to receiving important visitors. Those are the ones I remember.

NR: So you know nothing about this caller except that he was a player or an author—

TB: Oh he gave his name, Master Revill.

NR: Which you cannot call to mind, no doubt.

TB: Yes. But not perfect. Like a muddy reflection I cannot get it whole.

NR: Part will do.

TB: Let me see. What was it? Shagspark, Shakespurt, Shackspeer, something like that.

Once again I was playing Jack Southwold in *A City Pleasure*, the play about the country brother and sister who come to London and who are, it is revealed at the end, not really siblings and so may marry in safety. The play was a hit, a palpable hit, despite my predictions about it to Nell. It was

198

during this piece that I had encountered the Eliot family for the first time and, as Thomas Bullock had reminded me, helped to expose the false steward Adrian. All this only a few days earlier, but it seemed like another life. And that had led to the invitation from young William Eliot to lodge in his mother's and uncle's house to see if, by keeping my eyes and ears open, I might detect anything out of the way about the death of his father.

Well, I had found out things, unwelcome things. Like a foolish mariner that sets out on a bright morning across smooth glittering water, I started full of spirit and expectation. And before I knew it I was sailing beyond the confines of the harbour and out into the open seas and had no charts to help me while, overhead, the skies looked dark. For what I was groping my way towards was that the mysterious man who had called at the house on the afternoon of Sir William's death, the man who had eluded the distracted doorkeeper, slipped into the main garden and then somehow penetrated the inner garden, the man who had hidden himself up in the pear tree and carved his initials into the bark as he waited to drop on his victim like a thunderbolt, this man was none other than Master William Shakepeare, the principal author, joint shareholder and occasional player in the Chamberlain's Men. The carved initials had been given flesh, as it were, by Thomas Bullock's words, which could not but support the idea that Master Shakespeare had indeed haunted this house.

I had earlier conceived of Master WS as a murderer and a cheat and a rogue – just as I had seen him as a bishop, a prince and a king. He was all these things and more besides, because these were the things which he had made in the quick forge of his imagination. But now I began to wonder whether he might not be in reality what he had so successfully presented on stage in the persons of King Claudius or Richard III, a secret and a sly murderer.

The part of the crookbacked king brought to my mind a tale, a piece of gossip, which was given to me by Robert Mink. As well as his own lyrics, he evidently loves a naughty story. He wheezed with laughter as he told me backstage how, one day when *Richard III* was to be performed, Master WS noticed a young woman delivering a message to Dick Burbage so cautiously that he knew something must be up. "Or soon would be up," snorted Mink. The message from the girl was that her master was gone out of town that morning, and her mistress would be glad of Burbage's company after the play; and the tail of the message was to know what signal he would give so that he might be admitted. Burbage replied, "Three taps at the door I will give, and and then I will say, 'It is I, Richard the Third'." Richard was one of Burbage's biggest parts, according to Mink. "Women were drawn to his crookedness."

The servant girl immediately left, and Master WS followed after her till he saw her to go into a particular house in the city. He enquired about it in the neighbourhood and he was informed that a young lady lived there, the favourite of some rich old merchant. Near the appointed time of meeting, Master WS thought it proper to arrive rather before Dick Burbage. He knocked three times on the door, as agreed, and delivered Burbage's line about Richard the Third. The lady was very much surprised at Master WS's taking Burbage's part; but our author is after all the creator of Romeo and Juliet. The language of love and persuasion flows in his veins. You may well believe that the young lady was soon pacified, not to say satisfied, and both she and Master WS were happy in each other's company. And now here comes Dick Burbage to the same door of the same house, and repeats the same signal. Knock, knock, knock. And he delivers his line about the crookback king, little knowing that another has stolen a march on him. But Master WS, he pops his head out of the window and tells his fellow player and shareholder to be gone. "And do you know what he said to him?" said Master Mink, hardly able to get the words out for laughter, "'This is not your place, for William the Conqueror reigned before Richard III'."

As I sat with Messrs Tawyer and Sincklo in the tiring-house waiting for my entry in the last act of *A City Pleasure* I was musing over this story and wondering whether it was true. Didn't it contradict what Nell had said about the Chamberlain's Men? Wasn't Burbage a good, uxorious man? Was anyone what they seemed to be? If it *was* true, and not a piece of inventive, malicious gossip, what did it show about Master WS – nothing much, perhaps, except that he was mischievous and quick-witted (as I had seen for myself when he rescued me from the attentions of Adam the boatman) and that he might look out for another man's woman. Nothing much.

"Well, Nick, and how do you find our Company?"

It was Master WS, wearing a bland expression and his ordinary day-clothes. His voice has a country sweetness to it (how many in this realm are drawn to the great city as if by a magnet!). I was reminded of Old Nick's honey tones and how they made my hairs bristle, whereas with Master WS you at once trusted and liked the man. And this reminded me in turn that I was due to go back and see the apothecary after this afternoon's performance. But here and now I was face to face with this man whom, at that instant, I had been convicting in my mind of a stealthy murder.

"I am privileged to work here, sir."

"We are glad enough that you are with us. I have seen you play, let me see, three times now. And I have heard good reports from Master Burbage."

I glowed. A warm feeling filled me. How ridiculous that I could think that this civil gentleman, with his kindly brown eyes and slight country burr, was branded with the mark of Cain!

"And in this thing of Master Boscombe's you are . . . ?" he said, referring to *A City Pleasure*. I suspected that he knew and was asking for the sake of conversation.

"John Southwold, a citizen of London, a figure of fun though not to himself."

"It is a good piece," said Master WS.

"Oh it seems to me not so good," I said, meaning of course not so good as one of your own, but not having the courage to say so outright.

"How so?"

"It is clumsy," I said quickly. "For – for example, you can see straight away that the brother and sister are not brother and sister and that they will be married by the end of the piece."

"Of course you can," said Master WS. "A comedy must end with a marriage. It's a rule."

"And," I ploughed on, "it does not seem to my eyes a very deep satire. The audience enjoys the jokes. They laugh at the corruption and foolishness that the author shows them."

"Why shouldn't they?"

"But they do not understand that the author is showing them themselves. Holding the mirror up to nature."

Master WS half smiled in acknowledgement, I supposed, of my reference to one of his own lines.

"They think that the author is showing them their neighbours," he said, "and that is what makes them laugh."

"Then they do not understand properly."

"Everyone thinks that the satirist's darts are aimed at the man in the next room," said Master WS. "It is not in human nature for any of us to consider the same darts as lighting on ourselves. That is why we can all bear satire so *light*."

Again I noticed that deplorable tendency to punning. Accordingly, I tried to raise the tone of our dialogue with a classical reference.

"Then it is like Pegasus and the Gorgon."

"It is?"

"For Pegasus held up a mirror and deflected the glance of the Gorgon that would have turned him to stone. Just so each of us turns away the killing glare of the satirist."

"Very good, Master Revill, though I think that you mean Perseus. Perseus was a hero, Pegasus was a horse with wings."

This correction was delivered so gently that I did not feel more than faintly humiliated. I was eager to keep talking, or rather listening, to this quiet man. From his clothes and relaxed manner, he had no part in the afternoon's comedy and was apparently casting his eye backstage in the same way that a landlord might survey his estate.

"You mentioned rules a moment ago. The rule that comedy ends with marriage. What about tragedy?"

"A tragedy may *begin* with a marriage." And Master WS looked for a moment wistful.

"Discord in marriage, that is comedy, is it not?" I said. "The unfaithful wife, the cuckolded husband who may be dubbed the knight of the forked order – the man with horns is always a laughing stock." (I was thinking, on stage, yes; but I was also thinking of Sir William Eliot.)

"But what if he that was hit with the horn was pinched at the heart, truly pinched, and so ran mad?" said Master WS. "That might make a tragedy. Or if the wife accused of infidelity was innocent. That might make a tragedy."

"It sounds as if there are no rules then," I said, to draw him on. "These things are usually funny."

"Oh, there are one or two rules, if you want to call them that, though I prefer to say tricks of the trade. The kind of tricks that an alchemist might use – or an apothecary – in order to draw in an audience which is anyway willing to be seduced."

Was it my imagination or did Master WS's gentle gaze suddenly harden as he said "apothecary"? I fancied that he was looking very intently at me and I grew uncomfortable.

"As?" I said. "What rules of play-writing do you mean?"

"That nothing very important shall happen in the first few moments, while the audience is settling down to watch and listen. They must finish talking to their neighbours or swallowing their drink or lighting their pipes. Only when they have attended to their own comforts can they give their full attention to the play. And so the business played out on stage at the beginning should be small beer."

"Oh," I said, obscurely disappointed. I had been hoping for a revelation from Master WS, not observations on the eating and drinking habits of the spectators. He continued:

"Or – to give you an example from the other end of the action – before the climax of a play the hero shall withdraw from the action. The audience will not see him for the space of an act or so. That way, when he returns they are the more pleased at his return and the more sorrowful at his demise. Prince Hamlet is kidnapped on his way to England by pirates and we do not see him for a time. At the same time, the author must not make the fourth act overlong, in case the audience grows impatient for the hero's restoration."

"Ah," I said, wondering whether there was not real wisdom to be found after all in such small things.

"Now, Nick, I must not distract you because your cue arrives in a moment."

He clapped me on the shoulder in a friendly way and then went across to have a word with Messrs Tawyer and Sincklo. So absorbed had I been by Master WS's words and – to be truthful – so concerned had I been by the impression I was making on him that I had almost forgotten the play unwinding on stage. He hadn't though. I realised that, all the time we'd been talking in low tones, he had been listening to the lines that reached us from the far side of the tiring-house wall and assessing the time remaining before my next entry. Master WS must have an excellent working knowledge of *A City Pleasure* if he knew when a minor player such as myself was due to appear. And all this for a work not his own, and one that in my eyes had appeared to be a journeyman piece. I resolved to pay more attention, to try to work out for myself some of those things that he had termed the tricks of the trade.

After the performance I made my way across the Bridge and up towards Paul's. The streets were beginning to empty and I remembered the recent occasion when I had been convinced that I was being followed. This time I experienced no warning prickle, no sense of being observed. I felt inclined to laugh at my suspicions and the caution of hiding away under the slimy pillars of a pier on the river. Most likely the plump, respectable-seeming citizen I'd glimpsed was exactly what he seemed. Similarly with Master WS. This courteous and thoughtful man, with his fatherly concern for the younger members of the Company, how could he be other than what he appeared? Yet, as I walked up Paul's Chain, I thought too of how fond Master WS was of disguise and doubleness in his plays. He has told us himself how one may smile and smile and be a villain.

In Paul's the business of the day was concluding. Sellers and buyers were withdrawing to do battle again on the following morning. I thought of the young man that Nell and I had seen, fresh from the country and surrounded by coney-catchers like a solitary sheep among a pack of wolves. How much would he have lost in the card-game or whatever it was he had been lured away to, lost not just in money but in his good opinion of himself? Also forfeit would be his innocence about London. Unless he was unusually forgiving, he would never think of the town again except with anger and resentment. For a moment I felt ashamed of our bustling city and sorry for all the sheep that flock here to be shorn.

In the corner of the churchyard was the apothecary, Old Nick's. It crossed my mind whether I should have asked Nell to accompany me since it was she who had an "arrangement" with the old man. But Old Nick had been precise when he said that he wished to see me alone.

I pushed open the door of the shop. Inside, it was was even darker than on my first visit. The end of the day was overcast and little light penetrated through the squinting slit that passed for a window. After a time I could make out the recumbent shape of the alligator, together with the mermaid's tail and the unicorn's horn, all swaying gently overhead in the draught from the ill-fitting door. At the back of the shop on the wall hung the animal and vegetable materials, shrivelled or sagging, of Old Nick's trade. A glass item on the counter reflected a gleam of light.

I waited.

I cleared my throat.

"Hello," I said, my voice sounding oddly muffled. "Nick, Old Nick?"

He would make the same sinister entry as on my and Nell's previous visit, materialising gradually from the dust and darkness at the rear of the shop. Probably he was watching me at this very moment, his own wrinkled vision accustomed to the dark places where he did his dirty business. Probably he was waiting until my unease and discomfort had reached a level that would satisfy him.

I spoke the apothecary's name again, more loudly.

Silence. Silence in the shop apart from the odd drip of water and the occasional creak from the objects hanging from the ceiling. From outside, from the street, came the welcome shouts and shuffling sounds of ordinary life. I shivered. I would have left the dark shop if I hadn't had the feeling that to do so would be to show myself as a coward – and not just in my own eyes. I had a strong sensation now, when there was no one around, of being watched. Also, I reminded myself, I'd come to this place because Old Nick had summoned me and for a reason: to find out from the apothecary whether he'd discovered anything on the sleeve of old Francis's shirt.

Maybe, if the old man himself was absent, he had left a note, some indication of where he'd gone or what he'd found out. But even as I made up this idea I knew that it was not so.

If Old Nick had anything to reveal to me, he would do it in person. Nevertheless, to break the stillness, I began half-heartedly to cast around in the gloom, feeling rather with my hands than finding with my eyes, groping on the counter top, across the warped wooden floor.

To my surprise my search was soon rewarded. Tucked in the angle between the base of the counter and a floor-board was a small square of paper. I unfolded it and could see the marks of writing, but the light was too poor to make out what it said, or even whether it contained words or symbols. The chances were that it was some recipe, made of ants' tongues and maidens' tears, to cure the pox or love-sickness. As I was crouching over this little scrap of paper somebody tapped me on the back of my neck! I must have shrieked or shouted. Certainly I jumped several feet back towards the door. My heart was thudding furiously and there was a roaring sound in my ears. I had my hand on the door, ready to pull it open and dive out into the street, when a quieter voice inside, the voice of second thoughts, told me to wait.

The tap wasn't the tap of a person. Whatever had struck me on the neck was now sliding slowly down my backbone. My first idea was that it was the water which I had heard intermittently dripping in the darkened shop and which I had assumed, without thinking, to be the result of some half-completed experiment or spilled container. But now, even as the idea came clearly in words, I rejected it. Experiments aren't carried out on the ceiling, and this was where the drip had come from. And water is cold, particularly when it slides down the back of your neck. This little stream was slow-moving and neither warm nor cold. It shared my body heat.

I put my hand up to feel. Then I rubbed my thumb and

fingers together. They came away sticky and I knew why. Blood was dropping from the ceiling of the apothecary's shop. I looked up. My eyes were more used to the darkness now, but it was still hard to make out the objects that swung there. They were simply shapeless, and monstrous. The unicorn's horn, the mermaid's tail and the tortoise shells appeared to be implements of torture from hell. The alligator seemed to wink at me with his unmoving eye and I realised with cold horror that the shape suspended from the shop ceiling was no river-beast but a man's body. As quickly as I had decided that the shape was human came the certainty that, bundled together and trussed up over my head, was all that remained on earth of the wrinkled apothecary. He hung there, the blood in his veins gradually seeping on to the warped wooden floor.

"And so an end."

I startled myself with the sound of my own voice. I had time to consider that this was a strange thing to say – even time to reflect that perhaps it was a line from some play. It sounded like a play. It is strange what things will float to the surface of the mind when it scarcely knows itself. Then I had time also to consider that my voice was changed. And then I had further time to wonder whether this was, after all, my own voice or whether it did not belong to one of the shapes that seemed to grow out of the darkness around me. Even as I felt a blow to the back of my neck and others on my head, I was glad to solve this tiny mystery of whose voice it was. It belonged to one of the black shapes that was beating me. It was not my own.

And then everything descended, joltingly, into darkness.

ACT IV

*N*ow, *this business was not to be as straightforward as the killing of Francis.*

Francis was no more than a simple servant and easily ordered and led, even though at the last moment when he knew that he was going to die he showed unexpected spirit in trying to escape from me.

But Old Nick was a different kettle of fish, a much more slippery customer. I'd had dealings with him before of course. What man past a certain age in London has not needed the potions, lotions and ointments of such a master-mixer, either to stimulate the appetite before love or to cure its ravages afterwards? Also, he prepared much that was useful when slipped into a lady's cup.

Therefore it was with regret that I decided that Old Nick too would have to go. His absence will be keenly felt among men and women of a particular age and class. Nevertheless, only a fool hesitates between a lesser evil and a greater one – I mean, the loss of another's life or the loss of one's own. Because I am afraid that Master Nicholas Revill, in his blundering pursuit of Francis's shirt and the marks on its sleeve, may be coming a little too close to the truth. One thing may lead to another: a stained sleeve, the means of a secret murder, the identity of the murderer.

I have a less reasonable fear. I have seen for myself that strange facility which Old Nick the apothecary possesses – possessed, I should say. How, often, when he is grasping a fragment of clothing or a personal ornament (ring, brooch), he is able to track down something of the past fortunes or the future fate of its owner. He is like a dog put on the scent. Why, once when I wished to discover whether a certain lady was remaining faithful to me, I brought him an item of apparel which she had worn next to her body. He enjoyed pawing and sniffing at that, and then, tail up and nose to the ground, he was off. I was startled when he spoke in my lady's voice, and more startled still when the old man began to cry out in the words and accents that she was accustomed to use with me in the privacy of the bed. Even though the words and cries issued from his withered mouth, I felt myself becoming aroused to hear her in him.

When he had recovered I asked if he had seen anything in his fit. He told me that he could never see clear and continuous, but that it was like a landscape glimpsed during thunder and lightning: sharp, quick pictures that were gone before you were able to seize hold of them. Nevertheless he had, he told me, the sensation of being roughly but pleasurably used, and he sniffed again at the piece of clothing as though he would drink up her folded scents through his nostrils. "Who was using her?" I demanded. And Old Nick described the man, though imperfectly seen as through a veil of sweat and delight. All this was some time ago; I have forgotten exactly what the apothecary said. Perhaps I did not listen after I had heard enough to know that the man with my lady was not me. The answer I received was, as I had expected, that she had not remained faithful. Thus I had the licence to make my lady pay for her trangression and pay she did.

It was this facility in the apothecary to see and hear others over a distance of time and space, others whom he had never seen or heard in the flesh, that made me fearful in the matter of Francis's shirt. For I could not be sure what might be revealed as he smelled after the hapless servant. Nor was it sufficient to recover the shirt by stealth and leave Old Nick to his own devices. There was no telling what or who the old man might tell in turn.

I visited the shop in Paul's churchyard. I had recruited our false steward Adrian to stand guard over the door in case Old Nick and I should be disturbed. Ever since that business with Francis I have found Adrian to be more and more serviceable. He has evidently decided that his character is better suited to a life of out-and-out villainy than one of petty gains and thievery in an important household. In fact, he has acquired his own little band of disreputable followers. He grows into those traces of the demonic which he is fond of affecting: the black clothes, the black looks. Without boasting, I may say he aspires to the condition of ruthlessness and looks up to me as a model of what might be achieved.

Once inside the dark interior I call out for Old Nick and he appears, pat, from the back quarters.

"Oh, it's you," he says in that tone which tells me that I am not altogether welcome. His voice has a youthful sweetness and doesn't match its withered old source. Perhaps it is no more his, really his, than the voices which he produces during his fits.

"It is I," I say, "come to visit my old friend, Old Nick."

"What do you want this time? More of the mixture which will get your lady into bed? Or one that will get her out of it for good?"

"I require something for an enemy," I say.

"A love potion?"

"A poison."

"Who for this time?"

"The world."

"But you have already procured poison from me, have you not?"

In saying this he has signed and signed again the death warrant which I have brought with me, and yet does not seem to know it.

When I needed the mixture to pour down Sir William Eliot's ear, in imitation of the way in which the villain Claudius pours poison into the sleeping head of old King Hamlet, I naturally turned to Old Nick. Old Nick the master-mixer for love and death, he who will provide lotions and solutions for all events. But the apothecary knew me only as a pursuer of ladies, and I did not wish to reveal myself to him as a purchaser of poison. You see, I have some scruples. So I rented a dumb man in Shoreditch and instructed him to take a paper having my requirements written on it to Old Nick. And told him, be sure to bring back the same paper to me with the mixture. You see, I am careful.

So I thought I was free and clear. There was nothing to connect me to the purchase of the poison, the piece of paper being long since returned and destroyed, and the dumb man of Shoreditch being unable to reveal who sent him to fetch and carry.

But, in this case of murder, I have discovered that you are never free and clear. Once it is done there are a thousand subtle cords that bind you to the act, and each time you snap one you discover that you are still tethered to the deed by the rest. And new cords and cables seem to grow faster than you can break the old ones.

I wondered how the old apothecary knew, whether it was his power of seeing-through-touch. Maybe he had needed only to handle the note brought by the Shoreditch man to be aware of who had really sent it. But, however he knew of the poison which I had caused to be bought, here was another cable connecting me to the death of Sir William, and of Francis, too. A living cable.

He waits for me to say something.

I am surprised that this clever old man cannot foresee his own future — or rather its absence.

"You have a shirt of mine," I say.

"A shirt?" He pretends ignorance.

"Brought to you by a young player and his mistress."

"The whore Nell. I know her. But as to that shirt, it is not yours. It is a dead man's."

"He wished me to have it. He told me so before he died."

"The young player thought it was his. In fact, he brought it to me so that I could make a repair to the sleeve."

"But you are not a tailor."

"He wished to discover who or what had caused the damage to the shirt."

"All this to-do over a cheap item of clothing. It is not worth repairing. It should have been buried with the dead man."

"I would say it is worth a man's life," says the apothecary.

"It cost him his," I say.

"And others' besides? There was poison on the sleeve."

"Then it was your own," I say. "Your mixture."

"I know," he says. "There is no craftsman in London who has the skill to produce such a potent poison. I thought so when the shirt was first brought to me and a trial or two proved it."

"What else did you discover?"

"A frightened man in the dark called Francis. And another frightened one now."

"It is yourself you mean. You know why I have come."

"I can see what you are about to do."

"You are old and weak," I say.

"But I am not fearful as you are," says the impudent apothecary.

215

"Why don't you struggle or protest?" I say, curious and diverted for an instant, for he stands calm on the other side of the counter.

"To struggle against fate is futile."

"So this is your fate?" I ask.

"And yours," he says, at which I grow angry.

"I cannot see an end to this," I say, feeling the heat rising beneath my face. *"I want that piece of clothing."*

"It is here," says Old Nick, producing it from beneath his counter.

"Thank you," I say, grabbing the shirt with one hand and Old Nick with the other. I pull him across the counter, scattering boxes and glass-ware. When I have him on his front over the counter, I carefully place the shirt to one side, telling myself that this time I must remember to take it away. Then I place both hands round the scrawny neck of Old Nick and squeeze and squeeze. He is a tough old bird and my grip is awkward. Although he doesn't put up a great struggle it seems a long time before his thin legs stop flailing and his withered body stops bucking up and down on the counter-top.

Then I call Adrian from where he has been standing watch outside the apothecary's door. The man must get used to murder if he is to keep company with me. He swallows the sight of the body with hardly a gulp and then helps me to lower the alligator from its swinging perch. The alligator is hard and shiny and weighs little because it is hollow. We quickly bind up the withered old man and hoist him aloft in the beast's place. He must have been cut in the struggle by shattered glass because blood begins to drip onto the floor.

Adrian asks why we are doing this and I say it is my humour. I am reminded of Hamlet's stowing the body of Polonius in the lobby so that he can joke about it.

216

I tell Adrian that the corpse is expecting a visit from a friend of his, meaning Adrian's, and the thieving steward asks who and I say, "Master Nick Revill, the player" and even in the half-darkness of the dead man's shop I see the other's mouth twist in anger.

"Perhaps," I say, "you would wait here until he arrives."

I leave Adrian after giving him further instructions. As I walk briskly across Paul's I notice the innocent figure of Master Revill making his way in the opposite direction. I am careful not to be seen. Underneath my doublet is stuffed the shirt that belonged to Francis. I smile and smile like a man in love with this fallen world. I take pains to keep my hands clenched because there is blood on my palms.

*   *   *

Darkness.

A jolting darkness.

At first I thought that my eyes were tight closed and so made to unfasten them. Either they would not open or they were open already – I could not tell, it was so dark. I attempted to reach up with my hand from where it lay awkwardly under my body, but my hand would not move. My hands were joined together. Next I tried to shift my legs but they too were fastened to each other.

I considered whether I was dead. Close by me were squeaks and squeals and, more distant, thuds and murmurs. This must be the afterlife. Was I in hell or purgatory with gibbering spirits keeping me company, either in torment or in mockery? Well, father, I thought, you were right. Here it is, and here am I in it. I shall describe purgatory. Complete darkness. Your body unable to move but shaken and jolted painfully every moment. No other feeling but aches and pains in every limb. Something close and stifling lying across your face. And

217

tiredness, so that you want to sleep forever but cannot for the aches and pains and the jolting.

Nevertheless I must have slept – or somehow retreated from any knowledge of myself because, moments or hours later, I don't know which, I went through the whole process again of coming to, and being unsure of whether my eyes were open or shut, and attempting once more to move my hands and feet.

Around this time the thought came to me clearly that I was not dead but alive, in pain and bound up by the hands and feet. I couldn't see anything because there wasn't anything to see. The stifling cover over my face and body was a stinking hairy blanket. The jolting motion and the squealing noise were caused by whatever I was being carried in, a cart or wagon most probably, as it jerked across the ground. The regular thuds turned themselves into the sound of a horse's hooves. The murmurs were the low, occasional voices of the men travelling with me, my captors perched on the driving seat of the cart. The aches and pains in my body were proof not of the torments of hell but that I still had life.

I tugged at my hands but they were securely tied, I could feel the cord biting into my wrists and the backs of my hands. In my mind's eye I traced back the path which had led to where I found myself now. The visit to Old Nick's shop. The wait when I was convinced of being watched. The sight of the apothecary's body swaying from the ceiling. The voice in the darkness saying "And so an end". The blacker shapes growing up around me, blows raining down on my head. The descent into night.

As the conveyance bumped and swayed on its way I tried to order my thoughts. Whoever the man – or men – who had done this to me, he or they had presumably murdered Old

Nick as well. Although ignorant of the means by which the old apothecary had been forced through death's door, I couldn't doubt that he had been murdered and then grotesquely raised up into the place where his alligator normally hung. I was less certain about why he'd been killed, but the drowning of Francis, that poor servant's river-stained shirt, the strange death of Sir William Eliot, together with the play of Hamlet, Prince of Denmark, all these things bobbed in my mind like the confused flotsam of some sea-battle.

Why was I still alive? Where was I being taken, joltingly and painfully, in the back of a wagon under a stinking blanket? Since the individual who had disposed of Old Nick had taken me by surprise, why hadn't he made an end of me there and then, and left me displayed at the apothecary's? He might as well be hanged for two sheep as for one. Surely, since I was still living and breathing, it must be for a purpose. This gave me a little flare of hope. I was not required to die – or at least not yet. But then, I reflected, the hope that relies on the unknown purposes of a murderer must be slender indeed.

I twisted my head to one side, and winced as the after-pain of a blow forked down my side. I tried to peer under the blanket but there was not even the tiniest gap or cranny through which to see. Or if there was, it was night outside and nothing visible. I listened. No sound except the squeaking wagon and the plodding, panting horse, and the occasional murmured comment which I could not make out clearly. If I had been certain that there were people other than my captors at hand I would have called out. I would have cried, "Help! Ho! Murder!" so loudly as to be heard from Spitalfield to Southwark. But I feared there was nobody to listen. There were no street sounds, no echoes of our passage coming back from walls or houses. We must be outside the city. If I could have thrown off the filthy blanket I would have been able to tell from the quality of the air whether we were within or outside the city walls. The smell of London was the first thing that struck me when I came up from the country.

There are four main routes out of London and we might be moving on any one of them. North, into the flat lands beyond Finsbury Fields. Westward, down the river in the direction of Greenwich. Or perhaps eastwards – although on that route the cart would have passed through Holborn and Westminster, and a prudent driver might prefer to steer away from crowded places. These directions all involved traversing relatively law-abiding areas of the city.

On the other hand, if we had crossed the river either by the bridge or ferry, we would have moved south through my own patch of Southwark. This was no particular source of comfort. Were I planning to take someone prisoner and carry him off to a secret destination, this is the direction I would take. Everyone knows that the law and authority of the city do not stretch far on our bank of the Thames. Men and women who have stumbled into trouble recognise that they have a bolt-hole here. Even those on the right side of the law but afraid of its frown – boatmen, for example, or the owners of bearpits – feel instinctively that they are at home south of the water. Respectable figures like the players of the Chamberlain's Men are resident in Southwark. Master WS, he lived in the Liberty of the Clink, did he not? Though not Master Richard Burbage, no, he lived with seven little Burbages somewhere oh-so-proper north of the river . . .

So my muddy thoughts pursued their meandering course. I probably fell into sleep or unconsciousness again, from time to time. Master WS's bland, brown-eyed face came floating at me through the stifling darkness under the blanket. Something he had said when we were talking backstage at the Globe in what seemed to be another life. Something about an apothecary . . . and tricks of the trade. Why had he mentioned the word "apothecary"? I would ask Master WS the next time I saw him. But if this slow-coach didn't soon get to where it was going I would not be able to return to the Globe for the next performance of . . .

I couldn't remember what it was I was due to perform in . . .

Suddenly I was jolted awake by a violent lurch. The cart tipped to one side and shuddered to a stop. There was swearing up in front and the thwack of a whip being applied. Then shifting sounds as the men jumped to the ground and, shoving and cursing, struggled to get the wagon upright and on the move once more. After a time they succeeded. The wagon groaned as they resumed their places and we continued on as lumberingly as before.

But I was too preoccupied to wonder any longer where we were going or why I had been permitted to remain alive. The jolt, as the wagon fell into the hole, had been enough to bring something banging against my back, something which was evidently sharing my stinking blanket and which had been stowed a few feet off. I hadn't been aware of it until that instant. The stillness and stiffness of the object as it lay pressing into my back reassured me and I told myself that my bedfellow was a roll of rough cloth or a bundle of sticks and staves – or anything at all so long as it was not the truth. This truth I could now feel on my backbone. I was being jabbed at by stiff fingers. Fingers belonging to someone else.

Every time the wagon lurched I was prodded, as if in admonition. And then, underneath the animal stench of the hairy blanket, another smell crept into my nostrils. It was the particular scent of Old Nick – a compound of herbs, some sweet, some rank, and his own bodily self – and overlaying all this the scent of death. And I understood that the body which I had glimpsed swaying from the ceiling of his shop had been cut down and placed beside me in the wagon. And I turned very afraid.

Then we stopped.

Again the wagon seemed to lift itself up as the men climbed down. The next moment the blanket that covered me – us – was pulled aside. I don't know why but I had somehow thought that the hours had slipped away and that evening had shaded into night and night had grown into day again. We seemed to have travelled so long and so far. Even as I sensed one of the men groping for the blanket to throw it off, I prepared to emerge into the clear and cruel light of morning, blinking like a mole. But no such thing. It was night still.

However, my eyes were used to the dark by now. It was my element. And besides, there was a little light thrown at us by a sickly looking moon.

I saw two men at the foot of the wagon. They were gazing at its contents.

"He's out," said one.

"I shall light a fire under his feet," said the other.

I took only a moment to recognise the first voice as that of Adrian, the false steward in the Eliot household, the thief I had exposed as he prepared to steal my lady's necklace and blame it on dumb Jacob. Of course! What more natural in a man like him than that he should seek revenge on me, the player who had cost him his livelihood and the respect of his master and mistress. Seeing this, knowing who my enemy was, somehow brought a kind of relief even though I was trussed-up and helpless, lying next to the apothecary's corpse.

I groaned involuntarily.

"Still alive then," said the other man cheerfully.

"Get him out," said Adrian.

Together they reached in and seized hold of my bound feet and dragged me over the tailboard of the wagon. I thumped painfully onto the ground.

"And the other thing," said Adrian

Moments later the body of the apothecary was carelessly deposited next to me.

"Go and call," said Adrian. I sensed rather than saw or heard the second man move off a distance while Adrian stayed close. As far as I could make out from where I lay awkwardly, face half crushed into the earth, we were in a clearing in a forest. Pale moonlight lay across the grass and fallen leaves. A ring of trees stood guard around us. The air was still and expectant. The horse snuffed and shuffled. It must be hobbled.

From the edge of the clearing came the hooting of an owl, or a townsman's idea of what an owl's hoot should be. Ter-wit, ter-woo, three times repeated. I almost laughed. Obviously this was some prearranged signal to be delivered by Adrian's accomplice. I thought of Nat the animal man, the Southwark beggar who made the odd penny by imitating the cries of animals and birds. I remembered how, only a few days before, Nat had made the sound of a hyena for me in the Goat & Monkey, a screeching mirthless laugh; how, only yesterday, he had quipped with William Eliot about the mute unicorn. I wished I was there now, in the warmth and ease and companionship of the alehouse, or in the warmth and pleasure of Nell's bed. I wished I had returned with her to her crib, that I had not left her with an ill impression of myself. I wished myself anywhere but here in the middle of a dark wood.

The other man finished making his bird calls and was answered by hooting from farther afield. This was more convincing than the first call but to anybody who possessed country ears it was still no owl. My spirits, already low, sunk down even deeper. So there were at least three of them, three men who counted themselves enemies to me. Why stop at three? Might not the whole forest be full of individuals who hated me or could be hired by one that did?

I tried to see where Adrian was but he was out of sight, probably somewhere on the far side of the horse and wagon waiting for his minions to return. After a time there were whispers from the edge of the clearing and the next moment three shapes were standing so close to me that no more than their legs were visible. I played, not dead, but quiet, glimpsing things through a half-closed eyelid and hoping that if I stayed still I might also stay safe. I noticed one of the six legs swing back and forward and, at first without connecting the two, experienced a sickening blow in the belly. Trussed as I was, I doubled up on the ground and retched helplessly.

Through red-dimmed senses and past my wheezing breath I heard a voice say, "No, Ralph. Wait. Your time will come."

It was plain that Adrian was in command. So far I had heard not a sound from the third man, save for imitation of the owl. Adrian must have made some gesture because I felt hands fumbling at me.

I was hooked up under my bound arms and hauled into a

standing position. I fought to get my breath back. I spat and spluttered. With my hands tied behind my back I felt naked, though I was clothed, and open to harm. The other two men, who I couldn't see clearly, held me up. Directly opposite was Adrian the false servant, his countenance gleaming in the pale moonlight. His razor-like nose quivered. He sneered in a way that, had he been on stage, I would have condemned as unconvincing. The one-time steward was wearing the same gear as when I had last encountered him in the Eliots' private box at the Globe Theatre. A tall black hat and a dark cloak that, together with the sneers, signalled clearly: I am villain. Quake, all you who look on me.

I half expected him to rub his hands together with glee and – as if he had read my mind – this was the next thing which he did.

"Well, player."

For an instant I contemplated not recognising him. That would be galling. A villain demands a response. But he could see that I knew him. Saying nothing, I let my head droop in acknowledgement. I felt weak and beaten. I was weak and beaten. But something told me to play at seeming even worse than I felt.

"Oh, this is turning the cat in the pan," he said. "This is a change of fortune."

I still kept silent, partly because I could think of nothing to say and partly to deny him the satisfaction of an answer. He remained gazing at me for a moment longer, then turned away, motioning for us to follow. With my legs bound I was dragged by the other two across the rough tussocky ground. I wanted to say, "What about Old Nick? What about the apothecary? You cannot leave him lying dead and cold in the forest, for birds to peck at." When we left his corpse behind, I felt almost as though I was abandoning an old friend.

We were rapidly out of the clearing and into the forest. A thin light strained through the leaves from above and then was suddenly extinguished as clouds moved over the moon. By now my eyes were as used to the dark as they would ever become. We were treading some kind of path, a thread of greyer ground that wound among the boles and trunks. Ahead of us the yet darker shape of Adrian glided through the trees like an outcrop of the night. He was evidently familiar with the route. Neither of my companions was particularly nice or careful about our passage and my feet and shins were buffeted against roots and torn at by prickly bushes. I am sure they went out of their way to ensure that my head and shoulders collided with low-lying branches.

I was half hopping, half being hauled along like a sack. My two escorts were panting and sweating with the effort of carrying me, particularly the man on my left who was plumper and heavier than his companion. The one on my right was more wiry. His face seemed to be in shadow. He smelt woody and smoky. Several times one or other of them lost his grip and we had to pause while he got a firmer handhold. I would have suggested, conversationally, that it would be easier for all of us if my feet were unbound and I was allowed to walk. But it was plain that they wouldn't do anything without their leader Adrian authorising it and, no doubt, he thought that, with free feet, I would attempt to run away. As I would have done, given the smallest chance.

After we'd travelled a few hundred yards in this fashion Adrian made a decisive turn off the path. I saw a tiny light glimmering among the trees. Soon we arrived at what looked like a ramshackle hut, a darker shape in the enveloping darkness. A candle was burning in a gap between the intertwined branches of which the hut was made. I was pushed, almost thrown, through an open door. I landed face down on a scratchy mound of straw. I twisted round, spitting out fragments of it. The hut was small and barely enclosed my three captors as they stood upright while I sprawled on what I took to be a simple bed.

I suddenly understood in what sort of place I was and the probable identity of one of my escorts, the one who smelt and whose face was in shadow. As the greatest and most populous city in the world, London has more need of fuel than lesser towns and it is charcoal that is used in preference to any other. Our city is ringed about by charcoal-burners, men who live out in the woods where they ply their trade and who bring their supplies early in the morning to Croydon or Greenwich or Romford. There they sell their wares to the city colliers, who deliver sacks to the needy wives. The charcoal-burners are shy men, living more like beasts in the forest than like human beings in society, while their city cousins, the colliers, are crafty and think nothing of short-changing their customers by switching a larger sack for a smaller or filling the bottoms of them with dross.

I was convinced that this place where I lay bound and helpless was a charcoal-burner's hut, and the blackened, shadowy figure who had escorted me here together with the plump man was a charcoal-burner. For sure, I had smelt the woody, sooty scent on him but had not realised it for what it was.

This shadowy figure now scuttled about the hut in a way that suggested it was his own. He lit another candle from the one that had guided us there and placed them both on the earthen floor. The candles flickered in the draughts piercing the ragged sides of the hut. The shadows of the three men confronting me jumped and swelled on the walls and roof, which were crudely made of wattle and daub. Adrian seemed to swirl in his black cloak and hat, a dancing devil. The shadowy shape of the charcoal-burner was so encrusted with soot and grime that his features were indecipherable. He had long arms and his posture reminded me of a melancholy ape which I had once seen in a cage. The third man, the plump one, wheezed as he gazed at me with an expression hovering between hatred and satisfaction.

"Well," said Adrian, "we have met before."

"If you're going to take so long on the prologue," I said, "you may never get to the main action."

"We shall shortly move to the epilogue with no interim," he said. "Your epilogue, your exit."

Adrian accompanied these histrionic words with a leer. It is odd how even in a desperate situation – and this was the most desperate I had ever experienced – the mind can work clearly. What the false steward's expressions reminded me of was a line from Master WS's *Hamlet* about "damnable faces". Since I had played Lucianus, the poisoner in the play-within-the-play, and these were in fact the words that described my appearance, or rather *his* appearance, I suppose you could say I am something of an expert on looking horrid. And, in my judgement, Adrian was overdoing it.

"And so the whirligig of time brings in his revenges," I said.

"Sweet meat will have sour sauce," he said, and I saw that we might beat each other to death with sayings.

"Who are these gentlemen? Have they also got a grudge against me?"

There was a movement from the plump man. He had only recently recovered his breath after the exertion of dragging me through the forest.

"You are Master Revill, the player. Master Nicholas Revill?"

He had a thick, greasy voice, like his person.

"Surely you haven't brought me all this way without knowing who I am?"

Underneath my easy air there was fear. If I stopped to think I would start to shake, and a tremor would enter my voice. Accordingly, I said the first things that occurred to me, hoping to keep the fear at bay.

"Master Nicholas Revill, formerly of Ship Street?"

Ship Street. What was he talking about? That was where I'd lodged with the stuck-up Mistress Ransom and her overblown daughter, the one who tried to tumble me on her bed. Where I'd lodged, that is, until Nell had emptied a chamber-pot over the mother's head.

"Who are you? What do you want?" I said.

"Look on this as an action for breach of promise, Master Revill," said the plump man.

"I don't understand," I said, not having to play at being baffled.

"I am Ralph Ransom, brother to Meg, the simple virgin whose flower you cropped."

"Oh Jesus," I said.

"That is not the end of it," said the plump man. "In order to take from her that precious jewel which she could bestow once and only once, you also promised yourself to her in marriage."

"It's not true."

"You deny that you lay together?"

"I, yes, we never . . . she . . ."

"You came to her room, you spent yourself in extravagant words, she — oh foolish virgin, Margaret — took your forged notes as true tender and succumbed to your blandishments. You speedily untrussed and took down your hose, and my sister Margaret lost her honour to a man who possesses not a shred of that quality. She gave way, because you gave your oath that she would be your bride."

"This is absurd," I said, recalling all too clearly the scene in the woman's chamber, she all red smoke and fire and I wallowing under her like a bobbing bark in a tempest.

"There is more," said plump Ralph, determined to have his day and his say.

I groaned. In truth, I was in pain. The beating I'd received at the apothecary's, the jolting ride out of London in the back of the wagon, the prospect that I would end like Old Nick on the far side of death's door, all of these things afflicted me. And yet I played at being in a worse state still.

I groaned again and fat Ralph Ransom took this for a sufficient answer.

"You have abused my mother."

"I never touched her."

"Abused her most monstrously."

"Not a finger, I swear by my own mother."

"After deflowering my sister, you emptied the contents of your filthy chamber pot over my mother. Do you deny that?"

"I, well, it's . . ."

"She was covered in your piss."

"No, well . . . not . . ."

"A mother drenched with your waste, a sister defiled with your lust. Are not these good reasons for my hatred, Master Revill?"

I sighed.

"I know you for what you are," Ralph pursued, scarcely able to speak for the fury that had been building in him. "You are a filthy p-p-p-player, you are a dirty crawling c-c-c-caterpillar, a double-dealing ambidexter. You are a frequenter of b-b-b-brothels and houses of sale."

"That could be said of half the men in London," I said.

"You have as your trug or doxy or housewife, what you will, a woman called Nell? She is a notorious whore. You are her pimp or pa-pa-pa-pander."

Of what use was it to protest that Nell loved me and that I, in my way, loved her, and that whatever might be her relations with other men, with me they were unsoiled by the taint of money either offered or taken? So I might have said before yesterday, anyway. I gave up the attempt. These men had already convicted me. All that remained was the sentence.

"You know so much that you must have been following me," I said, lamely. And, indeed, I thought of the plump man who had been on my tail a few days before when I had left my Nell. I became certain that it was this individual who was now standing in front of me in the candlelit cabin.

"We have sniffed you out," said Adrian, who had been content to leave Ralph to batter away at me. "We have sniffed you out to your stinking lair. You have cheated and abused my friend Ralph through his mother and his sister as surely as you have cheated and abused me."

"Oh, you are a thief," I said, feigning a boldness I did not feel.

"Let losers have their words," said Adrian.

"You would have stole my lady's necklace – and loaded the blame onto poor mute Jacob too."

"You trapped me with a trick," he said. "You slipped a hair around my finger and said that it was one of my lady's when it was no such thing. Say that is not true, player, if you can."

How could I, when it was true, perfectly true? Never mind that Adrian really was a thief. I had used a subterfuge to trap him, as William Eliot had discerned. I'd dishonestly caught a dishonest man. There was a germ of truth in all their accusations and it was enough to dishearten me.

"What's *he* got against me?" I asked, gesturing with my head in the direction of the third member of this triumvirate, the long-armed and grimy charcoal-burner. Up to this point he had said nothing.

"He is in my employ," said Adrian.

The grimy creature nodded his head and smiled – that is, he opened a hole of a mouth. He had two remaining teeth at the top that huddled together for comfort.

"He is a man of few words," I said. "Is he dumb?"

"Nub is serviceable," said Adrian. "He lives in this forest."

At this announcement of his name and dwelling, Nub again performed a smile.

"Like a faun or a satyr," I said.

"Simple he may be," said Adrian, "but at least he is not a city fellow like you, player, full of deceits and trickery."

"I'm from the country myself." I tried to be jaunty but it is hard when your limbs are numb and your heart is dancing with fear. "From the West. I am a stranger to London."

"Why are we wasting time?" said fat Ralph to Adrian. "He keeps us talking to delay us."

"Waiting adds relish to the meat," said Adrian.

Of the three, Ralph was the most eager to exact revenge. Adrian, I judged, was no less enthusiastic to hurt me, probably to kill me, but he enjoyed his taunting and his hand-rubbing and his gleeful leers too much to get straight down to business as his companion wished. The other man, the ape of a charcoal-burner, was a hanger-on, probably vicious on request.

While we'd been talking I had been casting surreptitious eyes round the simple room, like a trapped beast. I was reclining awkwardly and painfully on a mound of straw, Nub's bedding, fit for a brute. My hands and feet I could scarcely feel, so long and securely had they been bound. I was sweating with fear although little gusts of night air entered through the many gaps and holes in the plaited willow of the hut walls. There wasn't so much a doorway as a place where a section of the wall was more tattered and incomplete than elsewhere. Small bones from the charcoal-burner's meals were scattered about. It was more like the den of an animal than the dwelling-place of a human being.

In the centre of the earth floor a pile of ash and burnt twigs lay heaped up together with the charred remains of some small forest creature; directly above this was an uncertain hole in the roof for the smoke to climb through. When I was forced, because of the discomfort of my position, to fall backwards on the prickly bedding from time to time, I glimpsed a single cold star shining far above the hole, hazed over by the smoke from the two candles. I doubted that Nub had ever been prosperous enough to possess a candle in his life. Adrian must have supplied them so that this absurd tribunal was not staged in utter darkness. Even as I looked up the cold star was snuffed out by a black curtain of cloud. That star was my hope, and now it was gone. The air grew even more still.

Fat Ralph was correct, of course. I was talking because I was frightened and because as long as I could get them to talk and keep them at it they were not doing anything worse, like beating me or killing me. Only two of them counted in this respect. The third, the charcoal-burner, showed no interest in my supposed crimes. However, as well as wanting to live a little longer, I was curious.

"Tell me one thing," I said, "before . . ."

"Before . . . before what, player?" said Adrian, practically hoisting himself into the air in his villainous dance of glee.

"Before the, ah, epilogue," I said.

"Your epilogue and your exit," said Adrian.

"Why did you kill Old Nick? Why did you bring him out here?"

"The latter is easily answered," said the false steward. "Old Nick, as you call him, was brought out here to keep you company. As long as the pit be big enough, what matter how many bodies it contain."

So they planned to do away with me. Well, that was hardly news. Yet there was something about hearing it cold that made me break out hot all over again. At the same time, like a bass accompaniment to the villain's threats, a growling broke out in the distance. Thunder. Once again, my mind reverted to Master WS, and how, often at some moment of crisis in his drama, he would interpolate a human storm with a heavenly one. Well, here was my crisis, and here was the storm, come pat. So Nature copies Art.

"And the first part?" I persisted. "How had the apothecary

deserved to die? Had he whored your sister too, Master Ralph? Or bepissed your mother perhaps?"

Ralph took a step towards me. His leg was already pulling back for a kick but Adrian put out a restraining arm.

"Later," he said. "I wish the player to know exactly what is due to him. I don't want him kicked insensible." Then, to me, "There is no harm in answering your question since your mouth and your eyes and ears will soon be stopped. Do you think you have seen all of us, player? Know that there is another in the shadows. It is with us even as it is with you theatre people. We are the ones on-stage – yet there is another off-stage who keeps his own counsel."

This was somehow not surprising. The whole tangled business was beyond Adrian's grasp alone.

"I knew it," I said.

"You know nothing," said Adrian. I sensed that the false steward already regretted saying what little he had said.

"He killed the apothecary, this individual in the shadows?"

Adrian seemed to want to withdraw his wicked and winking hints. For a moment his black cloak subsided into stillness, his tall black hat ceased to wag. He was silent.

"And Sir William Eliot, your old master. He was murdered, wasn't he?" I persisted, momentarily at an advantage. "But you didn't kill him. It was the man in the shadows, surely?"

From outside came renewed rumbling, as if some beast was roaming on the outskirts of the forest.

"I have said enough," said Adrian, now distinctly subdued.

"I am right," I said.

"Not a word more on that matter."

"You should beware, Master Adrian, that you never come into question for this. There will be no keeping silent then.

The name of this other mysterious man will be forced out of you under torture."

"He's right," said Ralph. "We must finish with this p-p-p-player now and send him off to join the apothecary while it is still d-d-d-dark."

He drew his hand across his double chins and gurgled, in what I assumed was a mime of throat-slitting. Like Adrian, Ralph Ransom was a poor player and would not have earned his keep on the boards. But Nub, that smoky charcoal man, again showed us his dark, almost toothless hole. Throat-slitting was a language that he understood and appreciated.

Adrian seemed to recover something of his old demonic self. His shadow grew on the wall as his cloak inflated and his sharp little nose quivered. The light from the candles wavered as the gusts of air through the wall-spaces grew stronger. The air was warm, like little draughts from the mouth of hell.

"To be brief, player," said Adrian, "we have sentenced you to death."

"A false steward, together with a fat woman's fat sibling and a mute charcoal-burner – you are no true court," I cried.

"We will do."

"B-b-but f-f-f-first , f-f-f-first—" stuttered Ralph. He was so angry, or excited at whatever was in prospect, that he was scarcely capable of getting the words out.

"Recover yourself, friend," said Adrian, patting him on the shoulder.

Ralph took several deep breaths. I almost felt for him as he struggled to calm himself.

"Think on this, p-p-p-player. We are not going to put an end to you without first p-p-p-purging you of your naughty p-p-p-part."

"You make no sense."

"Your vicious t-t-t-tool."

"I don't understand you."

But I was afraid that I did.

"You have shamed and beslubbered my sister with the seed of your instrument, with your silly weapon. Not c-c-c-content with that, you have monstrously abused my mother with the waste and outpouring from that same p-p-p-part."

"I never laid a finger on your mother, I say again. What happened was an accident. She chanced to be standing underneath the window when – when – it wasn't even me . . . And I never touched your sister with a will, either. Talk to her. She launched herself at me. She tricked me into entering her chamber—"

"*You* tricked *her* and you entered more than her chamber, p-p-p-p-player. And for that you will pa-pa-pa-pay."

"Jesus."

I was slick with sweat. The warm breath of the breeze penetrating the hut through its many crevices grew into a steady, somehow airless stream. Outside I heard the trees shaking their heads at the coming storm. Sweat ran from my forehead down my face, it gushed from under my arms. I began to shake. There was a flash outside the hut, followed seconds later by the thunder-crack. By the lightning, I glimpsed momentarily my three opponents, huddled about me. They looked human and not-human, like the wax effigies of the dead that you may see in Westminster Abbey.

"As you untrussed and took down your hose for your pleasure with this good man's good sister," said Adrian, "so we will now untruss you for ours." His voice was unsteady.

He was excited, as Master Topclyffe in the Tower was said to grow excited when he had a priest on the rack.

"Christ, no, wait."

"And after you have become our eunuch, after you have become a gelded player, the fingers will be removed from your right hand," said Adrian. "Then you will die."

I groaned because I was incapable of speech. My head pounded. The murderous, mutilating trio before me appeared to grow smaller as if I was viewing them down a dark tunnel. For an instant I thought that I heard light, pattering footsteps outside the hut, and my mind leapt at the hope of rescue, but another instant was enough to identify the sound as the rain, falling slowly, falling in single fat blobs.

"You trapped me with a trick," Adrian continued. "By sleight of hand you slipped a thread of somebody's hair under my finger and claimed it was my Lady Alice's. Because of you I was discharged from the Eliot household. Sir Thomas would never have discharged me but for you. Your hands are dangerous things and, like your cock, do harm to good and innocent people. Therefore, though the rest of your life be very short, your enjoyment of your organ of generation and of your fingers will be shorter still."

The speech came off trippingly, as though he had learned it by heart, had stored it up in that dark chamber ready for the occasion of its delivery. But there was still that tremor in his voice. The thrill of seeing another hurt, tormented. Or was it? A further flash of lightning and thunder-clap, and I could have sworn that Adrian flinched. Like many, perhaps he was frightened of a storm. But I could not see how to turn it to my advantage.

He motioned to the sooty charcoal man, as if to say "Now your time is come."

Through the haze that seemed to have filled the tiny cabin – a haze that may have proceeded from my own terror or from the smoky candles, or both – I saw Nub draw from somewhere among the dirty rags that hung off his person a long, rusty, curved knife. He loped towards me across the dirty floor and crouched at my feet. Obligingly, the lightning flashed once again and the thunder boomed out closer to. So, I thought, would this scene be staged: with noise and knife and quaking terror. Adrian and Ralph stood back. Evidently, like those citizens that crowd close to the scaffold to witness the agony of the dying, they were content to leave the dirty work to another but at the same time eager not to miss a moment's pleasure. The charcoal-burner cut the cord that bound my feet together and with his blackened claws threw my legs apart as casually as if he was dealing with a beast in the shambles. My limbs were numb, I could not move them.

This dirty man looked at me, and the red-streaked whites of his eyes stood out clear in his face. He smiled his toothless smile. If he had earlier reminded me of an ape, he now appeared to me with his two protruding teeth in the likeness of a rat. And like a great rat he started to crawl up my body, gripping the knife with one hand and fumbling between my legs with the other, deliberately protracting his pleasure and my pain. He had no liking for the subtleties of untrussing and pulling down my hose, not Nub. He intended to slice through cloth and skin and sinew and all, without discrimination. I writhed, I twisted, I dwindled, as it were, into myself but to no avail. He was wiry and strong. I was lying on my back with my hands bound beneath me. His weight was on the lower part of my body from which feeling had, in any case, almost departed.

But extreme fear may give a sharpness to the mind, even to

the senses. The haze over my vision cleared and I saw things clear, more clear than ever in my life. I saw the four of us as if from the outside, a frozen tableau, and here again a flash of lightning fixed us all in unmoving postures. In an instant I considered – and rejected – attempting to delay the charcoal-burner by pointing out that, if he did his worst there, where I lay on the pile of straw, the blood and mess would stain his sleeping-place. But that wouldn't bother a torturer and executioner.

"Wait," I said. My voice came out thick, as though my tongue had turned into a bolster.

"No more words, player," said Adrian from where he stood on the far side of the hut. Was he putting a distance between himself and the blood that was about to be spilt? "We have heard enough of you."

"This concerns your friend – the one who is off-stage – the one in the shadows."

I spoke as calmly and clearly as I could manage. Outside, the rain pattered steadily. My life depended on being understood. The charcoal man was still groping at my centre, questing after my fear-shrunken parts.

"He does not exist," said Adrian, almost calling across the space of the tiny hut.

"I have a message from him," I said.

I remembered the scrap of paper which I had retrieved from the apothecary's shop just before the ambush in the dark. The paper with the writing which it had been too gloomy to decipher. It was still in my grasp, actually in my hand. Like a dying man clutching at a straw I had clenched my hand over it as I was assaulted in the shop, and it had remained in my closed fist ever since. At least I hoped it had. The careless cruelty with which my hands had been wound round with cord might actually have helped to keep a grip on the fragment of paper. There was no sensation in my limbs now, but I recalled how earlier, in the jolting back of the wagon, I had been half aware of holding something. In my clear-sighted desperation I suddenly realised what it might be.

"A message?" said Adrian.

"He is t-t-t-time-wasting," stuttered Ralph. "Get on with it." This was directed at Nub, who seemed to be distracted by the conversation passing backwards and forwards over his black head. The curved, rusty knife stood erect in one hand while the other hand hovered above my groin. Possibly he waiting for the final word of command from Adrian. But Adrian was himself distracted by the noise from the black sky over the forest. He could not fully savour his revenge because he was somewhat fearful for himself. From the top of my great terror I looked down on his little fright. The other two had less imagination.

"In my hand I have a message. See for yourself."

I tried to speak with a confidence and sureness that I did not feel. But I am a player.

"Behind my back. In my hand I feel it still. I have a message from your friend in the shadows. I found it in the shop of the dead apothecary. It is important. He will not thank you if you don't recover it."

There was a pause while my life – to say nothing of my fingers and my private parts – hung in the balance.

"Turn him over."

Through the ragged door I saw lightning stab at the trees. I was roughly manhandled onto my front. I lay, face down, on the stinking, prickly pile of straw. Adrian's next words were covered by the thunder so that he had to repeat himself.

241

"Look at his hands. See what he is holding."

As if through a thick blanket, I felt a fumbling at my own bound and benumbed hands. There was a grunt from Nub which might have signified "here" or "see". I sensed rather than saw Adrian move closer to see what he had discovered.

"Bring it here."

Another grunt. The charcoal burner's black claws tugged and twisted at something that was in my own grasp. Thank Christ the scrap of paper was still there.

"Don't tear it, you fool," said Adrian.

There was more fumbling at my back. I hoped that, in the struggle to retrieve the note, my hands might be completely unfastened. No such luck. But in order to extricate the scrap of paper from where it was wedged between my hands and the cords that secured them, Nub had to pull at the ropes and the constriction on my lower arms became a little less.

"Give it to me."

Over my shoulder, I again sensed rather than saw Adrian as he reached out for the paper. There was a shift in the shadows thrown by one of the candles as someone, presumably Ralph, picked it up and brought a light to bear on this puzzle. I had no idea what was on the paper which I had been clutching for hours. It might be some recipe of Old Nick's, it might be a note of assignation dropped by a customer as he was paying for one of the apothecary's love-philtres, it might (for all I knew) contain the identity of the secret, off-stage man who Adrian had hinted at.

None of these questions was preoccupying me at that instant. I had at most a few seconds while the attention of my captors was distracted. Not the sooty, rat-like Nub of course. Reading and writing did not concern him. Even though I was lying on my front he continued to squat on my lower legs, knife in hand, ready to continue the business of emasculation once Adrian had given the word.

I heard the low breathing of the two upright men, a whispering below the pattering rain and the thunder-grumble. From this I could deduce that there was indeed something which concerned them on the scrap of paper. There were more whispers. I went limp. I groaned and my head fell forward onto the bed of straw. I wanted Nub to think – if he was capable of thought – that I had fainted from pain or fear.

"There are words here, player," said Adrian.

I stayed still and silent.

"Valerian, ipomea, agrimony, gall-bladder, ratsfoot, antimony."

I said nothing.

"Why, this is nothing, Nicholas."

"Look carefully, it is a code," I said. Anything to delay them for an instant longer.

"Well, code or no, we will decipher you first. Nub, unman Master Revill."

Nobody moved. I thought that most probably the filthy charcoal burner had not understood the meaning of "unman" – or "decipher", come to that.

"Turn him over and go on with your business." Adrian's voice was unsteady.

Nub raised himself off from where he had been sitting on my calves and prepared to heave me over onto my back. Even while the business was proceeding with the scrap of paper, I had been all ears for the advance of the storm. Fortune was with me. The patron saint of players (Genesius), to whom I had prayed for aid, was above, beyond the thunder and lightning but surely directing it. There was a flash of lightning almost directly outside and a deafening burst of thunder, as if the very fabric of the world had been torn in two, and straightaway a smell of burning in my nostrils. All were distracted. Each man, torturer and victim alike, cowered within himself.

I had an instant of opportunity, and an instant only. I was half turned over on my side, still shamming faintness. My legs were free, though without much feeling in them. My hands were bound yet not so tightly as before. Drawing my breath deep inside me, I jerked up my head, which had been lolling inertly, and struck out in the general direction of the charcoal-burner's face. I connected with his dirty nose or his hole of a mouth or some such – I cared not but was well pleased with the feel of the blow. He fell back and away from me and, by good fortune, on top of one of the candles. He may have been a little burnt and cried out in pain, but my ears still resonated to the thunder's voice. I flailed around and struggled to get upright. My legs were weak and I staggered, stumbled and almost fell, but then was upright once more.

Adrian and Ralph stood opposite. They had not moved during this moment's action, as if they themselves had just been transfixed by a lightning-bolt. Whether they were still deafened by the noise or dumbfounded by my sudden move-ment I do not know. Perhaps they were like spectators at an execution, ready for the pleasure of the event and never imagining that the condemned man might leap off the scaffold and join them in the crowd. I raised my head and screamed. A sudden shriek or scream can arrest and cow others, and on this night it seemed to me that I was the very epitome of the storm. Then I lowered my head and, with arms still tethered and on legs that were not yet altogether mine, I charged like a bull between my two tormentors. I was aiming for the ragged gap that served as a doorway to the hut. I butted into Ralph. He had a soft surface, and uttered a non-word that may have been "ouf" and was anyway blotted out by the surrounding noise. He dropped the candle, which promptly extinguished itself on the ground. I tore on through the entrance, ripping my clothing on the sharp twigs and branches that surrounded it.

Then I was free and in the night air. There was a strong smell of scorching and burning together from somewhere close at hand but I did not, in my dash away from the charcoal-burner's hut, see anything in flames. I was hardly conscious of the rain falling on my face, the continued darts of the lightning and the rip of the thunder.

I made my exit into the confusion of the night. I ran and ran and ran, as I ran once when I discovered the plague in my mother and father's village.

I zig-zagged among trees, blundered through low-lying bushes, crashed into unseen branches, slithered down slopes, splashed through streamlets. The lightning must have illuminated my course but, for them to see me, they would have to be facing in the right direction as the flash came. My only thought – no, it was hardly a thought, more the instinct of an animal for survival – was to put as much distance between myself and those three men as possible. While I ran, I struggled to loose my hands from the bonds which tied them.

You, who sit in comfort reading this and assessing possibilities and likelihoods, may wonder how a single, frightened, bound man may make an escape from three enemies who have their hands, wits and weapons about them.

As I am running, breathless, almost sightless, hands still bound, consider (in comfort) these things.

I am a player. I have to fence, to dance, to tumble about on stage. I am required to move quickly, sometimes while speaking lines which I have committed to memory. I can run if I have to.

Against me was a fat, wheezing individual whose legs would not carry him far without rest. Against me was Adrian, who might be thin and angry and was doubtless ready for the chase but who, unless he doffed his black mantle and high hat, would not make very quick progress through the forest. Besides, I sensed that he was frightened of the storm. And against me was Nub the charcoal-burner; he might be the most dangerous. The forest was his. But he was too stupid to do anything without direction from the other two.

Consider also. I was angry. That these three men should set themselves up as a tribunal, and judge me on false evidence, and sentence me to death, as Adrian had expressed it – all this filled me with a fury that was paradoxically hot and cold. I was like the storm. When I lowered my head and charged at my captors, I saw red in front of my eyes.

Consider further.

I was afraid. Not only was I faced with death – which they were not; I was threatened also with emasculation – which they were not. The latter is perhaps, in some eyes, a worse fate than the former. There must be many men who would sooner contemplate losing their lives than being forced to part with the very instrument that makes them what they are. So I had this advantage over the rogues who had taken me prisoner. I was desperate and had everything, or nothing, to lose. A cornered man has a strength which he may not know that he possesses – until the time comes for him to use it.

So I ran. My breath came in thick gasps. Sweat and rainwater gushed into my eyes and I couldn't brush it away. When I judged I'd put a distance between myself and the hut I stopped. I needed to catch my breath and to listen for the direction any pursuit was taking. I crouched down in the inky shadow of a great tree. It took me some moments to quieten my quivering, beating body sufficient to hear any other sounds. At first, nothing. Then, from a fair way to the left, in between the thunderstrokes and the lightning flashes, came a rustling and crashing through the underbrush. Perhaps a night creature but, more likely, one of the three men.

I tried to put myself in their position. I'd taken them by surprise and left them in darkness. Ralph would be winded after my collision with him, Adrian, already unnerved by the storm, would be thrown off balance because his carefully laid plans of torture and death had been disrupted. I had managed to strike Nub in the face but he was the kind to shrug off any hurt. Nevertheless I'd had a few moments' advantage while they recovered and rallied their forces, enough time to cover the yards of forest immediately beyond the hut. Anyway, had I been the hunter, I would have delayed setting off in pursuit and listened instead for the blundering noise of the quarry and watched for glimpses provided by the flashes. Only when his direction was known for certain by sound would I have set off, telling those with me to fan out slightly as they beat their way through the woods. This was what I assumed Adrian would do.

The night air and the rain cooled my throbbing face. Despite my sweaty self, I shivered. I knelt in the dark, like a true penitent.

My priority was to free my hands. My shoulders ached from my arms being forced behind my back for hours. Besides the pain, it is awkward to run with your hands bound behind you, particularly if you are making your passage through a fraught wood. You are afraid for your eyes and your face, you cannot balance yourself properly, you are unable to guard against a tumble to the ground. I couldn't cut my bonds. I had no knife – nor any means of holding one. Had I been able to find some saw-edged tree stump, I might have worked away at the cords until they frayed and parted. If all this were taking place in a play on stage, I would undoubtedly have found a cave to shelter from the storm in, a fire to warm myself by and a kindly old shepherd to provide simple country fare (and a beautiful daughter too). But it was still dark and I could not see any convenient tree stumps. And this was no play: there was a storm but no cave, lightning but no fire, and a trio of murderers rather than a kindly old shepherd (and daughter).

I had no choice but to writhe and twist and struggle with the ties that bound me. Like a man possessed, I rocked from side to side but was careful to stifle any grunts and groans, even though I considered that the swish of the rain would cover my noise. Nub had loosened the cords when he had snatched the scrap of paper from my grasp, otherwise I might not have succeeded in eventually freeing myself. My hands grew slick with moisture as I tugged and pulled. I felt the ropes slacken and give. A mixture of sweat and blood eased the passage of my wrists and hands. At last my hands fell free. They dangled at the ends of my arms like the belongings of another.

There was a pause in the thundering, which was in any case passing over. My ears still rang. Then my breath almost hopped out of me as an owl's hoots sounded close by. Ter-wit ter-woo, three times repeated. It was no owl, of course, but fat Ralph, signalling to his companions. Sure enough, some way to the front, there was an answering hoot – the same, only slightly more convincing version of the night-bird's cry which I had heard in the clearing by the wagon. So much for Nub. Finally there was a strangled croak from farther to the right, scarcely a bird at all or any creature known to God or man, and that I knew must be Adrian. I might have laughed out loud with relief and mockery but did not. Under the sound of the rain pattering on the leaves and dribbling from their branches, there was the noise of wheezing, again identifiable as Ralph. I breathed very shallow and huddled myself up on the ground into a kind of ball. I even shut my eyes because, like a child, I had a queer notion that if I could not see them they could not see me. Then there was a swishing and a crashing added to the wheezing as Ralph struggled, to the accompaniment of muttered curses, through the bushes and low branches to catch up with the charcoal-burner ahead. I guessed that the storm-tossed Adrian would also be striving to join his more nimble man.

Now I knew the whereabouts of all three. They were in front of me or making in that direction. Like a man at a crossroads I had a choice: to double back towards the hut, to follow in the track of my persecutors, or to turn to the right or the left. Or, simply, to keep where I was. Staying still would be the hardest. My heart was beating fast, every sinew in my body was tense with fear and expectation. I had to move.

But where? Although I thought that Adrian and the rest were in "front" of me and that the hut was "behind", I was by no means certain of the lie of the land. If you have ever been lost in a wood in daylight you will know how easy it is to draw circles with your feet while you think that you are ruling straight lines with your eyes. In the dark it is ten times worse. For all I knew, and especially in the rage and confusion of the storm, I might have gone round and about and ended up within yards of the hut. Nor could it be so far from day – so I reasoned to myself, the night had lasted a lifetime already, it could not be so far from day – and the dawn could expose me to my captors.

I had to hide somewhere. I did not relish spending several hours lying wet on the ground. I had the countryman's aversion to night and the open air and the foul weather. Were it not for the real terrors that beset me, I would have been afraid of all sorts of doubtless imaginary hobgoblins and foul fiends. So does a greater fear drive out a lesser.

When I judged that Adrian and Ralph and Nub were well to the front, I headed off to the right and, at a kind of queer, crouching run, entered what seemed a less dense part of the forest. I held out my hands before my face to protect myself and tried to run silent. When I began to lose my breath once more I stopped in a place where the trees were growing apart rather than all close-clustered. After a few moments I found the tree I was searching for. I reckoned it was safer to get off the ground where I might be found at any moment. Perhaps there was some remnant of boyhood here, some memory of hiding away from playfellows among the friendly leaves, of seeing without being seen.

My tree was large and generous in the spread of its branches, the lowest of which was almost within my grasp. I scrabbled for it and slipped. The bark was slimy and water pelted my upturned face. I tried once more, caught hold and swung by weakened hands. All at once the terrors of the night, the weariness, the hunger that I felt, seemed to overwhelm me. I dangled there from the branch, my feet grazing the ground, scarcely caring whether the others caught up with me or how they would deal with me if they did. I may even have lost consciousness for a instant. Then, from somewhere or nowhere, came a burst of energy and resolution, and I found myself straddling the slippery branch.

Sopping leaves and twigs scraped at my exposed hands and face. This branch might have been good enough for a boy to sit astride but it was too slight a place to give me much ease or concealment. A little further up and over I made out a more substantial perch. I scrambled to one side, pressing the wet, knubbly bark with face and chest, gripping tight with one hand while the other searched for purchase. In the end I manoevered myself across a great, motherly branch that would have held me and many another. Once there, I slumped forward, head on my arms, my feet locked in a tight embrace about the branch. Beneath me the water dripped to the forest floor. Lightning flashed, but now at a distance; thunder, having played its part, rumbled rather than roared.

I must have slept, if you could call it sleep. Slept and woken. Slept and woken.

The short remainder of that night was split into hundreds of little portions of time and those portions split into yet more portions, and in each and every one I spent some moments anxious and alert, and passed other moments when I would not have been able to say who or where I was. Call it sleep.

At one point something dropped on my back and scuttled off down one leg. I gripped tighter on my branch.

At one point I thought how this was the third time within a

few days that I had concealed myself in a tree. How I had spied on my knight and his lady in the garden. How, before that, I had climbed the pear tree and been on the verge of abandoning the chase when my eyes lighted on the carved initials WS. I wondered what Adrian had meant when he talked about another, a man off-stage who was directing their actions.

At another point I was woken by an animal cough. An eerie half light fell from above. The rain had stopped, but the air seemed to be saturated with moisture and strange, tiny, cloudy patches. I was cold and clammy. A finely-antlered deer was making his stately progress through the trees. Wisps of mist covered him up to his haunches so that he appeared as fabulous as a unicorn, a boat-like creature navigating the wood. A few yellow leaves spiralled down and vanished into the carpet of mist beside him.

Later I woke shaking. There was a stronger but still pale yellow light to one side of me, the right. Now, like a lodestone, I could tell in which direction I pointed. I was facing to the north.

Later still I woke and saw what had been concealed by night and the thick air. I was on the edge of a clear area of the forest and ahead of me was a vista like a picture in a book. The slanting sun struck at the towers and domes of a city and glinted off a river. Above, the sky was the clearest azure, promising a fresh day and forgiveness to us all. A solitary star, still visible in the west, was soon to be outshone.

I almost wept with joy.

We had not travelled so far after all. The direction we'd taken in the wagon had been south, across the river and then through Southwark, as I had suspected. I was up a beech tree in a forest on the gentle, sloping heights south of our city. I squinted and tried to make out the shape of the Globe theatre but in the rising sun everything danced and dazzled so much that it was impossible to discern particular buildings, however large.

At that instant, for me, London might have been the new Jerusalem, a city of gold and crystal. I felt I might leap from my perch and race across the fields and plains until I reached it. I had survived a night of terror, with nothing worse than bruises and scratches. I had outwitted and escaped from three wicked men who unlawfully sought my life.

I was alive.

There was a cough underneath my branch.

The deer, of course. An innocent creature of the forest.

But this was no deer, no simple beast. It was a human cough, it was Adrian the false steward standing beneath the tree.

At first I hadn't recognised him. From my position lying along the branch I looked straight down on the top and brim of his hat. This hat was so broad that it almost concealed the figure beneath. His breath plumed out into the cold morning air. Then he coughed again and shuffled a couple of paces forward.

My heart was thudding and my mouth was dry. I kept still. With luck he should move off. I assumed his two companions were within calling distance. When he went away I would jump down from the tree and run for my life, run for my city. It was just a matter of being patient – and still.

I continued to look at Adrian, at his back covered by the black mantle, at the hat which sat on him like a sooty chimney. But there is a strange sense in us, or in some of us, that says we are being watched even when we cannot see the watcher. Perhaps the poets are right when they poeticise about the threads of gold which connect them to their lover's eyes or the daggers which kill when she looks on them unfavourably.

Or perhaps I simply made a noise or Adrian was brushed by a falling leaf. For whatever reason he turned to look and I knew even as his head began to move round that he was aware that something was behind and above him.

I didn't take the time to think. If I had, various pictures would probably have flashed across my mind's eye to do with Adrian calling out for help and the other two joining him, and then all three trapping me up the tree, like dogs with a cat. And, if I had spent time thinking it out, that is probably what would have happened.

Instead I acted by instinct.

Before Adrian's head and upper body had completed a full turn I launched myself from the branch like a thunderbolt, like a dart of lightning. "Fell" might be more precise than "launched". I struck him somewhere about the middle before landing heavily and clumsily on top of him. He crumpled up and broke my fall. I did not pause to see what damage I had done to him. Frightened that he would call and bring on the others, I lashed out almost as soon as we had arrived on the ground in a tangle of limbs. I struck him about the face, I pummeled his back and shoulders. His hat had fallen off so I seized him by the hair and banged his head on the earth.

After a time I clambered upright. The red mist of anger that dropped before my eyes in the hut had returned and, through it, I cast around for a log or a stone, anything to strike at this man and crush him like a beetle. I found a fallen branch and swung it at his unmoving head like an axe. The branch must have been half-rotten – or my blows very forceful – because it snapped after ten or a dozen swings and I almost fell on top of him, carried by the force of my blows. That brought me to my senses and I staggered back against the trunk of the tree which had sheltered me and felt my gorge rise and I puked and was ashamed. Nub and Ralph were elsewhere in the forest. If anyone had been near they would have been alerted by the sounds of the fight and my gasping breath.

Nevertheless I had no time to lose. I knew what I had to do. Adrian was lying on his front, his legs in a strange, frog-like position. Blood covered the side of his face and was matted in his hair. The leaves and grass surrounding him were spattered with it. It was on my own clothing too as well as on my hands and, no doubt, face. I picked up his tall hat from where it had rolled into the undergrowth. Averting my gaze I plucked the black mantle from around his shoulders. He did not move. I was not sure that he would ever move again.

I had no time to be sorry. I scooped up Adrian's cloak and hat in my arms and, taking a deep breath, I set my face in the direction of London. The early morning mist had nearly burnt up in the heat of the rising sun. Ahead lay the city, not quite so bright and gleaming as when I had first glimpsed it from up the beech tree. The pure azure sky was streaked with cloud.

I ran downhill, clutching Adrian's garments. As I ran, tears and sweat streamed down my face. I had remembered the part that I was playing that afternoon at the Globe theatre. I knew what I had to do.

The play's the thing . . .

ACT V

Now Master Ralph Ransom he comes to me early in the morning in my lodgings as I am resting and preparing to go about the business of the day. Seeing him I expect him to report success in the matter of Master Revill. But first I am surprised not to see Adrian and say so.

Fat Ralph shuffles uncomfortably.

"Master Adrian is still there," he says.

"Where?"

"In the w-w-w-woods."

"Why didn't he come back with you?"

"He will never come b-b-b-back."

I struggle to gain control of myself, of my anger – and fear.

"And Master Revill, he will never come back neither?"

"He is spoken for."

I sigh with relief but suspect all sorts of things.

"Explain."

Ralph Ransom begins a long and complicated story of how they managed to surprise the player and take him off to the woods and how they met with Nub –

"Who is Nub?"

"*A creature of Adrian's. A d-d-d-desperate man. A charcoal burner.*"

"*I see.*"

But I am angry at the news. There are more and more people involved in this. Safety does not lie in numbers.

They carried Master Nicholas to some hut. He was bound hand and foot. They meant to play with him a little before they killed him.

"*And . . . ?*"

He had a message, Ralph said, a note. In his hand the player held a note.

"*Get to the point.*"

"*The p-p-p-point is, Master—*"

"*No names, not even in private. I have told you before. Simply tell me what happened.*"

"*In short, the p-p-p-player managed to run off while we were examining the note and our attention was d-d-dis-tracted.*"

"*And you caught him?*"

I begin to fear the worst. In fact I have feared the worst ever since Ralph put his fat greasy face round my door.

"*We p-p-p-pursued him. Adrian must have found him. Because there was a struggle.*"

Ralph's breath is coming thicker and quicker.

"*A struggle which Adrian lost,*" I say.

"*. . . In short, yes.*"

"*But Master Revill, he is spoken for, you said.*"

"*Oh, he crawled off into the b-b-b-b-bushes to die.*"

"*You saw him? His body?*"

"*Well . . .*"

"*Ocular proof?*"

"No, b-b-b-b-but Adrian gave a good account of himself, and inflicted some mortal strokes."

"On the body of a man you haven't seen and can't find."

"Adrian hates Master Revill. I hate Master Revill."

"Hatred by itself is not enough. It has to be accompanied by good sense."

"I am sure it w-w-w-was so."

"Wishers were ever fools," I say.

"What else c-c-c-c-could have happened?"

"Anything, you fool."

And then I change my tone because I have decided what I have to do now.

"Never mind," I say, "perhaps you are right and Master Revill lies even now in some ditch with twenty trenched gashes on his head, each one of them a mortal wound."

Fat Ralph sighs with relief. His blubbery shoulders seem to grow more rounded. He repeats himself.

"I am sure it w-w-w-was so."

"Let us assume that Master Nicholas is dead," I say cheerily. "We'll drink to that."

I turn my back on Ralph Ransom, telling him to make himself at ease, and go to my table and prepare two glasses of red wine. With a flourish I present one to him. I am reminded of the public display that King Claudius makes when Prince Hamlet is about to fight the duel against Laertes. How the King drops a pearl into the goblet which his nephew should drink from. How Queen Gertrude mistakenly picks up the goblet containing the pearl. How the King tries to prevent the Queen from drinking.

"Let us drink to . . . the end of our enemies."

"The end of our enemies," repeats Ralph.

"Now," I say, "this other man, this charcoal burner . . . ?"

"Nub."

"Yes, him. Is he secure?"

"Secure?"

"He will not talk."

"He cannot t-t-t-talk," says Ralph jocularly. *"Or if he did no one would be able to understand him. "*

"He is a foreigner?"

"He lives in the forest, it's the same thing,"

Ralph is now very much at his ease. So much at his ease that he begins, for the first time, to look round my lodgings. From his expression, which he scarcely troubles to keep concealed, I judge that he considers them rather meagre. True enough. I do not live as I would. I require more money, always require more money. This wooing of the ladies, it is a costly business. I am a generous fellow. Occasionally, I may take something from them in return for the expenses I am driven to (as I would have taken my lady Alice's pearl necklace, using Adrian as my instrument, had not the young player intervened) but I spend more than I get. That is the nub of the matter. And this word brings me back to the question of the charcoal-burner, and his silence.

"So no one will talk?"

"No one, oh no," says easy Ralph.

"Good," I say. *"Have some more wine."*

"Oh yes," says the dead man.

"I have a wine-supplier in Cheapside. Perhaps you have heard of him. He is French – Monsieur Lamord."

"Lamord," says Master Ralph, rolling the name round his tongue and pretending to a knowledge of vintners that he doesn't possess, although in this case there is no vintner called Monsieur Lamord.

"A strange name," I say.

"How so, Master—" *says Ralph, stopping when he remembers that I've forbidden him from uttering my name aloud.*

"In French, 'l'amour' means 'love'."

"Love, that's a fine name for a wine-seller," *says Ralph,* "though too much of one is the enemy of the other." *He sniggers. I notice that when he is relaxed and thinks himself out of danger he speaks smooth and without stuttering.*

"It also means something else if it is construed a little differently," *I say.* "La mort . . ."

"Yes?" *all unsuspecting.*

". . . means 'death'. So Lamord is love and death, two opposites in the one word."

"Very good. Ha ha. Lamord. Love, death . . ."

He glances at the wine glass which he has almost drained for the second time. Then he glances at me. Then his face turns grey.

"I cannot resist a pun," *I say.*

Ralph makes to fling the glass away from him but he is too weak, either through fear or through the quick-acting effects of the venom, and I am on him. He is already a dead man with what he has swallowed, but for the sake of completeness I hold the glass against his chattering lips and teeth, and force him to drink it to the very last drop. Some red wine dribbles down his chin and spills on his clothing where it looks like blood. He chokes and arches his back. Froth forms on the corners of his mouth. His eyes roll upward into his head. His hands clench and unclench on the arms of the chair.

When I am sure that there is nothing more I can do for him I lock the door of the room and leave him to die.

I cannot deny that this business is not going according to plan. By this time perhaps there is no plan. The murder of Sir William Eliot was carefully plotted and executed. It was an act of revenge, of mischief, and of other things besides. But with the other murders that have proceeded from that, I cannot say. Once you have embarked on this bloody course there is no turning back.

It is tedious.

Like in all human affairs, the more often it is done the easier it is done, with less scruple and heart-searching.

But it is also pleasurable. I had no intention of killing Ralph Ransom. The idea occurred to me as I was talking to him. With Francis and the apothecary, I set out to kill them. The player I left to others: obviously a mistake. But with Ralph there was the word, then there was the blow. I am like a fencer who cannot foresee the direction a bout will take, the moves of his opponent, the counter-strokes he himself will employ, but must rely only on his skill and quick wits. One day soon his arm will tire or his wits grow dull and he will lose, but until that time he loves his own craftiness.

These murderous actions, planned or unplanned, create their own consequences and sequels. Now I have to dispose of Ransom's body. Lug his fatness down the stairs and towards the river when the tide is high in the small hours of the morning. I could enlist someone to help me – Southwark swarms with the lawless and the desperate. But every accomplice is another mouth to feed or to silence. I shall do this alone.

As for Master Nicholas Revill, fat Ralph might be right. Perhaps the steward did inflict some mortal wound on the player and he is even now dying or dead in the woods. Or if he is not, then he might be scared for his life and have run away from London town. So there will be a gap in the play this afternoon.

But I expect to see him again. I will be prepared for that. I don't know what I will do but it will be something fitting.

*   *   *

"My God," said Richard Burbage. "What happened to you?"

He was preparing for his first appearance, all in black in the court of King Claudius and Queen Gertrude. In the background I saw WS looking curiously in my direction. He too was arrayed in his opening costume, the suit of armour worn by the Ghost of Hamlet's father.

"I fell into a fight."

Burbage looked slightly displeased.

"Did you win?"

"I suppose so," I said.

"I shouldn't like to see your opponent."

"I don't think you will."

"You've been away, Nick. And away in the wars to judge by the look of you."

This was Master WS, who appeared at my shoulder as soundlessly as if he really were the Ghost that he played.

"Away?"

"I saw you this morning on the back of a farm cart coming up from the country."

This was true. After quitting Adrian and gathering up his black hat and cloak (which I had brought to the theatre) I started to run for the town. Within a few hundred yards exhaustion overtook me. I stumbled and fell, and might have been lying there till this moment, had not a horse and cart trundled by. At first the carter suspected me for a thief and my ragged, bloody state for a ploy. I was able to convince him that it was I who was the victim of thieves, and he allowed me to slump into his conveyance. So I returned to London as I had left it, in the back of a jolting cart.

The carter was ferrying sackfulls of apples. Their sharp-sweet, heady smell crept over me as I lay huddled in the bottom of the cart, trying to make myself as small as possible. I drifted into an uneasy sleep, in which memories of stealing apples in Bristol orchards were wiped away by frantic chases through dark forests, A rat-like man was coming to cut off a tail which I had grown. My father's body went sailing through the air to land with a thud in the communal grave of plague victims. The cart went bumping on its way to the markets north of the river and I awoke just before we reached the Bridge. It must have been somewhere around this point that Master WS had seen me and my strange mode of conveyance.

"Yes," I said, "I suppose you could say that I have been away."

"Before the climax of a play the hero shall withdraw from the action," said Master WS, reminding me of his words on the previous afternoon, in what was another life. Although he was wearing armour he looked not warlike but melancholy, befitting a spirit come from the underworld with no happy news.

"We must speak after the performance," said Dick Burbage to me. "I have something to say to you."

"Yes, we shall speak," said Master WS, Burbage's fellow-shareholder.

A trumpet sounded the beginning of things. The musicians fluted and sawed from the gallery.

"I must be on," said Master WS. He vanished.

"And I," said Burbage.

I went to change in the tiring-house, although my entrance was many scenes away. Under the eyes of Alfred the tireman, I donned my costume as Lucianus, the poisoner in the play-within-the-play. I planned to add one or two items later, but needed to do it out of his sight.

My head was whirling with madcap schemes and plans. I think that I was half-mad at this time. Like a man in a maze I was struggling to find the centre, but in no very ordered fashion.

My reasoning went as follows: old Sir William Eliot had been murdered, of that there was no doubt. The circumstances of his death provided an uncanny parallel with the circumstances of old Hamlet's death in the play by Master WS. Both victims were sleeping in an orchard, both were taken by surprise, cut off without time to prepare for death. A poison was poured into the ear of the dormant King and the same method most probably employed on Sir William. There was a brother – Claudius, Sir Thomas – hovering off-stage and waiting to take up the reins of a impatient, lascivious wife, whether Gertrude or Lady Alice. There were sons, although each had reacted differently to the father's death: Hamlet was deeply unhappy with his mother's choice of a second husband and bitter because he sees the throne of Denmark slipping out of his grasp; young William Eliot was grieving for his father but claimed to respect (rather than suspect) his uncle and to love his mother. Nevertheless William had been troubled enough by the parallels between art and life to ask me to "watch and listen" in his own house.

I might have been inclined to put William's sense that all wasn't well down to fancy or imagination. Since he was afflicted by the need to model himself on Hamlet, what more natural than that he should assume his hero's distrust of the world, and the feeling that everything in it was rank and rotten, an unweeded garden? But the events of the past few days, from the drowning of Francis to my own scrape with death, had shown me that William's intuition was right. All was very far from being well.

The question I came back to, the one that I'd entered in Greek lettering in my notebook, was: who?

Who had been responsible for the death of Sir William, the death of Francis, the employment of Adrian and fat Ralph to kidnap and kill me?

There were two or three possibilities, as I saw it.

One was that Lady Alice had plotted to kill her husband – for the usual reasons, a jaded appetite and the wish for change. What I had seen of the couple from my vantage-point in the pear tree showed how she despised her first husband and was at one with her second. Some things would have been beyond a woman's strength, I judged, and she would have needed help, but when did a beautiful and dangerous woman ever lack a man's hands? She could have hired assistance, or been in league with Sir Thomas. An objection to this was the appearance of Adrian on the scene. Would he have been taken on, in this vicious capacity, by the woman or the man who had so recently discharged him from their service? Unless this was all a ploy. I went round in circles.

Another, stranger possibility was that son William had killed father William. *He* had hidden up the tree, *he* had scampered towards the old man's supine form, *he* had poured the deadly preparation in the porches of the paternal ear. There is no reason for thinking this, apart from the whisper in my innermost head that says that sons wish for dead fathers, and all so that they may have their mothers to themselves alone. If I examine the matter honestly, it was sometimes so with me.

A third possibility: the murderer of Sir William Eliot is none other than Master WS himself. I do not see our gentle, vanishing author wielding the knife or passing out the poisoned glass, but these feats of open or concealed violence he has done again and again in his mind's eye, for his pieces are full of death and villains and destruction. I could not help remembering those initials carved into the trunk of the tree in the Eliots' garden, or what the gate-keeper had said about the identity of the visitor who called at the house on the day of Sir Thomas's death. I could not but think of the odd comments made by Master WS, of the looks he has cast in my direction. Perhaps within him some barrier has broken down, and he no longer knows what is art and what is life. He writes a murder, he enacts one. Or he does it first, then he tells us of it. It is no longer enough that he imagine himself a homicide, he must play the part in truth and see where it takes him.

But I have to prove my case.

As Master WS may have taken a leaf out of his own book, as it were, so too will I. In our author's play, Prince Hamlet tests the King's guilt by showing him to his teeth and face the image or pattern of his crime. When the travelling players arrive at Elsinore castle they are requested, even commanded, by the Prince to stage a play which, in words and dumb-show, exposes the uncle's supposed deed. If he changes colour, if he squirms on his throne, if he hangs his head in shame, Hamlet will know him for what he is. He watches his uncle-father watching the play. Not trusting the testimony of his own eyes, he tells his good and faithful friend Horatio to watch the King too. But, in the end, there is no need because the entire audience sees what Hamlet sees.

Claudius runs from the play when it's hardly got going. As the poisoner (me, Lucianus) appears to work his wicked will on the sleeping king, mouthing threats and making damnable faces, the real King calls out for lights. Daunted by a play he is.

Frighted with false fire he is. In front of his court he flees. He is the man.

I planned something similar.

When I got down from the cart on the Southwark side of the Bridge that morning I first made my way to Nell's. Her reaction was like Master Burbage's.

"My God, you look terrible, Nick."

She had a little looking-glass and carried it to me. My face was a mass of bumps, bruises and scratches, from the beating I'd received and from my headlong flight through the forest. There was blood there too, and on my hands and clothing. Adrian's as well as mine. My limbs ached and my wrists were badly chafed from the effort of freeing them from the ropes. I considered making some reference to our last meeting, in the Goat & Monkey with William, and to the way in which I had snubbed her because she was pursuing her trade with young Eliot. But I did not want to reopen old wounds – I had enough fresh ones.

Nell brought some water in a pewter bowl and a cloth and gently wiped away the mess around my face. I winced and drew my breath in sharp. She applied salves and ointments, of which she always kept a plentiful stock. Is there a mother in every woman?

Unlike a mother, though, Nell did not question me, at least not then. Perhaps because she deals so much with men, and with our strange and shameful needs, she is content to let things go unexplained. Instead, she chattered on about the remedies she was applying and how this one was compounded of rue and sanicula, and that one was made of strawberry leaves and fennel and mercury mortified with *aqua vitae*, you understand . . . What I understood was that my Nell was a country girl at heart and knew the remedies of the fields and forests. I also understood that she'd spent plenty of time in Old Nick's company. She was using expressions that were not natural to her. Her patter and expertise must have come, in part, from him. I wondered whether to tell her of the old apothecary's fate, trussed up and dead in the place where his alligator had hung. I wasn't certain of the nature of the relationship between Nell and the old man, whether their "arrangement" was for business or pleasure. With a whore, of course, the one may be the other. On the whole I thought the news of Old Nick's demise could wait. Sooner rather than later there would be a full accounting, after which she would know all.

I was grateful to be lovingly tended and, as I lay on the bed that we sometimes shared, I felt myself slipping into an exhausted sleep even as she talked away. But I couldn't allow myself rest – the play had not yet run its course.

"Nell . . . ow—"

"Don't talk, Nick. Let me finish."

"This is important. It's – oof – to do with what happened."

"I'm not asking any questions, Nick. Keep still."

"I will tell you everything later. But there is something – ah – I want you to do."

"It's a bit early in the day—"

"It's – ouch—"

" – and you're in no condition for that."

"It's not that."

"What then?"

"I want you to go to the playhouse."

"To ply my trade?"

Nell picked up some of her customers at the theatre,

although I had asked her to keep away from the Globe, at least for as long as I was working there.

"No, to watch."

"Are you in a play?"

"Yes. I am Lucianus, nephew to the king – and a poisoner."

"Oh, that play."

"That play. But I don't want you to watch that play. The play's not the thing. I want you to watch someone watching it."

"This is deep, Nick. Perhaps you have a touch of fever and are not altogether sure of your words."

"I am altogether sane. (Although I am by no means sure that I was at this point.) Listen. I wish you to observe someone and to see how they respond to what is happening on stage."

"But *you* could do this."

"I will be watching someone else. Besides, Nell, two pairs of eyes are better than one. I do not trust my senses. I am stumbling in the dark."

"You are not well, Nick."

I was moved by her words and, more, by the way that she uttered them.

"Scratches and bruises only. My mind is clear. Nell, do you ever think of leaving London?"

"Whatever for? How would I do for a living?"

"There are men and towns everywhere, if you are determined to persist in your course of life."

"Why, you know London has more men – and more of them rich ones – than any other town. And you know what they say. Fair wenches cannot want favours while the world is so full of amorous fools. Where could I find such a good place again?"

"*Good*, Nell? Good for trade perhaps, but is it for *your* good?"

"How solemn you sound, Nicholas. What has happened to you that you've turned moraliser?"

I thought of the deeds of the night before. I saw the body in the wood, but kept silent.

"I've been thinking that I may not be welcome here much longer. I might return to the country."

"Not with me for company, my dear. Or not until I'm too dried up and raddled for the sacking law."

"Sacking law?"

"Whoredom. Were you going to ask me to go with you?"

"No . . . well, not exactly. I just wondered . . . Look, to come to the business in hand. That play. There is a performance this afternoon."

"Which I should go to but which I shouldn't watch."

"You are often at the playhouse but not for the action on stage, I think."

"True," she said. "But you want me to watch a watcher, not catch him for profit."

"Watch a watcher and give me your opinion."

"A whore's opinion. What did you say to me the other day, 'My trade is rather more respectable than yours, I think'?"

I saw now that it was not always to my advantage that Nell recalled my words. I felt priggish, particularly as she uttered this in a fluting voice which suggested the puritan. That wasn't how I'd sounded, surely?

"I would value your opinion," I said, as Robert Mink had said to me in the matter of his verses.

She did not reply.

"Please," I said. "I am sorry for my thoughtless words to

you as you were going about your business. In the Goat &
Monkey."

"Those I have forgotten. Very well. I will do this for you –
but you must promise me one thing, Nick. Not to try and
reform me."

"I wasn't trying," I said. "I merely asked if you ever wanted
to leave London."

"It comes to the same. Do not become like the Puritans and
the moralisers who believe that women like me must have sin
beaten out of them by the beadle. Or, with you, it would be
the softer kind – the ones who believe we must all be unhappy
at our work and will leap at the chance to turn honest . . ."

"I never . . ."

". . . as if we could earn a quarter as much in any other
trade. If you men would have us reform you must stop visiting
us first – yes, and paying for the pleasure too."

"I'm sorry I ever mentioned it," I said. And I was too.

"Now tell me what you want of me this afternoon," she said.
So I did.

The next step was easier than I'd expected. From Nell's I
crossed the river to the Eliots' house. William was curious as
to where I'd been the previous night and even more curious
about my battered state. I palmed him off with some story
about an argument, a fight, typical behaviour among the
raffish players, didn't he know.

"I will be leaving soon," I said. "My contract with the
Globe is coming to an end because Jack Wilson is returning."

This, by the by, was more than I knew, although I did
know that my days must be numbered. They certainly would
be by the end of the afternoon.

"I will be leaving London too," I said.

I was surprised to hear myself saying this.

"I am sorry for that," said William. "I have enjoyed your company."

"Thank you. And I yours."

"You have learned nothing in my uncle's house?"

"I'm not sure. Perhaps I can tell you later, after this afternoon's performance. You will be at the Globe?"

"I could not miss the Prince of Denmark," said William, "though I must have seen him live and die a half dozen times."

"And my Lady Alice?"

"My mother doesn't like the play, as you know. Too many words and too many memories stirred up. Probably the very reasons that I like it."

"Could you persuade her to attend? It will most likely be my last performance. And I have other reasons . . ."

"I will try."

"Sir Thomas?"

"My uncle is away on business."

"Is he in Dover?"

"He has business there, yes, I believe."

So all was arranged.

And now I stood waiting to make my entrance in the dumb-show.

"How are you, Nicholas?"

I turned round and there was Master Robert Mink, looking as affable as ever.

"My, I wouldn't like to have been your opponent," he said casting his eyes over my visage.

Despite my best efforts at face-painting it was, I suppose, still obvious from close to that I had disgraced myself in some apprentice-style brawl. In a way this suited the villainous role which I had to play, but I still grinned sheepishly at Master Mink.

"No questions," he said. "You young men! Sudden and quick in quarrel, as our friend says." He nodded in the general direction of the stage, meaning Master WS.

He was costumed as the Player King, a part that was well fitted both to his bodily size and his good-natured authority. In the dumb-show, and then in the play-within-the-play, he must suggest a weary wisdom. When his Queen announces that she will never marry after his death, he knows that she protests too much. She will do what she says she will not. A royal widow does not sit long with an empty throne for company. Thinking of which, I cast my eyes in the direction of the box occupied by Lady Alice Eliot and William. I could not see them and had to hope that they were visible from the vantage point on the other side where I had secured a seat for Nell.

"Well," said Master Mink, "and you are enjoying your time with the Chamberlain's Men?"

"I fear that my time is almost over."

"Jack Wilson is coming back?"

"He is sure to be, soon. His mother must either be dead or have decided to live a little longer."

"I am glad that he is to return. He is a good player, although I am not sure that you don't have – ah – darker looks than Jack and so are more apt for darker parts."

"Master Shakespeare was kind enough to say something of the same sort when we first met," I said.

"Did he now? Well, he is the best judge of these things, I suppose. Anyway we shall be sorry to lose you."

"Thank you," I said, reflecting that this was a fine day for compliments.

"Before you leave you must visit my lodgings. You have not yet heard my Lover's Triumph."

"No, I have not."

"My lodgings would be better than the Beast with Two Backs. We would not have to depend on the stumbling service of Gilbert the potboy. I have a fine red wine that I'd like your opinion of."

"I would be honoured."

"And now I must take a few moments to myself. I always do this before I go on stage."

He removed himself into a corner. Meantime I fumbled in the sleeve of my costume for a speech I'd penned earlier. This is the very same device which Hamlet uses, a speech of some dozen or sixteen lines planted in the play to expose Claudius. Well, I did not pretend to be Master WS and would not dare to hold up my poor candle to his blazing sun, but I congratulated myself that I'd managed to add a few lines in the style of what Lucianus delivers when he is about to pour poison into the ear of the Player-King (Master Robert Mink). These lines would hint at the real-life mystery and murder of Sir Thomas Eliot.

My plan, as should be evident, was to confront those whom I considered might be responsible for this foul deed.

To wit: Lady Alice Eliot, spied on by Nell in the audience.

To wit: Master WS, spied on by myself from the stage.

(It was a pity that Sir Thomas was absent in "Dover" but I believed that, if he were guilty, he shared that guilt with his wife, and that therefore, if she were exposed, so too would he be.)

All this might seem to strain belief. Why should a man or woman spill their secrets because they see them played out on a stage? But I had authority for what I was doing, the authority of the Prince of Denmark himself, for:

> I have heard
> That guilty creatures sitting at a play
> Have by the very cunning of the scene
> Been struck so to the soul, that presently
> They have proclaimed their malefactions;
> For murder, though it have no tongue, will speak
> With most miraculous organ.

Adding lines to plays is common enough. The broader clowns in the other companies did it all the time, even if the professionalism of the Chamberlain's Men kept Robert Armin, our company clown, within bounds. Nevertheless, what might be tolerated in an older player would not be allowed in a snipper-snapper like myself. Even if nothing untoward occurred as a result of my own little lines-within-a-play-within-a-play, I would be cast out of the Chamberlain's for impudence, for incompetence. I would never work with such a company again. Most likely, I would never act again.

I would go back to the West Country and, like the prodigal son, turn into a keeper of swine.

I would go back to my own land and follow my father into the church. Without his certainty and his charity, I would become a sexton and dig graves.

But the play had not yet run its course. I had to expose a murderer.

I wasn't relying on my feeble words alone. I slipped on the cloak and hat that belonged to Adrian, the false steward. They were his badge or emblem, the mark by which he was most surely recognised. Like the cuts and bruises on my face, they sorted with the part I played. That I was wearing a costume not issued by the tireman would also be held against me, I thought, as I rapidly adjusted Adrian's mantle. There was dried blood around the collar.

And now I must be on. I slept-walked through the dumb-show. I went through the wordless motions of pouring poison into kingly ears, and pouring another kind of poison into the ears of the widowed but receptive queen. All this time I was in a frenzy of impatience to reach the main action so that I might speak the lines I had composed. It would most probably be the last thing I said on a public stage. I was conscious of banks of faces in the boxes and galleries, of shifting bodies in the pit. The day, which had promised so fair early in the morning, had grown dull. Sullen clouds hung over us and I felt the odd drop of rain.

As I came off after the dumb-show I saw Master WS looking at me most strangely. He had no part in the play-within-the-play or in the court scene in which it unfolds, but he was due on very shortly afterwards, a visitor in Gertrude's bedchamber where the Ghost appears – though only to Hamlet's eyes – for the last time. Master WS had removed the armour worn in the opening scenes on the castle battle-ments and was garbed in a night-gown. Now he is to become a wistfully reproachful Ghost, dressed as he might have been in life had he visited his wife's chamber. He stretches his arms across the divide between the living and the dead but the Queen does not see him.

I noticed that Master William Shakespeare, the Ghost in a nightgown, was looking at Master Nicholas Revill, the player-poisoner dressed in a dead man's mantle. He was wondering why I wasn't wearing my proper costume. He was wondering where he had seen my outfit before. He began to make towards me, but at that moment I heard my cue.

The Player Queen has just wished a good sleep to the Player King,

> Sleep rock thy brain,
> And never come mischance between us twain

and when she exits I enter. As I did my fear dropped away. I became master of the stage. There was a appreciative intake of breath from five hundred people, the little gasp of satisfaction that comes from seeing a villain about to do his worst. While Hamlet flew around talking to Claudius and Ophelia in state of high old excitement, I stood rubbing my hands and pulling naughty expressions.

On the line "leave thy damnable faces" I stepped forward to the recumbent body of Master Robert Mink. He was on the ground with his back to the double audience, that is the court audience of Elsinore and the real audience in the Globe. Before lying down to sleep in his "orchard" he had carefully laid his crown to one side. As I moved forward, I threw covetous glances at this golden ring. I crouched down and reached out a finger towards it, tentatively, as if it were a hot pan. Then I stood upright, fumbled beneath the cloak for the phial of poison and spoke over the sleeping king. I noticed

Master Mink regarding me with his open eyes.

With a trembling excitement I got to the end of the bit written by Master WS.

> Thou mixture rank, of midnight weeds collected,
> With Hecat's ban thrice blasted, thrice infected,
> Thy natural magic and dire property
> On wholesome life usurp immediately.

At this point I should have poured the poison into the sleeper's ears. Instead I went on:

> This cloak I wear's the colour of my heart;
> A dead man's gown, it serves to hide my art.
> This poison too is death to all it touches,
> He who mixed it now its power avouches.
> It well behoves the murderer to beware,
> The schemes he lays may bring him naught but care.
> I murder now, but inward know full well
> That all such deeds but speed my path to hell.

Then I bent forward to deliver my poison. And several things happened at once, some of them expected, some not. What should happen as the poison is poured is disarray. My lord Hamlet speaks quickly to King Claudius and the rest, explaining how this is only a *play* they're watching. But his words have no effect, and the guilty King shouts for light and dashes for the exit.

What actually happened was this: the players who made up the court spectators, including Dick Burbage as the Prince, at once realised that I'd started to improvise. I sensed rather than saw their slightly puzzled looks and altered postures. What does this provincial lad think he's doing? How dare he tamper with the lines written by Master WS, author, player and chief shareholder! Where is he taking us? And, if they were listening to the words I was uttering, they would wonder what I was talking about. The references to Adrian the steward, to Old Nick, the dead apothecary, the warnings to the murderer that all his acts serve but to enmesh him more helplessly in the nets of hell, all this had a private meaning that was far from the purpose of the speech as written for Lucianus, nephew to the king. What the Globe audience made of it was anyone's guess. Probably hardly a one of them noticed anything was amiss. You'd have to know the play very well, as William Eliot did, to be aware of this little straying from the path.

In any case Burbage and the others retrieved the situation brilliantly, as you'd expect. Hamlet spoke his lines, Claudius panicked and headed for the exit. The agitated court dispersed. The overlooked players slunk off, puzzled at the extreme expression of kingly disapproval which their drama had provoked.

I've left the most important detail till last.

As I delivered my own inferior lines and leaned forward to discharge the poison into the sleeping king's ear, I saw Robert Mink's eyes fixed unblinkingly on me from his position on the stage floor. He took in my tall black hat, he took in my sable-coloured mantle. Like the other players he was aware that I had departed from the text in the lines which I uttered. Unlike them he did not seem baffled. Then it shot through me with the speed of an arrow.

He was the murderer!

Master Mink, who had given me the note for my Lady Alice on my second afternoon in the theatre. Who had hidden

up a tree in an orchard in the springtime and secured the death
of Sir William, her husband and his rival. Who had enticed
poor innocent Francis to his death. Who had put an end to
Old Nick and hung him up in the air. Who had urged false
Adrian and fat Ralph and dumb Nub to do away with me
most viciously. And all this for the love or lust of Lady Alice,
so that he might possess her or her property, or both. Just as
Claudius slays his brother so that he may lay his hands on wife
or crown, or both. Had I not seen, during our meeting in the
Ram, how he regarded himself as a true (and spurned) lover?
For sure, the fervour and the self-pity with which he had
delivered the Lover's Lament had not been counterfeit. Had I
not also witnessed his casual malice, the way he held the
unfortunate potboy's hand over the candle? Master Mink, I
saw clearly (even though my brain was wild and whirling), was
that most dangerous kind of man who is all sweet and easy on
one side to conceal what is crabbed and angry on the other.

This takes many minutes to commit to paper but so fast is
our understanding sometimes, that all these things I knew for
true in less time than it takes to say "one".

I believe too that my state – exhausted, cut and bruised,
newly escaped from the threat of emasculation and death, red-
handed with the blows inflicted on the false steward Adrian,
conscious that my time with the finest, most noble company
of players in the world had now run its course and that I
would in future live my life as an humble swineherd, away
from the terrors and temptations of this busy city – I believe, I
say, that my strange state of mind and my fatigued body gave
me an especial understanding. Standing not quite at right
angles to the world, I saw more clear what was the case. And
the case was not good.

This "understanding" passed between us, Revill and Mink, without words, and Master Mink, he looked both sad and glad. Sad that his secret had been discovered yet also glad to have been found out.

Then he was up and off, escaping like Claudius from the unearthing of his crime. Yet to any onlooker his departure was simply in character. Like the rest of the players he departs quickly but quietly, to avoid the King's anger and also to leave the stage free for Hamlet and Rosencrantz and Guildenstern.

As I made my own way off stage I heard the scene taking its predestined course, with the prince mocking his one-time friends and exulting in the certainty of his uncle's guilt.

I too had found a guilty man, but in a quite unexpected quarter. I thought of my stupidity in assuming that Master WS might be a villain, I thought of the way I had told Nell to fasten her gaze on Lady Alice. I wondered what to do next.

Now that I had discovered to my own satisfaction who had first forged this chain of killings I felt a strange responsibility for him. I saw Robert Mink exit not just the stage but the theatre itself and before I knew it I was outside in the street too. He set off, without a backward glance, down Brend's Rents, the lane which runs past the towering white walls of the playhouse. He was still wearing the costume of the Player King, although without the crown. He ran the risk of a great fine if he was found out for this offence. But his hurry showed how he had already been found out, and in a rather greater matter than the taking of a costume.

The rain that had been hanging over our heads now started to fall in earnest. This was no fierce storm as on the last night, but a weeping in the heavens rather than their anger. Truly, Nature fits herself to us. Mink turned down one alley, then another, moving with steady purpose. Perhaps he was making for his lodgings. The alleys soon became slick with mud and churned-up waste as the rain drove along them. I had not taken off Adrian's hat and mantle. The first kept my head dry but the second soon hung heavy and wet. Still Master Mink did not cast his eyes over his shoulder. He was heading for the river, I realised. There were several sets of steps nearby which served the theatres and bearpit and other places of pleasure.

He reached the open riverside and I heard him hail a waterman. I could, perhaps, have run and caught him up but instead I moved more slowly. The rain was coming down thickly now and the far bank was a blur. As he was about to embark, he turned for the first time and saw me, but without surprise, as if he had known all the time that he was being followed. He seemed to be waiting. Then his gaze shifted to my right.

I turned and saw Master WS approaching. He was dressed in the night-gown he wore for his third and last appearance as a Ghost.

"Wait, Robert," he shouted. "Master Mink, stay!"

But, as if that were the signal he'd been waiting for, Mink leaped into the waiting boat and pushed off from the steps. Almost at the same time he bent down and seized the standing waterman by the legs and jerked him up and out of his own boat. The man fell into the river. Like most of his kind he was probably no swimmer and it was lucky therefore that he landed in a shallow spot and was able to flounder and wade his way to safety.

Master WS seized me by the arm and pulled me in the direction of the river. The wind was coming colder off the water, blowing gusts of rain and spray in our faces. Waves slopped at the piers of the steps. Anybody already out on the river now would be heading for shelter, if they were sensible, and I doubted that any boatman would take a fare in this weather.

Master WS called to a boat that had just pulled in. The fare from the other side of the river scuttled off, pressing payment into the boatman's palm, and ran up the steps to get out of the wet.

"No sir, not in this," called out the boatman.

"He's taken my boat, Adam. The bastard, the cock-sucking arse-wipe, the triple-turned turd."

This was the ferryman who had been so rudely ejected from his own craft, now back on shore, and standing beside Master Shakespeare and me, as witnesses to the offence against him. He was dripping from his immersion in the river and the rain. He was a powerfully built man. His chest heaved as he bellowed out these choice descriptions of the boat-robber. If Mink hadn't taken him by surprise, the boatman looked as though he wouldn't have been bested.

"Not Adam Gibbons, is it?" said Master WS to the ferryman who'd just docked, half shouting to make himself heard above the roar of the wind.

"Depends who's asking."

The boatman was bobbing on the choppy water and his head jumped up and down above the top of the steps.

"Adam Gibbons, the master boatman?"

"Took my boat, he fucking did," bellowed the voice of the mariner beside us.

Adam the boatman was more interested in the compliments flying through the air than he was in the grouses of his fellow-sailor.

"If you say so, sir."

"We have met, boatman. You said that if I ever needed a boatman for something special, I should just bear old Adam in mind."

Recognition dawned in the streaming, upturned face of old Adam as it emerged into view above the steps. The water ran down his beard like rain off thatched eaves. Recognition dawned in me, too. This was the boatman who'd nearly throttled me when I'd accused him of being a pleonast. That last occasion Master WS had saved my life. Now it looked as if he was trying to endanger it. I might have more than one life, like the cat, but I did not consider that I had more than one in a single day.

"Beg pardon, sir, didn't recognise you in that . . . that . . . them night-clothes."

"That boat is my lifeblood and my livelihood, Adam. Bleeding bastard cunt's taken my liveli-fucking-hood," said the ferryman whose boat was now bobbing away. Who would not recognise the authentic, oath-ridden tone of the Thames boatman?

"Well, now is the time for something special, Adam," said Master WS, ignoring the desperate bellows to one side of us. In the midst of the downpour and the noise of the wind, there was in WS's voice a note of good humour, even amusement.

"We require you to pursue the boat that belongs to your fellow. We need the man who stole it and your fellow, he needs his boat back. Will you help us?"

Up and down bobbed Adam's head.

"I don't know, sir . . . this weather . . ."

The wind took his words and hurled them round about. Whitecaps were forming in the middle of the river. Spray spattered the platform where were stood. Inwardly, I withdrew my notion that Nature or Providence matched their weathers to our moods or needs. This looked like an unwise moment to launch onto the Thames. I could see Master Mink pushing, pushing, pushing his way up and down and through the waves towards the far bank – though he had not yet succeeded in rowing far.

"I'll make it worth your while, Adam."

"Well, sir . . . that depends what my while's worth, don't it."

The boatman's head bobbed.

"It will be a measure of your great skill."

"No flattery, sir." The head bobbed again.

"I am sure you would like to help your poor robbed fellow here . . ."

"No charity neither." The head bobbed once more.

"Or are you like one of these fresh-water mariners, whose ships were drowned in the plain of Salisbury?"

I was still trying to work out this jibe and wondering how Master WS got away with it whereas I was handed a throttling for trying to be clever, when old Adam's face bobbed up for the last time.

"Hop aboard."

"And me," said the other boatman. "Let me get my hands on the fucking cunt."

"No room, Ben," said Adam. "Only these two gentlemen here."

He obviously hadn't recognised me. I would willingly have surrendered my place on the rocking, pitching boat to Ben – or to the archangel Gabriel for that matter – but Master WS seemed determined that I should accompany him. He stepped in first and I followed in an awkward movement that was something between a step, a scrabble and a jump. To move from the relative solidity and safety of the stairs to this narrow, swaying craft, to know that only a thin skin of wood separated me from the green slopping waters of the Thames, was to experience, and for the second time in little more than twelve hours, a powerful fear for my life. As I got down almost on a level with the tide, the river seemed to expand and fill the horizon, and I entered a watery universe.

I am no fish, I cannot swim.

On the bank, Ben the boatman was shouting obscenities into the teeth of the wind and waving his fist at his own distant boat, or rather at its occupant. Adam pulled out into the bouncing waters. Master WS and I huddled on the seats in the stern. I pulled my – Adrian's – hat lower on my brows. WS was bare-headed and the rain beat at his large balding brows, but he did not seem to care.

"Good, Adam, good, master boatman," he muttered by way of encouragement to the grizzled greybeard wielding the oars. WS's face still showed traces of a ghostly painted whiteness and his sodden night-gown clung to his under-garments. I realised that he must have sped out of the theatre after us as soon as he had completed his final appearance as the Ghost. The play would continue whatever the weather. The players were partly protected by the stage-roof, while the better class of spectators sat snug in their boxes and galleries. The groundlings in the pit endured the rain as stoically as an army on campaign, appearing to enjoy the vicissitudes of the elements.

As far as I was able to see through the rain and spray the river was almost empty of smaller boats. This made it easier to keep sight of Master Mink in his stolen craft. I had crossed the river often enough by ferryboat but always when the water was, by comparison, like a millpond. Now I recognised for the first time the force and fury of which this great broad slippery fellow was capable. The jumping and bucking of the little ferryboat was like being on a mischievous horse, and reminded me of my fear the first time my father had put me astride one.

"We are gaining," said Master WS. "This is excellently done, master boatman."

It was true that Mink's boat seemed a little nearer. The figure of the rower was furiously plying the blades. Sometimes one of the oars flailed helplessly in the air, at others it was buried deep in the frothing current and Mink had to twist his body to retain hold of it. Like us, he was bobbing violently up and down, and either his motion or his diminished size against the river and sky – or perhaps the frantic futility of the to-and-fro action – made me think of a small child on a hobby-horse. It was plain that he didn't know what he was doing and that matters were slipping out of his control as we approached the middle of the river where the current was strongest. At this difficult pass Adam's skill showed through. He was strong in the chest and arms – as I knew to my cost – from years of pulling people from shore to shore. More important, he knew the river and its moods inside out, backwards and forwards, top to bottom, and although he mightn't have ventured out in this weather from choice, now he was here he knew how to ride the waves. He knew when and where to thrust his blade deep into the swirling flow, when and where to withdraw it so that it just skimmed the spume.

I found that my own alarm had blown away, as if in the wind. It was partly the horrid fascination of watching an individual in much greater difficulty than ourselves on the water and partly the sense that we, Master WS and Master NR, were in the hands of a man who knew his trade and acquitted himself skilfully. I began to think that WS's compliments to the boatman had not been so extravagant after all, and that, were we to survive this enterprise, I would treat this class of men more respectfully in future.

Adam glanced round over his shoulder to check our progress. He turned back and bared his teeth at Master WS in triumph. Suddenly the distance had narrowed sharply. Caught by some miniature whirlpool or species of eddy, Master Mink's boat was moving in slow circles while we continued to plough through the waves as slow but remorseless as fate. If Mink had noticed us he didn't give any sign. He was more concerned to regain control over his craft. But his oars hardly connected with the water. Like a pair of giant wooden scissors, they cut the turbulent air.

Master WS stood up in the stern beside me.

"Careful, sir," cried Adam, but Master WS, he paid no attention to the boatman's caution.

Cupping his hands around his mouth he called out Mink's name. Once, then again.

Despite the usual gentleness and evenness of his speech he could, as occasion required, throw his voice so that it landed like a dart at the back of the gallery. This he did now. Mink must have heard because he stopped agitating his oars and looked across at us. Distracted, his grip on one of the oars slackened and it slipped itself from the rowlock and floated away out of reach. His small chance of escape vanished with it. All the time the gap between the two boats was closing. It might have been an illusion, but it seemed to me that out here at the midpoint of the river the water was less broken and choppy than it was inshore.

"Robert," called WS again when he had got the other's attention. "We must talk, you and I."

This was such a ridiculous thing to say, in the middle of a rainstorm, in the middle of rough water, that I almost burst out laughing.

"Bring us closer, boatman Adam."

Adam swung and twisted and turned his blades with the dexterity of a swordsman until our boat approached nearer to Mink's. Master Mink, like the two of us, was still wearing his costume. He was a very bedraggled and woebegone Player King, just as Master WS was a damp Ghost and I, I was a sorry poisoner.

"Can we attach ourselves to him?" WS asked Adam. "A rope or a hook?"

We too began to circle slowly, caught up in the same fluvial eddy. A strange calm had settled over the scene. I glanced up. The clouds had torn themselves apart in their brief fury and now, in their exhaustion, patches of impossible blue showed among the dirty white. Adam reached beneath his seat and grabbed a coil of rope from some nether compartment.

"Fasten this to the sternpost, sir, and then let him catch a-holt of it."

To the mariner's manner born, Master WS slipped the looped and knotted end of the cable over our sternpost and, alerting Robert Mink with a shout, tossed the coils to the other boat. Mink might have chosen to ignore the shout and the rope spinning through the air but instead he chose to be helped. Seizing the other end of the cable he swiftly secured it to one of the thwarts before passing it round the sternpost in his, or rather Ben's, boat. Now, joined by a cord, the four of us began a stately rotation, the two ferryboats dancing on water that sparkled and gleamed in the newly emergent sun. The skill and mastery of Adam Gibbons kept both craft in the same position relative to each other. A half dozen yards separated us. The far banks were a slowly shifting backdrop.

Robert Mink's plump, affable face appeared no longer so well-fed or friendly. Replacing it was no expression of evil, such as would have suited a man who had commited at least three murders; nor any sign of remorse, as would have befitted a penitent; but instead a curiously affronted look. Now occurred the following dialogue, as calmly as if the three of us were sitting in a tavern after a performance. I call it a dialogue because, although I intervened once or twice, the main business was between Robert Mink and William Shakespeare, as will be clearly seen. The role of old Adam, meantime, was to lead us slowly round and round in the freshly washed sunshine and to see that we came to no harm.

"Well," said WS. "Dick Burbage will not be pleased to see three of his costumes walking away like this."

"Nicholas is wearing no costume, but a dead man's clothes," said Mink.

Master WS looked down at where I sat hunched and shivering on the stern seat, wrapped in Adrian's mantle, topped by his hat.

"Why, so am I," said Master WS, plucking at the sleeve of his ghostly night-gown and referring to the late King of Denmark. "I am dressed in a dead man's garb."

"Ever the jester," said Mink. "Like your Yorick."

"But this is no jest," said WS.

"No jest," said Mink. "I have been out and about killing people. Why, I killed one this morning at breakfast."

I started shaking and could not stop.

"And I killed one last evening at supper-time and hung him up in place of an alligator. Master Revill knows who I mean."

My teeth began to chatter . . .

"And another I killed one night by these very waters. He had a dirty shirt and would not keep it clean."

. . . and chatter.

Around us circled the watchful buildings of London, the palaces and the stews, the theatres and temples.

"For the first I was up a tree. I entered through the husband's door and waited up a tree. I watched until he was asleep in his hammock. Then I poured it all down his ear. Guaiacum paste and mercury. Because his wife said she wanted me. She gave me the key to her husband's door. I had the key from her but she did not open up to me. She preferred the brother. She tricked me."

"This is all a play, Robert," said Master WS, gently.

"No play but still your work," said Mink. "The other one now, Francis, he got it on his sleeve so that was the end of him."

"This is my play which you have been playing in. You are sick in your mind."

"No play, I tell you," said Robert Mink, "although there are almost as many dead as at the end of one of your pieces." He laughed. "My dead will not rise up for applause and a little dance. Clap and see."

He gazed about as though he expected an invisible audience to respond. Then, as if he was urgently seeking to convince us, he said: "You are looking for Master Ransom? You see, I have names. I can give you chapter and verse."

"Who is he?" said WS.

"Your young player there knows who I mean."

"He is a c-c-c-confederate of that gentleman's," I said. "He tried to d-d-d-dispose of me last night."

"He will bother you no more," said Mink. "It was he I had for breakfast."

"You are sick, Robert," said WS. "You don't know your own words."

"I am as sane as you are. I am in earnest."

The boats bobbed about. In the distance I could see the tall houses on the Bridge.

"If you killed him as you say, where is the body, then?"

"In heaven. Send thither to see. If your messenger find him not there, seek him in the other place yourself."

"Ah," said WS, ruefully. "You are in earnest."

"But if you find him not within this month you shall nose him as you go up the stairs to my lodgings in Swan Street. I, for one, do not intend to return there."

"No, you are on the way to Tyburn, Robert," said WS. "You shall go to heaven in a string if this is true."

The water had grown calmer and the sun was out but I could not stop my shaking.

"All of this, it was your handiwork too, playwright," said Master Mink.

"How so?"

"I mean that I signed your name to it up a tree and so made it yours, and I gave your name when I was asked who I was by the doorman. And, in doing so, I became you. So it was your handiwork."

I thought of the initials on the pear-tree bark; of what Thomas Bullock the gate-keeper had said.

Master WS looked shaken. A cloud passed over his normally placid features.

"Why?"

"Do you remember what you were called by Robert Greene when you were first up in London and writing plays and playing in plays?" said Mink to WS.

"Yes."

" 'An upstart crow', was it not?"

"Oh yes, and Shake-scene and so on," said WS, in a way that suggested that he had never quite put such early insults behind him. These matters were still talked of in the theatre fraternity.

"Did you hate those who laughed at you?"

"I do not find it easy to hate," said WS mournfully. "Though I do know that Robert Greene died destitute in a shoe-maker's house near Dow-gate. His landlord had to pay for his winding-sheet."

"That will not be your case, I think," said Mink. "You will not die in poverty, unregarded."

"No," said Master WS. "I do not think so."

"I am a poet too," said Mink. "Young Master Revill there, shaking in the stern beside you, he has heard some of my verses."

"Y-y-y-yes." For some reason, my eyes began to water, not for Mink but for myself.

"I recited to him my Lover's Lament. That was true verse, it was no feigning."

Slowly now, slowly, our boats circled each other, like two watchful dogs who know that, sooner or later, they must fight.

"What did you think, Nick? Tell me what you thought of my verses."

"They – they – were – b-b-b-b- "

"Bad?" said Mink. He spoke in simple curiosity.

"B-b-beautiful," I finally forced out the lie between my gnashing teeth.

"You are lying, Revill. No lies now."

"T-t-t-true though."

"A pity then," said Mink. "For I had invited you to my lodgings to hear my Lover's Triumph. Oh, and to poison you afterwards."

Tears flowed down my face.

"There is no escape for you either, William," continued Mink. "For I wrote a tragedy once. It was called *The Tragical History of Sulla, Emperor of all the Romans*."

"I saw it," said WS. "At the Curtain."

"The Red Bull."

"The Red Bull, then. But it was not by you, it was by – let me see – I have it, Robert Otter. Though, come to think of it, I have never heard of that author before or since. Master Otter." He paused, then said with a note of weariness, "Oh, I see. Otter – Mink."

"Never heard of again, that is right. Otter is well buried or drowned."

"But I did see your play, your *Sulla*."

"You were fortunate because it received only one performance."

"Many good plays go unappreciated and receive a single performance."

"Oh, my tragedy was appreciated – but not as a tragedy. It was greeted with howls of derision, as you will surely remember if you were there. There were tears of laughter, screams of glee. People pissed thermselves laughing. It should have been called *The Comical History of Sulla, Roman Fool* . . ."

"The people are not always good judges. Why, in a future age, they may play your *Sulla*—"

"There will never be another performance because the people were right, it was no good. It was no tragedy. Come now, playwright. Give me your honest opinion of my play, if you really attended that performance."

There was a pause. The sunlight glanced off the water. I waited, with indrawn breath.

"It was no tragedy," said WS. "You are right, and the audience at that performance was right to respond as they did. I didn't piss myself – but I laughed long and loud."

"You see," said Robert Mink, almost triumphantly. "I cannot write verses. I cannot write a tragedy neither. But I can create one. I can do in real life what you only do on paper. So who is the better?"

Then Mink did an extraordinary thing, or a thing even more extraordinary than what he had already done. He bent down and retrieved from the bottom of the boat a crown. It took me a moment to recognise it as the prop which he had been wearing in the part of the Player King. Because he was no true king, but merely a player playing a king in the play-within-the-the-play, the crown did not match Claudius's for heaviness and splendour. Instead it was a piece of trumpery, lightweight, crudely gold-painted. It was meant to signify to the audience "king", simply and without more ado. He must have tucked it away somewhere in his costume, as he hurried

296

from the theatre and then out into the alleyways down to the river.

"Who wears the crown?" he said, grinning. "Tell me, who wears the crown?"

"You do," said WS. "It is yours."

"Sir! Sir!"

All this time Adam Gibbons had been quietly dipping and splashing his oars to keep the two boats on a parallel circular course. I don't know whether he was listening to the conversation between the two players or – if he was – what he made of it, but now a more pressing consideration had come up. I'd been so engrossed in what I was hearing and in my own shivering, quivering state that I'd been only a quarter aware of our surroundings.

"The Bridge, sir!"

We were caught up in a gently revolving eddy but, as well as making slow circles, we were also travelling downstream with the current. The tide, which must have been at its height when we boarded Adam's boat, was ebbing and our two roped vessels were going downriver with it. When, minutes before, I'd glimpsed the buildings of London Bridge, I'd not grasped how close we were running to it. The great starlings or bases that supported the piers, nearly two dozen of them, loomed close. The spaces between the piers gaped like so many hungry river mouths. The merchants' houses above looked more like cliffs of wood than human habitations. The roaring, which we must have been hearing for the last few minutes without properly attending to its cause, and which was produced by the constriction and the forcing of the waters through the piers, seemed to grow deafening.

Now, it is possible to pass through the arches – but the

prudent traveller disembarks well before reaching the Bridge and continues his journey on foot. And you can be sure that any boatman making the passage would expect extra for his pains and the risk he takes. With our two boats the risk was considerable. We were still joined by rope. Robert Mink, disappointed tragedian and multiple murderer, was no oarsman. In fact, he had only one oar remaining.

Master WS spoke. He mixed firmness and persuasion. "Now, Adam, there is still time but we run the risk of being carried away on the tide or, worse, of being battered against one of the piles. Only your strength and skill can save us now."

He neglected to mention, by the by, that it was his own skill – with a silver tongue – that had persuaded Adam to take his boat out in the first place and so put himself, and the ferryman, and me, all at risk. But Adam did not appear to harbour any resentment against this man who might be leaving a boatman's widow and children unprovided for in this harsh world, or depriving the English stage of its finest adornment, or snuffing out the life of an obscure West Country parson's son turned player.

"Pull, man, pull. Robert Mink, you have an oar. Use it!" Half crouching in the stern, Master WS issued orders and encouragements. Adam Gibbons dug into the task with a will. His back bent and straightened, bent and straightened, his breath came thick and short, sweat poured down his face and dripped off his beard, still matted with the rain. If Master WS was fearful he didn't show it. I wondered that he didn't seize a oar for himself and begin to paddle – the thought occurred to me to do it – and then I realised his thinking was clearer than mine. Adam was the expert here, his was the skill and strength. If we were to be saved at all it would be by the boatman.

Despite his best efforts, however, we were drifting closer to the Bridge. The roaring of the waters was growing louder, the cliffs of houses rising higher, the gaps between the piers gaping wider. White, knife-like crests formed as the water pushed against the outworks of the great piers. Cords of sinew stood out on the oarsman's neck and temples and arms. The rope between the boats was taut. In the background Master Mink was making motions with his remaining oar. I shut my eyes. When I opened them again, our position seemed unchanged.

And then I understood that our boatman was winning the struggle. If we had not put a distance between ourselves and the Bridge we were, at least, no closer to it. The size of the piers and the buildings surmounting them remained constant. I silently willed him on, with clenched hands and gritted teeth. All the time Master WS spoke encouragement and praise. Slowly, slowly, we pulled away from the Bridge, against the current; slowly, slowly, we struck out on a diagonal for the southern shore.

But then we seemed to, as it were, leap forward. The reason was not far to seek. Robert Mink, understanding that Adam was succeeding in the task of drawing us back towards dry land and safety, had unhitched the rope that fastened his craft to ours. As the gap between the boats widened he shouted out again, "Who is the better, playwright? Who is the better?"

He stood unsteadily in the little ferryboat as it was borne back and away by the current towards the Bridge. By twisting round in the stern, WS and I had a good view of what happened next. Adam kept tugging on his blades, ferrying us to *terra firma*, unable to see much of what was taking place over our turned shoulders. Probably he wouldn't have been interested anyway. Just another accident on the river. An unskilled sailor. A dry-land mariner.

Mink's craft, bearing him alone for captain and crew, dwindled in our sight. He continued to look in our direction, rather than at the course on which the current was taking him. He was washed nearer and nearer to the Bridge and I thought that he would slip between one of the central arches like a morsel of butter down a gullet. Once beyond them, if he did not capsize, he might well be able to make for the shore and the wilds of Essex or Surrey. But at the last moment, rather than capsizing, his little boat swerved and smashed hard into one of the great piers. We were too distant to hear anything apart from a far-off scraping and cracking sound above the low thunder of the descending water. The bow of the boat tilted and upended as if it the waves really intended to swallow it in one gulp and I thought I saw a small figure topple into the fast-flowing stream. The dot of a head was visible against the blue sky between a pair of arches. Then the head vanished as swift as if it had been wiped away.

I wondered what had happened to his poor trumpery crown. Then I surprised myself by discovering fresh tears coursing down my face.

"Come, Nick," said Master WS, as we reached dry land. "There is still a little business to conclude for this day."

And business there was.

The sun was shining as we raced through the streets, WS in the lead. Steam rose from the gutters and rooftops.

I was alternately sweating and shivering when we reached the Globe, and everything seemed to be occurring in a dream from which I would surely soon awaken. Somewhere on the way I lost my – Adrian's – tall, villainous hat. His cloak still clung to my back.

By the time we arrived in the tiring-house the bloodbath was done. Hamlet had finished his duel with Laertes and both had been mortally wounded. The Prince had witnessed his mother take a fatal sip from the poisoned chalice prepared for him. King Claudius had seen all his schemes unravel in front of his face, as his Queen died and his nephew compelled him to drain the remains of his own poison draught.

Now Hamlet is left alive for a few moments, long enough to request loyal Horatio to report to a wonderstruck court the truth behind these strange and terrifying events. Now the poison from the venom-tipped sword has the upper hand of Prince Hamlet; now that fell sergeant Death strides in to make his last arrest.

All is done.

Almost.

There is the little matter of the late arrival of the ambassador from England with the news of yet more deaths. Minor characters, ones whom Hamlet has brushed from his conscience.

I tottered on stage, a weary English ambassador, exhausted no doubt from my urgent passage across the North Sea, my breakneck gallop across the Danish plains, my rapid entry through the portals of Elsinore. Perhaps my appearance, battered, rainswept, sweat-sodden, surprised beyond surprise, made up for a somewhat wooden delivery.

The sight is dismal,
And our affairs from England come too late.
The ears are senseless that should give us hearing,
To tell him his commandment is fulfilled,
That Rosencrantz and Guildenstern are dead.
Where should we have our thanks?

Then I remained, grinning inappropriately like an ape, as Horatio talked of casual slaughters and Prince Fortinbras of Norway talked of his rights of memory in the Kingdom of Denmark. Then the soldiers were bidden go shoot their pieces in honour of the late Prince.

Then we faced the applause, and we had our music from the gallery and our little jig, and after that I knew no more.

Epilogue

The final accounting. Two brief scenes.

Lady Alice summoned me to see her in her closet. She was writing at a desk, or pretending to, a piece of stage business. A fire of sea-coal burnt in the small grate. All the warmth of our previous encounter together, when we had exchanged lines from 'Venus and Adonis', all that warmth, I say, seemed to have migrated from her and lodged itself in her little fire. Certainly, there was none left in her manner towards me. A nipping autumn had established itself; the last shreds of summer had been scattered in storm and thunder.

"Master Revill, I hear you are leaving us."

"Yes, my lady. I have found lodgings on the other side of the river again – among my own kind."

"I suppose that is best."

"Now I am staying on with the Chamberlain's Company," I said, to lead her on, to be questioned and complimented.

But Lady Alice was unconcerned at my changing fortunes. That was not why I had been called to see her.

"Robert Mink was of your company, was he not?"

The news of Mink's death, or more precisely disappearance, in a river accident, was widely known. He had had a following among women of a certain kind, as I had discovered at the requiem mass sung for him, women not quite respectable, though not unrespectable neither. If Lady Alice had been among their number, however, she would certainly have stood out by reason of her rank.

"I believe that you know that Master Mink was one of us," I said. "You must have seen him – on stage."

"You have heard that Sir William, my first husband, could not abide plays and players. Yet even so, I did occasionally attend the playhouse, with William or my brother-in-law. So I must have seen him there, but never in this house. Sir William would not have borne that."

I, by the by, had never hinted that Lady Alice had seen Robert Mink anywhere, let alone in her husband's house. Master WS's lines about the lady protesting too much came into my mind. I did not reply.

"They say that women are like wax. Quick to take any form imposed on them, true or false. But there are some men like that too. A hint or a word is enough for them to build up a castle in Spain."

"Sometimes a key will do," I said, and Lady Alice pretended not to understand, but went back to attend to her writing.

Without waiting to be dismissed, I made to go. I no longer needed the patronage of the Eliot family, in fact I wanted to rid myself of all of them.

"Anything else you may have heard—"

"Yes?"

" – is false, and slanderous."

"Of course, my lady."

"Nicholas," she said, trying a different, gentler tack. "I came to see you when you were lodging here one evening."

She spoke as if her visit belonged to another age rather than little more than a week earlier. "I may have thought that you were here for a purpose, but I realise now that I was mistaken. You were here simply because of my son's generosity."

"As you say."

"It is easy to misconstrue others' motives."

I saw that we might go round in circles all day, so I said farewell and asked after Sir Thomas.

"Sir Thomas?"

"Your husband."

"He is in Dover, I believe," she said, "about his business."

As I walked from the closet I heard behind me the sound of her pen furiously scratching at paper.

"You're staying?"

"For the time being."

I felt sheepish.

"So all those words about wanting to leave London, and go back to the country and live a simple life away from the flesh-pots and wanting me to give up my trade and cover myself in sackcloth and ashes . . ."

We were in bed, as you might have guessed. Where else would you have us at the end of the story?

"Nick, your country is here. Feel."

"I was sick, I didn't know what I was saying."

"These little fits of sorrow, I know them well."

"I suppose your customers have regular attacks."

"Only afterwards, never before."

"And you, Nell?"

"Oh, even I am not proof against them. But I harden my heart and sit them out."

"Women are good at that."

"So tell me, Nick, did she know?"

"Who?"

"Lady Alice Eliot."

"You saw her in the Globe. How did she respond?"

"I couldn't see her well. It was getting overcast. The rain was starting to fall. And those boxes, it's not easy to see clear inside."

So that part of my plan had been hopeless from the beginning. Even if Lady Alice Eliot had been shaken enough by what she saw on stage to give herself away by a change of expression, by an altered complexion, by an abrupt gesture, it wouldn't have been seen by Nell anyway. And as for my belief that WS lay behind the crimes . . . I blushed and grew hot in memory. Fortunately, he suspected nothing of my suspicions, or if he did he was tactful and generous enough not to mention it.

(Indeed he and Dick Burbage had been masters of grace and courtesy when they asked me if I wanted to extend my contract with the Chamberlain's. That was what they'd wanted to talk about after the ill-fated performance of *Hamlet.* It took me the best part of a week to recover from that and from my adventures in the forest and on the river, but when I returned, expecting a dismissal, I received an invitation instead. "What about Jack Wilson?" I said. "For I am only filling his shoes until he returns from attending on his mother." "We are prepared to find another pair of shoes for you, Nick," said Burbage. "I was much struck by the way you returned to the theatre to give your last lines. That is the first and last requirement of the player, that he should appear on cue – even if he is dead or dying."

"Besides," said WS, "we have a space now with the sudden departure of Robert Mink."

"A tragic madness," said Burbage, and I wondered how much Shakespeare had told him.)

"Nick, did Lady Alice know?" said Nell again.

William Eliot had wanted to know the same thing about his mother. "Did she know?" This is the very question that Prince Hamlet asks of Gertrude. Does she know? I had no answer. Robert Mink's story that he had been tricked or betrayed by a woman who had given him a counterfeit key to the garden but not the key to herself might have been so much fantasy. "A castle in Spain," as Lady Alice said. It was certain that the player was driven by a queer desire to emulate in reality what he had only seen played on stage. Even as Master WS's *Hamlet* was being rehearsed by the Chamberlain's Men, Robert Mink, the Player King, was enacting the crime that underlies that tragedy, a garden murder. He had secreted himself up the tree, he had scratched the letters WS into the bark, he had slaughtered old Sir William with an arcane mixture (guaiacum paste and mercury) bought of the old apothecary. Remaining in his strange perch to witness the finding of the corpse, he had seen Francis by moonlight wipe his shirt-sleeve across the dead man's face. In fear of discovery he had disposed of the servant, then of the apothecary, and had given orders that I was to be put to death. Finally he had killed one of the men who had set out to kill me. Ralph Ransom's fat, deceased self was found in the player's lodgings in Swan Street.

"I don't know whether she knew," I said. "I have seen her only once since that afternoon."

"She may have known and not known." said Nell.

I didn't understand this but let it pass.

"And what was in the note?"

"The note?"

"The piece of paper you picked up at Old Nick's."

"I don't know that either," I said. "Or rather I didn't understand it."

"But what did it say?"

"Does it matter?"

"It could be important."

I struggled with my memory. I was naturally reluctant to revisit the charcoal burner's hut where, as the storm crept up outside, I had so nearly lost manhood and life and all. Nevertheless, at Nell's behest, I strove to recite the words that Adrian had read aloud.

"Valerian, ipomea, er, ag-something, ag-ag-ag- "

"Agrimony?"

"Yes, agrimony, then gall-bladder, I think . . . ratsfoot . . . and, er, antimony."

I was rather pleased with myself for reproducing so exactly what had been written on the apothecary's note. Then I noticed that Nell was laughing, to herself.

"What is it? I can tell you, it wasn't funny out in those woods. You nearly didn't have me – or this – to toy with any more."

"Poor Nick," said Nell.

"That's better," I said.

"Old Nick, I mean, the apothecary."

"Well," I said, annoyed, "he is in the woods now and will never be out of them again."

I thought of the rat-like Nub and wondered what he and his tribe of charcoal-burners might have done with the bodies of the aged apothecary and the false steward. They could have been left for forest animals to pick over but somehow I doubted it. There was always the risk of discovery, of investigation, even in those lawless wastes. I thought that Nub would probably know what to do. At any rate, I wasn't going back to find out.

"A harmless old man," she said.

Not so, I thought. A supplier of poisons. A maker of arrangements.

"Nell?"

"Yes."

"The arrangement that you had with the apothecary, what was it?"

"Jealousy?"

"No, but tell me."

"Sometimes, Nick, a man comes to me and he has lost the will and cannot go. You understand?"

"Of course. Though that is not my case."

"No, it is not your case. But for those who cannot go, what striving and misery there is. The cursing and the grief of these men and not all of them old neither. There is a real sorrow. All your repentance is nothing to it. You know what they say, old jades whinny when they cannot wag the tail."

"Old Nick, he was one of these?"

"No, he was ever more of a watcher than a doer. But he asked me to try out certain preparations on the old jades. Those words that you've just said, that list, they were a preparation. An infallible preparation to make men go, and go again."

"What, valerian and agrimony and the rest?"

"Yes. When your pistol will not discharge."

She could hardly speak for laughter.

I was not pleased and by my look must have said so.

"Nick, you do not reform me with these puritan glances. Where is the harm? These things were for our profit – and pleasure. Old Nick was pleased because he was making money. I was pleased because I too made money out of the old jades and they were pleased, oh how they were pleased, by these preparations and mixtures. Where is the harm?"

"No harm," I said.

"But you do not really think so," she said.

"Pleasure and profit as you say," I said.

"And it is not your case. For sure, you do not need these preparations, this valerian and agrimony and all," she said, grasping me.

"Oh no," I said, feeling the old Adam rouse himself from slumber and stretch and look about himself, "it is not my case at all."

Other fiction titles available from Robinson Publishing

Crocodile on the Sandbank   Elizabeth Peters   **£6.99 [ ]**
The very first Amelia Peabody adventure, which introduces the dashing Emerson and a rather lively mummy . . .

The Curse of the Pharaohs   Elizabeth Peters   **£6.99 [ ]**
The second Egyptian murder-mystery with Amelia Peabody and Emerson – this time they investigate the strange murder at Luxor of an eminent archaeologist.

The Falcon at the Portal   Elizabeth Peters   **£6.99 [ ]**
The eleventh in the series, and more mystery and danger for our intrepid heroine in the Land of the Pharaohs.

Arms of Nemesis   Steven Saylor   **£6.99 [ ]**
Intrigue in Ancient Rome, as Gordianus the Finder investigates a murder that involves the household of Rome's wealthiest citizen.

The Venus Throw   Steven Saylor   **£6.99 [ ]**
Following the violent death of the philosopher Dio, Gordianus is hired to investigate – by a beautiful woman with a most scandalous reputation

A Murder on the Appian Way   Steven Saylor   **£6.99 [ ]**
Amidst a city torn with riots and arson, Gordianus is charged by Pompey the Great with finding out what really happened to a murdered politician.

Robinson books are available from all good bookshops or direct from the publisher. Just tick the titles you want and fill in the form below.

TBS Direct
Colchester Road, Frating Green, Colchester, Essex CO7 7DW
Tel: +44 (0) 1206 255777
Fax: +44 (0) 1206 255914
Email: sales@tbs-ltd.co.uk

UK/BFPO customers please allow £1.00 for p&p for the first book, plus 50p for the second, plus 30p for each additional book up to a maximum charge of £3.00

Overseas customers (inc. Ireland), please allow £2.00 for the first book, plus £1.00 for the second, plus 50p for each additional book.

Please send me the titles ticked above.

NAME (Block letters). . . . .
ADDRESS . . . .
. . . .
POSTCODE . . . .
I enclose a cheque/PO (payable to TBS Direct) for . . . .
I wish to pay by Switch/Credit card
Number . . . .
Card Expiry Date . . . .
Switch Issue Number . . . .